G000272558

BETWEEN
SEAN
CATT STATES

WWW.SEANCATT.COM

BOOKS@ROUGHIMAGE.CO.UK

Between States

Copyright © 2015 Sean Catt

Published with the assistance of Actual Books LTD. www.actualizeselfpublishing.com

Cover art by Rhys Wootton. www.rhyswootton.com

Cover art copyright © 2014 Rhys Wootton

Typeset by Blush Book Design in 10pt Adobe Caslon Pro. www.blushbookdesign.co.uk

Paperback ISBN: 978-0-9929046-8-5

eBook ISBN: 978-0-9929046-9-2

A CIP Record for this book can be found at the British Library.

"*They say when you look in dark places you find dark things. And trust me; I have been in some very dark places.*"

Jake Palmer

UTAH RUNNING

THE PICKUP SWERVED OFF THE HIGHWAY AND SLEWED TO A HALT ON the shoulder. Its passenger side wheels juddering as the tires scrabbled for grip in the gritty desert soil that had insidiously invaded the edges of the cracked grey asphalt.

A small cloud of brown dust billowed up and hung fleetingly in the scorching noonday air before a gentle breeze allowed it to drift lazily across the front of the stationary truck. On its way over some of the heavier particles settled, momentarily helping to conceal the rust patches that clung like oversized gravel rash scabs to the weathered pale blue paintwork.

Swiveling round to look out the rear window Jake winced as a number of joints in his back popped, reminding him he really needed to get out and stretch his legs. Through the rear window he caught sight of the hitchhiker jogging towards him. The guy's open white shirt flapped at his sides, while the large camo duffel bag slung over his left shoulder bounced up and down against his back.

What had he just done?

Jake's road rule number one:

Never pick up hitchers. Not ever!

And now in the middle of nowhere, well somewhere in the middle of Utah, to be precise, he sat doing exactly what he promised himself he'd never do again.

As the alarm bells in his head started ringing in earnest, Jake's mind slipped into complete turmoil. Half of it was all set to do the sensible thing and drive off, while the other half which had succeeded in gaining control over his motor functions refused to have any part of it, and stubbornly refused to respond.

Man, this is gonna turn to shit!

Just like everything always has, and just like everything always will.

You're a loner for a very good reason. So just go!

Besides, do you care if he thinks you're a total douche bag for making him run up the road before driving off?

The guy had almost reached the truck, but still Jake's internal conflict raged.

He'd decided a good while ago that he needed to avoid having company like the plague, it being far better for everyone that way, especially him.

Come on! Do something!

His inability to react rationally still paralyzing him, he watched as the guy tossed his bag into the back of the truck.

Shit!

Noticing Jake looking at him through the dust covered window, the guy grinned and gave a two handed thumbs-up. A few seconds later as the passenger door opened, Jake's stomach performed a double backflip with half pike. A sudden wave of nausea swept over him as the potential consequences of his indecisiveness finally dawned on him.

As he looked across the cab, a young slim guy with several days' stubble and a tangle of unruly dark brown hair that fell low over his forehead stood there framed by the open door. Flicking the bangs up out of his eyes the guy beamed broadly at Jake, then bounded up onto the bench seat, the huge grin still firmly fixed on his face.

Damn! The guy smiled a lot. And right now, Jake really didn't need cheery companionship. Still he'd made a solemn promise not so long ago to remember 'That no man is an island', even him, and he felt obligated to keep his word.

"Hey thanks dude, I honestly thought I'd be walking all..."

The hitcher's voice trailed off and the smile instantly fell away as he stared across the cab at Jake who returned the surprised look for a few seconds, now acutely aware of why his 'spidey sense' had managed to get itself so on edge.

Jake then impressed himself no end by managing to come up with a more or less coherent opening response far quicker than he expected.

"Well, couldn't leave you out there in the middle of God knows where, not in this heat. You know, mad dogs and Englishmen and all that."

He groaned inwardly at the last part, did he really say that? His ability to disengage his brain, engage his mouth and say the dumbest things never ceased to amaze him.

So there they sat, gawping open mouthed at each other like two goldfish in a bowl. Noticing the hitcher's hand maintaining a firm grip on the door handle Jake sensed the guy was trying hard to think of a damn good reason why he shouldn't just get straight back out again.

As for Jake's passenger, even a half decent reason to get back out the cab just as fast as he climbed in would do. He could then wave goodbye, and forget the whole thing had ever happened. But seeing as no one else had bothered to stop for him today, he really couldn't come up with any sane or rational reason to go back to walking in the blazing sun. Exhaling noisily through his nose he forced the smile back onto his face. Then letting go of the door he stuck his hand out at Jake and nodded.

"Hi, I'm Billy, thanks for the ride, much appreciated."

Jake smiled back, and then lying through his teeth replied, "Good to meet you Billy. I'm Jacob, but everybody calls me Jake."

Everybody… Yeah right, Mister Popularity… Not!

Still, he'd become pretty adept at the whole lying thing; having had more than enough practice doing it to himself.

He shook the offered hand, Billy's firm grip and the handshake were positive enough, though clearly not an overtly 'pleased to know you buddy' one. Not really all that surprising though given the circumstances, still at least it wasn't one of those limp, clammy handshakes that give you the shudders and makes you want to wipe your palm dry on your jeans as soon as you let go.

Retrieving his hand Billy went to pull the door shut. As he yanked it closed, the hinges, rusty through lack of use creaked in protest then let out an almighty cracking noise.

"Don't worry," Jake said laughing, "It does that, never fallen off… Not yet anyways."

Not waiting to see if Billy found his lame attempt at humor funny, he slammed the column shift into drive and punched the gas pedal, the V8 engine snarled in response. The surge of power to the rear wheels causing the old '87 Chevy Fleetside to snake its way along shoulder. As it ran over the rumble strip, the body briefly drummed and vibrated before it lurched its way back onto the highway.

It being his truck, Jake felt obliged to talk first.

"So, where you looking to get to?" he enquired as casually as he could so as not to initiate a protracted dialog.

Billy shrugged, "Kinda depends which direction you're headed and how far you're going."

Jake pondered on his reply for a few moments; he didn't want to let on that he planned on going to the California coast, as he really did not want a passenger all that way, especially this one.

Half-truth time. "I'm thinking about heading down to Vegas."

"That's cool." replied Billy, "I'm looking to get to L.A, but anywhere heading in that direction would be good."

And with that the conversation promptly died. The further they drove, the more difficult it became to break the uncomfortable silence. After twenty minutes or so when an exasperated Billy couldn't stand it any longer, he blurted out what he'd been dying to say since they'd met.

"Dude, I know you know what I am. I saw it in your eyes as soon as I got in, but I gotta admit I'm confused as hell. Your smell is… well… well it's so different, it's not like any wolf I've ever come across."

Billy knew if truth be told; he'd had no dealings with any of his kind whatsoever outside of those in his old pack back in Colorado. And since being on the road if he picked up the scent of another shape shifter in a town or truck stop he made sure he stayed well downwind and avoided them at all costs. Something that had worked pretty well for him up until now.

"It's like… Well it's just… Oh hell, I don't know what I mean! It's like it's softer, if that makes any sense?"

"Yeah I even got told once it's almost feminine." Jake replied, smiling at Billy's attempt to describe his scent.

"Oh, I didn't mean anything like that." Billy quickly added, hoping he hadn't got the guy pissed.

Jake grinned for a second then responded. "It's okay, I know what you mean," He glanced back over, "So I'm guessing you've never come across a cougar before then?"

"Holy Hell… You're a cat?"

Stunned and rendered speechless at the revelation, Billy's mouth dropped open for several seconds before it snapped shut.

The guy's naivety and his almost comical shocked reaction amused Jake, however he refrained from laughing as he had a feeling his traveling companion would simply see it as having fun poked at him, so he just nodded instead.

Once Billy had regained his composure he let out a low whistle.

"Wow! Obviously I've heard about feline shifters, but we got told they're seriously rare. One of the pack teachers I had as a kid even said they were just a myth of some of the Native American tribes."

Jake wasn't sure he liked the idea of some mutt shifter going about telling people his kind were nothing more than someone's folklore.

"Hmm, well I guess we're both figments of the imagination to most out there eh? A werewolf and a werecat, real nightmare stuff."

Billy's eyebrows furrowed and met in the middle as he tried hard to emphasize the disdain in his voice.

"When I was with the pack we were taught that we should always be proud of our shape shifter heritage, and that werewolves are just the invention of superstitious European peasants and Hollywood scriptwriters."

He then went quiet as he decided he'd probably come across more like some prissy school mistress than a proud wolf shape shifter.

Jake shrugged. Great, this guy really needed to lighten up and find himself a sense of humor, and that coming from him that was saying something.

"Fine! Shape shifters then, I'm not gonna get all bent outta shape over it. Far as I'm concerned it's just semantics. But I am interested in to why you keep referring to your pack in the past tense; I thought with you wolves the whole pack thing was for life?"

As he glanced back over, he both saw and sensed Billy become uncomfortable.

"Hey, I didn't mean to pry buddy, just forget I asked."

"It's okay, it's all ancient history now I hope. A number of pack members decided to make their dislike of what I am very vocal and public. It ended up getting so bad I decided I would be best off away from all of them, so I left."

As he'd only known Jake for barely half an hour he decided he had no real obligation or even any desire to explain that his 'leaving' actually amounted to sneaking out of the ranch where he lived in the middle of the night. Oh yeah, 'ranch', ha-ha, good name for it, a more fitting description would be 'prison camp'. The inner compound that contained the ranch buildings had heavy duty electric gates and a guard patrol at night made up from the unmarried guys who lived in the bunkhouse. The boundary bordering the remote road that led past the ranch had an eight foot tall wire fence topped off with razor wire hidden from view behind a screen of trees and bushes. Most of the rest of the boundaries had barbed wire and post fencing. Billy always felt the only things missing were searchlight towers with machine guns.

"Of what you are?"

Jake felt he had a pretty good idea as to the answer even before he'd asked the question, and should have done the sensible thing and kept his big mouth shut. But as usual his dumb cat curiosity felt obliged to make him to pursue it nevertheless.

"Yeah, it seems my 'coming out' magically turned me into a different person to the one I'd been before anyone knew I was gay. Overnight I became some sort of social outcast to be avoided at all costs. Then it didn't take long for the snidey remarks to start, and over time they became more and more hurtful until they grew into open hostility to me by some, while others just shunned me. A few of my friends supported me to start with but it didn't take long before they too turned away as they came under more and more pressure from the others. Even my own father couldn't deal with having a faggot for a son."

Jake winced at the use of the term 'faggot' and the deep anger that spat the word out.

"Look, I'm really sorry. For people to be so judgmental like that is just wrong. I just want you to know that I'm…"

Billy held his hand up between them cutting Jake short.

"Look, no offence dude but I really don't need anyone's sympathy, or especially their pity, however well-intentioned. So can we leave it there, okay?"

He really didn't feel in the mood for some complete stranger and a straight one at that trying to be all touchy feely and 'understanding his hurt'. He still felt bitter at the world, shape shifters in general and the bigoted haters in his pack in particular for not being able to accept him for who and what he was. Well maybe not pissed at the whole world, but definitely all shape shifters, period.

Suppressing his yearning to let rip at the guy for cutting him off like that, Jake turned his attention back to the near empty highway ahead, his eyes focusing in on the point where the road disappeared into the haze just below the horizon.

Who did this guy think he was, talking to him like that anyway? And in his own truck too.

Yep, it's all going to hell in a hand basket already, you never learn do you?

God made cats solitary creatures for a reason you know, dumbass!

Just get rid of him at the next town or truck stop. He's bound to find a ride there with someone, even if he has to whore his ass to some big hairy trucker.

Sat the other side of the cab Billy realized all too late he shouldn't have snapped at the guy so, after all he did stop to give him a lift, when every other vehicle had just driven by or hooted and waved at him as they drove past. Which were all better than yesterday, when he'd had the well-aimed remnants of a burger hurled at him by some laughing brat in the back of a minibus.

It would serve him right if Jake just stopped the truck and threw him out on his ass. Time to suck it up and apologize.

"Dude, Look I'm really sorry. I shouldn't have let go at you like that."

Jake slowly shrugged his shoulders and kept his attention fixed on the road ahead.

Billy turned away and looked down at his lap.

Damn! Way to go Billy!

Maybe it would have been so much better if this guy had just simply driven past too. Billy considered asking Jake to stop the truck and let him out, but a ride sure beat walking along some desert highway in the blistering heat of the midday sun, even if no one spoke the whole way.

For his part, Jake needed a cigarette. Yes, he knew he'd promised himself to give up, and when he reached California he would most definitely stop. But none of this stress was his fault; he'd done nothing to deserve it. He grabbed a crumpled soft pack off the dash. Shaking the packet nothing appeared, so he shook it again, harder this time, still nothing. In desperation he held the battered pack between the steering wheel and his left hand and poked his right index finger through the hole in the top and felt around.

Nothing. *Great!*

"You can have these if you like, I don't really want them."

Jake looked across at Billy who held a cigarette pack in his hand. Billy went on to explain he'd bought them at the last truck stop he'd been at. Somewhat ashamedly he admitted that he'd intending to start smoking just to spite his father, but had only managed to smoke part of one before it hurt his throat and made him feel sick.

Then pulling a shiny new chrome Zippo out of his pants pocket, Billy offered it to Jake.

"You can have this too, if you like, I've got no need for it now. I bought it on impulse at the same time 'cos it looked so cool. But I didn't know you needed to put lighter fuel in it. I kept trying to get it to work until some old guy pointed out it must be empty and offered to fill it up. I think he felt a bit sorry for me."

He passed the lighter over to Jake, though it took two attempts to convince Jake he didn't want anything for the cigarettes or the lighter, and that they were a contribution towards gas costs.

Holding the lighter up Jake checked out the black silhouette print of three vultures perched on a tree branch. It certainly looked seriously cool, he could see why Billy had bought it. One handed he flipped the lighter open, and under his big thumb the wheel rasped against the flint, the resulting shower of sparks ignited the fumes with a gentle *'phut'* which became a wide yellow flame. He lit the cigarette then listened as the lighter snapped shut with a satisfyingly solid clunk.

Jake hesitated just before dropping the empty pack on the floor. He suddenly felt uncomfortable with openly displaying his increasing slobbishness by adding yet further to the detritus of his life strewn across the cab floor. Though it did seem a bit late now to pretend he hadn't been living in the truck for the past few weeks as the dash lay buried under almost as litter as the floor, and the cab had started to smell noticeably funky. So instead he scrunched the pack up and shoved it in his jeans along with the lighter.

As they drove along Billy glanced across at his companion who'd once again fallen silent. Only then did it dawn on him that the guy was actually pretty good looking. So as nonchalantly as could, he wedged his back into the corner of the cab so he could see the road and at the same time be able to check out Jake without it looking obvious, or so he hoped. Maybe the journey wouldn't be so bad after all.

Guessing Jake to be in his early to mid-thirties, that put the guy about ten years or so older than himself. Jake's distinctive hair had caught Billy's eye as soon as he'd got in, dark blond where it had been cropped short at the sides, giving way on top to longer, almost honey colored hair in a wide shaggy Mohawk, it kind of gave the impression of being like a lion's mane. Billy felt pretty sure cougars didn't have manes but it definitely suited him. The guy also sported several days' worth of stubble, not enough to make him look overly unkempt and scruffy, but enough to give him a certain ruggedness. Moving down he could see powerful arms covered in dense blond hair sticking out of a tight black tee shirt stretched over wide shoulders and a deep chest. And oh man, the guy's thighs filled his black stonewashed jeans to the point where the strained seams looked fit to burst.

However, the face held Billy's attention more than anything else, the expression seemed almost sad and lonely, and he felt sure he could see the distant, solitary look of Jake's cat form in it. The fact Jake had small ears that ever so slightly stuck out, and a wide button nose all seemed to reflect the guy's cougar side. But something about the guy made Billy think some profound underlying hurt went deep into Jake's soul, not any one thing Billy could easily put his finger on, or describe, he just felt it. Billy also suspected that the human Jake sat next to him wasn't so different to his animal side, being extremely private and independent. Shame the guy had to be straight, a shifter and flat out grouchy; otherwise, he could definitely be into older guys and this one in particular.

Up to now Billy had never given much thought about the type of guy he felt attracted to most. His virtual incarceration at the ranch meant he'd had no chance to find out up close and personal, not even so much as a clumsy fumble in a parked up car. This just left him to drool over a number of characters he'd seen on the TV in his room. And having been home tutored since his mother's death he'd never even got the chance to experience post football game showers in high school.

And every red blooded male's god given right to ceaselessly surf the net for porn had been denied him as the computer in the ranch house sat on a small desk in a corner of the large dining area for everyone to see. Plus it had some sort of filter on it that meant his access to all the marvels the World Wide Web had to offer had been restricted to the sorts of sites most ten year olds would dismiss as majorly boring. And to top it all off he had to be the only person on the planet with a smart phone whose contract didn't include internet access. It was a downright depressing thought, but considering everything not surprising, that at twenty three he was still a virgin with anyone but himself.

Oblivious to the scrutiny Jake bent his wrist back, hung his arm out of the window and flicked his cigarette butt out into the wind. Then turning to Billy threw him a much needed conversational lifeline.

"Would you like the radio on? I'm 'fraid most of my CD's and the player got stolen a while back in St Louis so I've just the original radio left."

"Yeah, sounds good."

At least they were still on speaking terms, which Billy hoped meant the journey wouldn't continue in sullen silence. The pair spent the next couple of hours tuning backwards and forwards between stations. Gradually their chatting about their favorite music and bands became slightly more animated and friendly, little by little the tense atmosphere in the cab started to ease. But not to the extent that either of them wanted to participate in any improvised sing-a-long duets.

During yet an another seemingly unending commercial break on the station they were listening to, Jake explained he'd been on the road since early morning and wanted to make South West Utah by late afternoon then find some out of the way motel to stop at so they could shift. By this point the desert would have turned greener with trees and shrubs as they climbed higher into the mountains, and hopefully they'd get the chance to run.

Billy agreed with the plan saying he too needed the release of shifting to his animal form. He also realized that the full moon that coming night would likely be responsible for the pair of them being irritable and short tempered. Well definitely him, but as for Jake… Clearly the guy didn't need any external influences to make him grumpy.

Okay, Billy knew that like all shifters the pair of them could shift whenever they liked, and if necessary could fight the need to shift on the night of the full moon. But for some reason the full moon had a compelling influence over shifters; it fired you up inside and made demands on you to shift that were so potent many couldn't fight it, and most didn't want to resist it, happy to totally immerse themselves in the freedom and delight of their animal form.

However, he remembered all too clearly one full moon night about three years ago when after yet another blazing row with his father he'd refused to shift and run with the pack, instead locking himself in his room. As the night progressed the urge to shift tore at him, turning him ever more aggressive and maddened with rage. Shortly after midnight, he literally started bouncing off the walls as he threw himself at them in blind fury, anything standing in his way falling victim to a frenzy of destruction.

In the morning he woke up on the floor to find he'd completely trashed his room. Hardly anything had survived intact, from the smallest of shattered toys to the shredded mattress and bed linen. It hadn't been so much what he'd done that worried him, but the fact his memory of what had gone on during the frenzy of destruction remained ominously blank. How could he have caused all that damage and not be aware of having done it? But one look at the bloodied mess of shattered and swollen knuckles on his hands that would need a shift to heal confirmed that he alone had been responsible for the devastation that surrounded him.

Amazingly his old man didn't blow a blood vessel when he surveyed the damage that including furniture smashed to matchwood and gaping holes in the drywall panels where sconces had been torn from their mountings, leaving power cords hanging down like dead snake's tongues from the holes. After silently looking around the room nodding, he simply told Billy to give him a list of everything that needed replacing before walking away.

As Billy's father reached the door he turned, and waving his finger for emphasis addressed Billy, "And now you have some idea of what you will be ultimately capable of once you're taught how to channel your anger properly."

With that he walked off ignoring Billy's pleas for further explanation.

Since that night he'd asked his father on numerous occasions what he'd meant, but each time his father refused to elaborate further apart from saying that a time would come when the right person would make themselves known to Billy and teach him what he needed to know. Billy filed the memory away again at the back of his mind; happy to forget it as he was so excited about shifting and didn't want to depress himself thinking about his father or the pack.

When you ran free under a full moon in your animal form something very special, almost magical happened, a feeling that wasn't there when you shifted at any other time. And for the first time ever he would get to get the chance to run without either his father or some other wolf keeping a close watch on him, controlling where he went and what he done. His old man may have well saved all the effort and just harnessed him to a running line in the compound.

Billy spotted the road sign for the town first, saying that he reckoned Milton sounded like the kind of place that ought to have a motel. Jake agreed it had to be worth a look, plus he needed gas soon. Out in the middle of nowhere open gas stations could be few and far between, many having gone bust and been abandoned. As such he didn't like dropping much below half a tank if he could help it. Exiting the highway they took off down the two lane blacktop that led towards the town.

A mile or so on they spotted an old weathered billboard advertising the delights of the '7 Oaks Motel'. Its claim to fame being that it professed to be the 'cleanest in town'. Jake said they'd still check the place out, although judging by the state of the hoarding he didn't hold out much hope of it still being in business. As they approached the outskirts of town they came across a much smaller wooden roadside sign for the same motel and a gas station which looked somewhat newer, raising their hopes of the place being open.

At first glance Milton appeared to be typical small town America, but then as they looked closer the signs of significant decline which had obviously started a good few decades back could be clearly seen every-where. On the sides of brick built commercial buildings, the painted on advertisements for businesses long since gone had succumbed to the sun and weather, leaving them almost unreadable. A number of empty store windows still sported yellowed and faded 'closing down', 'everything must go' sale banners.

A good majority of the houses had an air of sad neglect about them, their peeling paint and unkempt front yards all contributing to the overall appearance of a town that had hit hard times. The whole place had a tired, shabby feeling to it, almost as if the people there had simply given up.

It seemed that even commercial developers had taken one look at Milton and deemed the place not worth investing in. And so it had escaped the usual plethora of strip malls full of used car dealerships, gas stations, fast food outlets and discount warehouse stores gracing its outskirts.

Driving further into the town itself an eclectic assortment of mis-matched buildings bordered the typically wide Main Street, in front of these stood parked a collection of mostly older cars and pickups. Out front of the stores weeds grew freely in the sidewalks that consisted of cracked concrete and herringbone pattern bricks, the later obviously from a more affluent time in the town's past. On the sidewalks people stood or sat around in two's or three's, all talking about nothing of any great consequence, as they so often do in small towns.

Billy watched through the open passenger window, as heads turned to look at the unknown truck as it drove past. Jake scowled behind his sunglasses. He just out-and-out hated the whole small town thing where you're born, get schooled for a while, marry some local girl, and then slog your guts out until the day you drop, when they planted you under the sun baked ground in some cemetery on the edge of town. Just like so many generations of your kin before you, and the ones that are destined to follow after you.

As they approached the sheriff's office near the center of town, they spotted two deputies who looked to be in their early thirties sporting marine style haircuts leaning against one of the two police cruisers parked outside. As they passed by the deputies turned and followed the pickup's progress.

"Sure hope they're not gonna hassle us," remarked Billy.

Jake grunted and said that he wanted to stop at a store and buy some food and drink, plus he needed cigarettes, but not wanting to risk any potential closer contact with the police maybe they should just carry on to the motel.

Billy nodded in agreement; they didn't need to eat now as hopefully they'd get to feed later as there would likely be something to hunt down.

Just before the sidewalks finished and the buildings started to die out at the far side of town Jake spotted a small rundown looking general store on the right, he pulled over and parallel parked in front of it.

"I'll just dive in there quickly." He said pointing to the store door, "I don't think the police are interested in us or they'd been up behind us by now."

He walked out the store five minutes later carrying a brown paper bag containing a few groceries, a carton of cigarettes and two chilled bottles of Coca Cola, only to be confronted by the sight of a police cruiser parked slantways across the front of the truck. One of the deputies from earlier stood leant against the pickup's passenger door looking through the open window. Jake could see the guy's right hand resting on top of his gun, the holster's thumb break already unsnapped, giving him a fast straight draw.

Shit!

They really didn't need this, and he especially didn't need it, and with that his heart sank. As he approached the pickup, things suddenly became a whole lot more complicated, for the underlying scent coming off the deputy was distinctly wolf. Either hearing or sensing Jake's presence behind him the deputy turned and moved away a little from the pickup's door so he had a clear line of sight of both Jake and Billy, his right hand never leaving his pistol grip.

Jake could see this going down one of two ways, either the 'Howdy doody fellow shifters, real nice making your acquaintance, now you have a nice day y'all' way. Or more likely, it would be trouble, with a capital 'T', especially once the deputy realized he was a cat. For even in the big, bad world of grown up shifters who should know better, cats and mutts didn't play well together, to the extent open hostility often occurred between the species. So much for minority groups sticking together for the common good. Still what could you expect from canines he mused? Any species that went around deliberately sniffing each other's butt holes to see what they'd eaten for breakfast had some serious issues.

He walked around the back of the pickup to the driver's door, at which point the police cruiser's passenger opened and another officer got out. Going by the uniform, this one had to be the local sheriff, a stockily built guy probably in his early fifties with greying hair in a buzz cut, as he put his campaign hat on Jake could see the underarms of his tan shirt were already dark with the day's sweat. The mean look on his face and the absence of a goodies basket suggested this wasn't a visit from the town welcome committee. Jake opened his door, placed the grocery bag on the seat next to Billy and climbed in, but before he could close the door behind him the sheriff moved into the way and pulled it wide open.

"So what you two boys doing in my town then?"

Jake turned to face the sheriff and just about stopped himself from physically recoiling.

Whoa!

The guy had breath that could drop a charging steer. Not only that, the son of a bitch was another wolf. And going by his attitude and bearing he had to be either a pack alpha, or some wannabe with delusions of grandeur, hence the 'my town' line.

But despite what he felt about these two local representatives of law enforcement, Jake sure as hell didn't need any trouble with some bunch of hick shifters in the middle of nowhere. Not a situation that would ever have a good outcome.

Sensing Jake's discomfort, Billy answered the sheriff, explaining they'd come from Colorado (partially true, as he had) and were headed for California, and they just wanted to get to the motel, have a shower and get some sleep before heading off in the morning.

The sheriff stood staring at Jake, then looked at Billy, "Your friend with the pretty hair here a mute then boy?"

Jake could feel his adrenalin levels climbing and his fuse shortening, but he knew the asshole would keep probing until he pressed the right buttons and evoked a reaction, so he needed to keep his temper bottled-up at all costs and hoped the guy got bored quickly.

"No Sir... I can talk just fine, didn't wanna be rude and butt in."

The sheriff leant in even closer, his face now right in front of Jake's and inhaled deeply through his nose, his eyes flashed open wide and a surprised look shot across his face, only for it to leave again just as quick. His eyes narrowed to slits, the disdain on his face now unmistakably clear.

Jake managed to glean some little enjoyment from the fact that it had taken shit for breath a good while to work out he was a feline, something that would no doubt embarrass the guy as it made him appear slow witted. Maybe he could blame it on allergies blocking his nose up thought Jake.

"Y'all be gone from here by lunchtime tomorrow." He jabbed his finger in Jake's face, "You hear me now boy? I don't wanna see you two back here in town again."

Jake envisaged the sheriff standing in the middle of Main Street in Stetson and spurs opening his musical pocket watch and counting down the final seconds to high noon.

Then almost as an afterthought the sheriff added, "I won't tell you not to run tonight, as that just wouldn't be right. But mind you don't stray too far from the motel."

Billy replied, "Yes Sir, we'll stay close by and be long gone by lunchtime."

Billy and Jake nodded in unison just to confirm their clear understanding.

They sat and watched as the sheriff and deputy walked back to their cruiser. As the deputy reached the driver's door he turned to face them, put two fingers to his eyes then pointed straight at them, the fact he would be watching them clearly spelt out. With that he got into the cruiser which then reversed out across the road, lurched to a halt, turned around and headed off at speed back into town.

Jake slammed his door shut so hard it made the open window glass rattle. He felt sure the sheriff's stench had been permanently ingrained on him and his clothes. Damn, he really needed a shower now, maybe two.

"You know they were both shifters don't you?" Billy asked.

"Yeah, I caught the deputy's scent as I walked past him, though once in the truck I could only smell the sheriff."

"Yeah talk about overpowering. You reckon he's got distemper?" Billy grimaced comically, "And that deputy acted kinda weird too. You know, like real creepy weird. Just kept asking me what city you and I came from and why we were here, when I told him Colorado Springs, he started going on about city kids thinking they're so much better."

Billy held his index finger up to the side of his head and drew circles with it, indicating he thought the deputy to be pretty much bugged out.

After managing a halfhearted laugh, Jake took the two Coke bottles out of the bag and passed them over to Billy.

"Fraid they didn't have anything stronger." he explained, the tension in his voice still clearly evident.

He then pointed at the glove compartment.

"Bottle opener's in there... somewhere."

Billy rummaged about in the clutter that filled the glove box to overflowing and eventually produced the bottle opener holding it up in a mock show of triumph; he flicked the caps off and passed one of the bottles back over.

Holding the bottle to his lips Jake let the dark, sweet drink run into his mouth, it bubbled and frothed against his tongue and the roof of his mouth, as he swallowed it felt cool and soothing against his dry throat. Leaning back against his door Billy very nearly dropped his bottle as he gawked open mouthed at the sight of Jake's Adam's apple bobbing up and down as he gulped down his soda. It had never crossed his mind that somebody could look sexy drinking.

No, No, No!

He really needed to stop having those sorts of thoughts about the guy, he didn't even like him that much.

Once they'd left the town behind them, the mood in the truck lightened again, and in a little over a mile they came to the motel and a neighboring gas station.

"I'll get gas now rather than in the morning," said Jake, "I don't want to be here a minute longer than I have to, and I definitely don't need any more dealings with Sheriff Shit-kicker."

Billy nodded his wholehearted agreement with that sentiment. He'd never had any contact with the police before in his life, and going by this experience he definitely didn't want any again.

Jake slowed the pickup and pulled over onto the gas station forecourt. As he approached its three rusty and mismatched pumps he heard the classic 'ding ding' of the forecourt bell as he ran over the thin black rubber tube that stretched out from both sides of the central cement island the pumps stood on. On stopping, he caught sight through the passenger door window of tattered handwritten signs wrote in broad black permanent marker that were stuck to each of the pumps with several layers of yellowing Scotch tape. Lifting himself up on the seat he leaned over to read the notes.

NO SELF SERV

NO CHEKS

He smirked, not just at the misspelling, and the fact it looked like a three year old had scrawled it, but underneath someone had added in much smaller, very neat handwriting

Sorry no credit cards taken

Thank you

Then in the very bottom right corner they'd drawn a tiny flower on a curved stalk; this addition had a distinct female touch to it, definitely not the work of some hairy assed tractor mechanic.

Sitting back down he caught sight of a skinny young girl of maybe eighteen or nineteen stood in the store doorway watching them. Jake stared back at her out of his window for a good few seconds. When it became obvious she wasn't going to do anything, he decided to get out of the truck to go find someone who would serve him.

As he stepped down out of the pickup the girl ran gawkily from the store, her red plastic sandals slapping against the ground, she then disappeared into the adjacent auto repair shop. Hoping she'd gone off to get someone, he leant back against the truck door, crossed his legs and folded his arms in a display of mock pique. It then occurred to him that in all likelihood the flowers and neat handwriting on the signs were hers.

A minute or so later she re-appeared alongside a thickset middle aged man in grimy, oil stained brown bib overalls, his face almost matching his overalls in terms of ingrained dirt and grease. The mechanic hadn't even made it to within ten feet of the pumps before the pungent aroma of stale sweat, chewing tobacco and gear oil coming off the guy assaulted Jake's nose.

As the man reached Jake he spat out a dark brown gob of saliva on the ground by the rear tire of the truck then wiped his shovel sized hands on a piece of rag hanging out of his hip pocket.

"Yeah?"

The guy's attitude and tone didn't exactly radiate warmth and hospitality.

Jeez, what gave with the people around here?

Jake thought it would be more fitting if they changed the name of the town from Milton to Misery.

"Fill it up with regular, please?"

Jake deliberately added and emphasized the 'please', he had been brought up to be polite and he'd be damned if this bunch of hayseeds were going to drag him down to their level. As the man started to pump the gas, Jake looked back over to the repair shop where the girl still stood by the large wooden doors, her attention equally divided between watching Jake and looking down at her feet as she drew patterns in the dust with the toes of her sandals.

Out of the corner of his eye a sudden movement caught his attention, turning his head towards the store he saw the deputy from their earlier encounter with the sheriff step into the doorway from the relative darkness of the store. He could see the guy eating something, cramming the remnants of it into his mouth he chewed a few times then still with his mouth full called out, emitting a spray of crumbs.

"Hey! Stacey-Leanne. C'mere and fetch us another of those jelly donuts."

Jake watched the girl dejectedly trudge back to the store. He could see her thin, pale green summer dress looked faded and the tattered hem that finished several inches above her knees exposed spindle like legs ingrained with dirt. Reaching the store she attempted to get through the doorway back inside, but the deputy refused to move aside. Instead as she started to squeeze past he thrust his body outwards pressing his groin and stomach against her, pinning her against the door frame.

In an attempt to break away from his unwelcome attentions she tried to move back out from the doorway. But as she managed to struggle free he grabbed her pitifully thin upper arm and pulled her back to him. This time she didn't try to resist, she just stood there, head bowed in silent submission. Judging by her reactions Jake decided this had to be a scene that got played out all too often.

Poor kid. Christ, he wouldn't be surprised if the asshole didn't turn out to be her cousin or even her brother-in-law.

"Thirty five bucks."

The words jerked Jake back from his thoughts. As he pulled a wad of bills from his pocket he instinctively glanced at the pump and noticed the gas came to just under thirty four dollars. As he counted the money out he couldn't resist a silent chuckle at the guy's nerve to round up the price to the nearest five bucks. Once he'd paid, the mechanic tucked the money into his bib pocket then walked off back to the repair shop without saying another word, or even bothering to look over at the girl. Jake turned back to the store and saw the girl had gone but the deputy still stood there, now leant against the front of the store, his arms folded across his chest as he glared over at Jake.

Not your fight buddy, just get in the truck and go.

But somehow, he couldn't shake off the terrible feeling that what he'd witnessed wasn't just for the immediate amusement of the deputy, and later as mental stimulus while the creep jacked off, it had also clearly been some perverse attempt at a show of dominance for Jake's benefit.

Getting back into the truck Jake slammed the door shut in anger and rested his arm on the window opening.

He turned to Billy, "You know, I'm solely tempted just to drive on to the next town, but it could easily be another two or three hours to somewhere big enough to have a motel and then we'll likely be back down in desert again."

Billy agreed they were pretty much stuck here.

As Jake went to start the engine someone forcibly grabbed his left forearm that rested on the door. Looking at the hand he followed the arm back up the rolled up tan shirt sleeve to the face of the deputy. The sneer from earlier was still there, but now a real malevolence could be seen behind it.

"Just you remember I'm watching you two city boys. Watching you real good."

City boys? Didn't Billy say the guy had been going on about city boys earlier?

Jake stifled a laugh, why did this guy have such a hang up with people from cities?

"Yeah, we remember."

The open sarcasm in Jakes voice clearly hadn't been appreciated as the next second he felt the cold steel of a gun barrel rammed hard against his left temple. The deputy carried on pushing until he'd forced Jake to turn his head away and face straight ahead.

Bad move that Jacob, should have kept your big mouth shut.

"I'm in a mind just to shoot you both here and now. And there ain't no one gonna miss you or make any fuss about it this time." Threatened the deputy.

Jake guessed the deputy carried a Glock 22 and knew only too well that even a shifter couldn't survive a .40 caliber hollow point to the head.

As much as it peeved Jake he knew the guy was right. And with the sheriff being a shifter there would be no reports filed, so with nothing on record there would be no questions asked. Within in a few hours he, Billy, and the truck would have all magically disappeared, never to be seen or heard of again.

Whoa! Hang on, 'this time'?

What exactly did that mean? Did this guy have previous for offing people for no good reason?

Okay, in case he did, Jake needed to suck it up big time.

"We know you could Sir, but we aren't out to bother anyone and I didn't mean any disrespect to you. All we want to do is get to the motel, sleep and be gone first thing in the morning, like we told the sheriff."

The deputy lifted the butt of the gun up, so now when he twisted the barrel around against Jake's head the front sight dug into the skin too.

"You want me to let you go? Maybe I will if you beg me real nice. Or maybe I won't."

Despite Jake's lightning fast reactions he had no chance of getting out of this one. The deputy still had a firm grip on Jake's forearm, and Jake knew the split second the deputy felt his arm muscles tense there would be a good chance of the guy pulling the trigger believing Jake to be about to try something. Even if he did managed to duck and get his head clear any shot would likely hit Billy instead.

"Please, just let us go." Jake pleaded pitifully.

A hollow laugh came from the deputy.

"Guess I should let you go then, before you piss your pants. You about to piss yourself aren't you boy?"

If it got them out of this mess Jake would do just that. Hell, he'd done a lot worse in his time.

"Yes Sir."

The deputy stood there savoring every last cruel moment of his intimidation of Jake. He then dragged the gun across Jake's temple so he could see the indented circular red welt left by the pressure of the barrel against Jake's skin and the small crescent shaped graze caused by the front sight. Slowly he ran the tip of his tongue across the inside of his top lip then back again, letting out a small excited sigh through his partially open mouth on the last pass.

Holstering his gun, the deputy turned and sauntered off back to the store, nodding and mumbling to himself.

Goddamned city kids coming into our school showing off, trying to impress everyone.

Well you ain't so big now are you?

You gone got a good ole country ass whoopin'.

Made you bleed and made you cry.

And now you gonna go running off home to your momma.

We sure showed them didn't we Jabbo?

Coming into our school thinking they're all so high and mighty cos they come from the city.

I whooped these ones real good. Just like you always saying we should eh Jabbo?

But I remembered like you told me, not to do these ones so bad we have to go hide them in the dump too.

I done good this time didn't I Jabbo?

Jake's brow furrowed so much his eyes reduced to slits.

"Yeah fucking hilarious... Asshole!" he muttered once the deputy had disappeared back into the gas station store and well out of earshot.

He didn't like being called 'boy' at the best of times and especially by someone the same age as him.

"Do you think he really would have shot us?" Billy asked, his voice having gone all shaky.

Jake opened his eyes fully again and looked across at Billy. The guy's scared expression said it all. Billy obviously needed some reassurance.

So once more Jake done what he excelled at, and lied. "Na, he was just messing with us. I reckon it gave the bastard a boner too. I'll guarantee you he's nothing more than a bully. And he has a badge and a gun to make him feel even more of a man."

"Yeah you're probably right." replied Billy. "I can't believe how cool you were with him pointing his gun at your head; I would have freaked or shit myself for sure."

Jake could see he hadn't totally convinced Billy, who kept worrying his bottom lip with his teeth. Billy then went and clinched it with a, "Do you think we should go Jake, just get outta here and find somewhere else to stay?"

Although it would be the wisest move, Jake wasn't ready to let some dumbfuck of a local deputy drive him out of town with his tail between his legs, so to speak. His pride simply wouldn't let him give in that readily.

"I think he's had his fill of humiliating me." Jake replied trying to sound reassuring. "Besides, once we're in the motel and out of his sight I'm sure he'll forget all about us and go find something or someone else to amuse himself with."

As they pulled up outside the motel Jake's heart really started to sink, he felt it wouldn't take much more for it to disappear without trace beneath the dark waves of his despair. Outwardly the place appeared to be as rundown as both the dilapidated sign they saw for it on their way into town and the adjacent gas station. Jake also seriously doubted its assertion to be the 'cleanest in town'. But as it appeared to be the only one actually in town, its cleanliness became a moot point.

The long, low single story concrete block building comprised the office and a string of ten rooms leading off to the right. Their orange doors and dark brown frames that faced directly onto the parking lot had weathered to a dull matt finish. At least no one could complain about false advertising. Honestly, could his day really get any shitier? Oh well, on the upside at least the sign said open, and there was always a slim chance the rooms would be okay. He hoped.

Billy looked at the sign in the window beside the reception door that proclaimed,

ALL ROOMS $40 / NIGHT

Shoving his hand into his jeans he pulled out a small wad of cash. Holding it in his lap, he looked down and gently let a soft, slow sigh out through his nose, he reckoned at most he had a little over three hundred and fifty dollars left. In total he'd managed to find nearly four hundred in his father's wallet and bedroom, plus he'd got eighty bucks for his mountain bike at the truck stop, he had asked for a hundred, but the guy instantly beat him down and Billy caved in within seconds. He'd never had money of his own, as his father deemed he didn't need an allowance. Anything he needed like clothes or books had been bought for him. So he needed to find a job, any job, as soon as he reached California, what little money he had left wouldn't last him more than a week or so at best.

Glancing across Jake caught Billy's reaction to the amount of cash he had in his hand and guessed that the all the guy's worldly possessions were in the bag he'd slung in the back of the truck and in his hand. Putting two and two together, Billy had obviously left the ranch in one hell of a hurry, the result of which meant the guy had to be well on his way to being broke. There had to be a whole lot more to the pack story than Billy was letting on.

The next step would be a big one for Jake, did he get his own room and the two of them shift separately, or should they stick together for the night. Basically it boiled down to which would be the lesser of the two evils. Shift with a virtual stranger so they could protect each other, or shift alone out in the woods.

Considering what just happened with Deputy Dipshit at the gas station he didn't feel too keen to go it on his own for once. Plus a little voice in his head kept hammering away, '*Remember Jake, no man is an island, even you.'* Sure Billy had some issues, but that said they were without doubt nowhere near the scale of his own, plus his gut told him Billy seemed genuine and all being well, trustworthy.

Decision made.

Now he just had to hope he wouldn't live to regret it, or not live as the case may be.

"I'll get a twin room, that way we can split the cost. I don't know about you, but I really need to shift tonight, try work off some of the aggression in me. So being together will also make shifting safer too."

"Thanks, dude." said a now much relieved Billy. "It definitely makes sense to keep an eye out for each other."

Extracting a crumpled twenty from his wad he passed it to Jake who headed off to the motel office.

Jake's offer to shift together had taken Billy by surprise, especially after their stormy start, but the guy had been right about it being the sensible thing to do, the change left a shifter totally vulnerable for a good hour or so. In the pack they'd shifted in groups so there were always fully changed shifters either in their animal or their human forms who could protect the ones shifting.

Billy wondered how cats being solitary animals protected themselves; he guessed they must hide away in their own secret dens, or if they were travelling having to hide in strange empty basements or abandoned buildings, maybe even in caves. Although over the past few months when the rest of the pack shunned him he'd felt lonelier than ever, but he'd never physically been alone until he'd left the ranch. There'd always been other pack members close by, or at least within earshot, he just couldn't imagine what it would feel like to be that alone. It then dawned on him that it would be that way for him now, at least for the foreseeable future.

As Jake walked up to the office he noticed that what looked suspiciously like a chunk of automobile gearbox casing propping the door open. Though someone had painted it white and stuck some plastic flowers in the top in an effort to make it just that little bit more stylish. Once inside a quick glance around confirmed his worst fears. It seemed like he'd travelled back in time and had ended up on the set of some bad nineteen fifties/sixties Sci-Fi 'B' movie. Now it just needed a man to enter stage right in a rubber suit spray painted silver and wearing an oversized helmet complete with the obligatory eye slit pretending to be a robot.

But there were no robots, aliens or flying saucers, instead a woman in her fifties with a pinched face and a cheap local beauty salon perm sat behind the imitation wood grain front desk that separated the office in two. Its faded gold quilted front had definitely seen better days, though probably none of those had been in the last twenty years. Without even bothering to look up at Jake, she carried on thumbing through a magazine and talking on the phone.

"Listen Ruby honey I have to go for a moment, there's someone here. Don't you go away now 'cos I need to tell you what Nancy Bishop's daughter has been and got herself into, and with the youngest of the Maguire boys too. You know the one... Yeah that's him, the one that's not quite right in the head."

With that she carefully put the handset down and briefly peered over her tortoiseshell cat eye glasses at Jake before looking back down at her magazine again.

"Hi, twin room for the night."

"No twins, just doubles." The woman answered curtly before she licked the tip of her index finger, rubbed it once with her thumb and turned another page with deliberate slowness.

Jake scowled, "Okay, if that's all you've got we'll take a double."

Looking up again she sighed, her face showing her annoyance at the intrusion into her conversation. She turned the register round for him to sign and tapped it with a fingernail.

"You both have to sign."

Jeez! Fine!

He shook his head. Had he ended up in some kind of personal purgatory? Jake Palmer's very own living hell, destined to spend the rest of his miserable life in crappy little towns getting shit off everyone?

No, he had to think positive; everything would work out just fine in the end. He just needed to get to California, that's all, no biggie.

After walking to the doorway and gesturing for Billy to join him he returned to the front desk.

"That'll be forty for the room, and it's two dollars each for towels if you want them, TV takes quarters."

Jake handed over the money and took possession of the room key that hung off a chipped pale blue plastic tag with a large embossed gold number 8 on one side, it reminded him of a worn out rectangular casino chip. The woman reached down then passed him two virtually threadbare white towels that smelt heavily of cheap detergent. He handed them to Billy, plonked the room key on top and stomped off back to the truck in order to park it outside their room.

Still fuming from his encounter with the motel's own living embodiment of a gorgon Jake threw his and Billy's gear bags onto the bed then unzipping his pulled out his toiletry bag, some clean boxers and another pair of black jeans, grabbed one of the towels and made for the bathroom. His plan being to scrub himself clean of the sheriff's stench he felt still clung to him and his clothes.

However, the sight of the bathroom left him doubting he'd be feeling clean anytime soon. The vanity sink set in a chipped and worn faux marble laminate countertop had a rust ring in the bottom from the continually dripping faucet. The once white plastic shower curtain had yellowed with age along the bottom where it hung in the stained tub. Several pale green tiles had at some stage in the past come away from the walls and been stuck back with silicone caulk that had oozed out round the edges and never been trimmed off.

If he had a pair of flip flops with him he'd be wearing them in the tub, and the thought of what lurked under the drain strainer made him shudder. But he needed to get clean, he felt so dirty. He stripped, had a pee then reluctantly climbed into the tub and showered.

Three washes later Jake felt almost clean again, he dried himself off then cleaned his teeth twice, just to be sure. After a frantic hopping about fit trying to avoid treading on the cockroach that had almost run over his foot, he put his clean clothes on then went back into the bedroom congratulating himself for not screaming like a little girl at the evidently premeditated killer cockroach attack.

He looked at Billy, smirked and nodded back towards the bathroom.

"All yours. Enjoy."

"Thanks dude." replied Billy.

Getting off the bed Billy grabbed the remaining towel, bundled his toiletries and clean boxers on top of it then headed to the bathroom stopping briefly at the door to look back at the still smirking Jake. Why the smug grin? What did he know? Deciding to stop being so paranoid, he walked in and closed the door behind him.

Jake waited, sure enough the expected 'Urgh! That's disgusting!' came from behind the bathroom door.

Hmm, just wait 'til Mr Roach comes back with his buds, Jake mused.

Still grinning he lit a cigarette with his shiny new lighter, and finding the old pack in his pocket screwed it up and threw it at the round metal waste bin, which made a satisfying metallic clang as the pack hit the side. Looking around he spotted a matchbook in one of the nightstand ashtrays, he picked it up, dark green and red lettering on the front proudly advertised 'The Hill Top Hotel Chesterfield'. He wondered if the '7 Oaks Motel', in glorious uptown Milton even had its own matchbooks let alone seven oak trees.

Putting the matches back he went and sat down on the doorstep, and resting his elbows on his drawn up knees he supported his chin on the heel of one of his palms. Looking across the parking lot, he could see where dirt and windblown litter had accumulated in the corners of the cement block curbing, while the profusion of scrubby looking weeds bordering the lot had trapped numerous bigger pieces of garbage. Looking out towards the road he could see a black power cord coiling its way up the neon sign, the last foot of which hung out limply from the rusty white pole like a snake with its back broken. And except for some obviously abandoned sedan sitting on four flat tires in a corner of the lot, there was just his and one other vehicle parked there. As the other vehicle wasn't there when they'd turned up, he assumed it had to belong to someone just arrived. He felt a little disappointed to think he and Billy weren't the only guests anymore.

Just a few short months before the death of his folks in a propane gas explosion and resulting fire that left their Kansas farmhouse nothing more than a pile of shattered lumber and gray ash, he'd left the farm and small town America for the lure of a life surfing and bumming around in California. Once settled in on the coast, he'd sworn on everything any twenty three year old holds true that he'd never again be found in any backwater shithole. But once again he found himself in a crappy little town along with the hicks, the heat and the dust. What depressed him more than anything was the promise he'd made himself all those years ago stood little chance of being honored anymore. Not now he had no real control over his life, thanks to his paymasters.

And to make things worse, he knew exactly what was coming next. When his stupid mind got itself into this sort of funk the memories of how he'd ended up like this in the first place always came slamming back to haunt him. He lit a second cigarette off the first one, rested his chin back on his hand and waited for the waking nightmare to start once more.

True to form, the memory of his parent's burial service in Garden City came back to him, a surreal and almost indecently quick affair that had consisted of a single coffin.

As the funeral home owner Mr Paulson had attempted to explain to him before the service started. "I'm really sorry son but because of the intense heat of the fire there… err… Well, there wasn't much left besides ash."

Paulson stood well over six feet six tall and his long gaunt face had an unseasonal pallor to it. He put his hand, with its boney fingers and long well manicured fingernails, on Jake's shoulder and patted it before continuing, "Well, we all thought it for the best if they shared a single coffin."

He removed his hand. "But they are next to your grandparents here," he gestured across over the coffin to a pair of adjacent headstones. "Your grandpa had the foresight to buy four plots some little while before he passed over."

Then with just the merest hint of a smile he added, "Which of course still leaves one spare plot."

Jake looked up into the guy's face, but before he could ask anything the minister standing next to Paulson added, "Of course you will want to be with the rest of your family when the Good Lord calls."

Jake again tried to speak but not being able to think of any words to convey what he wanted to say he simply stayed silent.

The undertaker held his arm up and tapped his wristwatch, his fingernail making a chinking noise on the glass, "Shall we Minister? We do have Miss Monkton at three thirty."

By now, a small group stood gathered round the grave. They comprised of the minister, four pallbearers and Paulson, two neighboring farmers with their wives, plus Jake who stood there still forlornly clutching a ten dollar bunch of flowers he'd bought from a supermarket on his forty minute walk across town from the Amtrak station to the cemetery.

As he had no idea where his maternal grandparents or his two uncles and aunts lived there hadn't been any way he could let them know about the funeral. So he had no family to turn to share his grief or comfort him. He'd never felt so alone in his life as he did right there stood in that edge of town cemetery with its patchy brown grass scorched from the long summer sun.

After the twenty minute service when everyone had shook his hand said 'What a darned shame it had been' and wandered off, he took two of the larger flowers from the bunch he'd bought and left one on each of his grandparent's graves. Sitting down with his back against his grandpa's headstone he watched as a guy with a mini digger filled his parent's grave in. When finished the gravedigger took Jake's flowers and carefully placed them on the mound of bare earth. He nodded respectfully to the grave, and then at Jake, who nodded back. The guy climbed back onto the digger and Jake watched as he drove off the grass onto the roadway. Once the noise from the engine had faded, and he sat there in silence it finally sunk in that everyone he'd ever truly loved had gone out of his life forever and he'd never see them or be able to hug them ever again. He wondered at what age you became too old to be considered an orphan.

After leaving the cemetery he found his way to his parent's lawyer's office in order to sign papers regarding the sale of the farm and the transfer of money to his bank account. He thanked Ed Morley the lawyer dealing with his parent's estate for arranging the funeral and buying his return train ticket. He also found out that Morley had gone to college with Jake's father and the pair had both met their wives there. Morley offered Jake a room for a couple of days if he wanted to meet up with old acquaintances, but Jake politely declined the offer as he felt he hadn't been expected to say yes. Anyway, nothing remained for him here anymore; he just wanted to get back to California. He regarded that to be his home now.

Jake had walked almost clear across town when a dark colored delivery van pulled up to the curb some way ahead of him. He watched bemused as two guys both for some reason wearing black beanies in the summer heat got out and struggled to unload a large cardboard box, which they placed on the sidewalk between the front passenger door of the van and the side door. The two guys then unloaded a second similarly large box which they stood the other side of the door nearest to the approaching Jake.

Having already lost interest in the unloading of the van he went back to his thoughts once more. He nudged his backpack strap further up his shoulder and started debating whether he should buy another pack of batteries for his Walkman in case the spare ones he had with him didn't last the three hour wait for his train and the twenty seven hour journey back to L.A. He'd just made up his mind he should buy at least a couple more packs and get some food for the journey when he reached the van.

As he walked past the first box and drew level with the open side door he turned his head and out of renewed curiosity glanced into the van just as the two guys who'd unloaded the boxes lunged at him grabbing his arms. Before he could get his head round what was happening, they'd thrown him inside the van causing him to land hard on the floor face down, his fast reflexes just managing to protect his face from connecting with the ridged metal floor. And as for the world outside, the two large boxes either side of the door effectively hid Jake's abduction from casual view, leaving no one any the wiser.

Jake attempted to get up, but a guy in a black ski mask shoved him back down, the force rolled Jake over resulting in him ending up on his back. The guy in the mask then pinned Jake down, while behind his head Jake heard the thud of the sliding door slamming shut.

"Go! Go! Go!" A voice near him barked.

Hitting the gas the driver swung the van out into traffic, the squeal of the van's tires quickly followed by the aggressive honking of several car horns. As the van swerved wildly a second time another masked assailant who'd been attempting to pull a hood down over the struggling Jake's head lost his balance and went flying, cursing loudly as he crashed heavily into the rear doors. In the confusion Jake heard someone shout "For Christ's sake hold him still! And get that fucking hood on him!"

As Jake realized the beanies the two guys had been wearing were actually rolled up ski masks, somebody grabbed his arm and knelt on it in order to hold it out straight and still. He instantly forgot everything else going on around him as he lay there waiting to feel a bone snap in his forearm from the concentrated weight of someone kneeling on the center of it. There then followed a sharp sting on the inside of his arm by his elbow joint, and he instantly knew they'd injected him with something, but he was determined to fight whatever had been pumped into him and fight to the last.

Jake woke to find himself with a pounding headache, his nose squished up against something and a tongue that felt like a piece of carpet. Lifting his head he saw that he was in what looked suspiciously like some sort of interview room with glass smooth light gray walls and a white tiled floor. The dazzling shadow free lighting from four large recessed fluorescent lamps set in the white ceiling physically hurt his eyes to start with, making him squint and shade them with his hand.

Looking down he saw he'd been stripped completely naked, he presumed that had happened while he had been unconscious. He guessed his backpack along with his Walkman, wallet and cell phone were with his clothes, or rather he hoped so. But oddly his captors hadn't restrained him in any way, not that he felt much like getting up and strutting about butt naked. In fact he thought if he stood up he'd throw up.

Taking in his surroundings he saw he'd been sat at a large heavy looking metal table a good six feet long and four feet wide with a large bottle of water placed in centrally in front of him. His face having rested on the table whilst unconscious had obviously been responsible for the nose squashing and the small puddle of drool. There were two aluminum chairs, the one he'd been sat in and one the other side of the table. Grabbing the bottle he gulped half the water down in one go, then catching his breath looked up and spotted a pair of CCTV cameras with little red lights on mounted high up on the end walls. The only thing missing was the one-way mirror wall that they had in all the TV cop shows. Once his stomach had stopped churning over he stood up and walked to the door. He felt obliged to try the handle despite knowing full well the door would be locked. Despite yanking the handle several times the door refused to open for him, so he sat back down.

After what seemed like hours with no one coming in to question him, he began shouting at the cameras, demanding to know why they'd kidnapped him and were holding him against his will. Suspecting the cameras were being monitored he decided to get someone's attention by wedging one of the chairs under the door handle, and make them ask him to let them in. He'd still been mulling the idea over when the door burst open and two large men in dark suits, and wearing ski masks creepily patterned to look like skulls dragged him out of the room, only to dump him in an identical sized room a few doors down a long featureless corridor. In this room however the table and chairs were missing, instead it contained a stainless steel toilet, with no seat or toilet tissue, a coarse brown blanket on the floor and two more ever watchful cameras with their little red LED's glowing brightly.

He wrapped the blanket around his shoulders, had a piss, then sat down in a corner his back cattycorner against the two walls and tried to sleep. It seemed like he'd only just dozed off when the men in suits and ski masks came back and pulled him up off the floor before he'd even had chance to stand on his own. One of them tore Jake's blanket off throwing it onto the floor, as they hauled him back to the interview room he noticed they were both wearing black running shoes that looked so out place against the smartness of their suits. After they'd dumped him in the chair and left, he noticed a full water bottle had replaced the empty one he'd left on the table. Again he sat there for what felt like an eternity before the masked men returned. As they pulled him out of the chair he grabbed the water bottle from the table, but one of the men snatched it from him and threw it back on the table, they then dragged him off and once more threw him in the other room.

Over time this behavior developed into a routine of sorts, although randomly there'd be a cold TV dinner sat on the table in its plastic tray waiting for him, but no fork or spoon. He guessed they must have considered he could use them as weapons or to self-harm. So he ate with his fingers licking them and the tray clean when finished, all very caveman. But that wasn't nearly as degrading as having no toilet tissue or a sink. He wondered how bad he'd have to smell before they'd let him have a shower.

After what must have been a good thirty or maybe forty times of swapping rooms, he'd lost count a good while ago, he found himself back in the interrogation room. However, this time no food or water waited for him, instead another coarse brown blanket had appeared, this one spread over the table. As he walked around the table trying to figure out what was going on, a tinny sounding voice spoke above him. He looked up at a small white grill in the ceiling which he figured to be a loudspeaker.

"Shift now… Lie on the table and change to your animal form."

The voice didn't come across as angry or demanding; just cold and totally devoid of any emotion, something Jake considered to be much worse and a lot scarier.

Jake shouted at the loudspeaker. "Who are you? What do you want with me?"

The speaker remained silent for a few minutes, then;

"Shift to your animal form now."

"I don't know what you mean! Tell me why I'm here."

Again the speaker stayed quiet. Jake sat down and folded his arms across his chest in a petulant display of defiance.

This time it wasn't long before the two men returned. The door burst open and the first one in yanked Jake off his chair and in the same movement swung him round backwards against the wall knocking the wind out of him. Jake staggered forward only for the second one to punch him in the stomach making him double up in pain. As he stood bent over gasping for breath they kicked his legs away from under him causing him to land hard on his right hip, the impact jarring through his body.

Then as he attempted to get back up the two men grabbed him under the arms, dragging him out of the room face down and head first, his lower body weight taken on his knees. Flung through the doorway into the other room, Jake landed in a heap on the floor. He looked around for his blanket, but they'd taken even that away from him. The introduction of deliberate, measured violence and now the lack of a blanket to wrap himself in suggested either a disturbing change in their tactics, or he was being punished for his display of defiance.

Crawling into the corner he drew his legs up and looked at his bloodied knees cut and grazed by the joints in the tiled floors. He started to sob, why were they doing this to him, what had he done to them? It didn't take long before the sobbing had turned into full blown crying. He'd never hurt anyone, never done anything bad, this had to be a case of mistaken identity. Somebody else should be here, not him.

Just as he'd almost cried himself to sleep, an ear-piercing whistle filled the room, clamping his hands over his ears Jake shook his head and screamed at them to make it stop, but of course it didn't. Now even his sleep deprivation had been stepped up a notch. Eventually the whistling noise stopped. He leant back against the wall and waited for the men to drag him back to the interrogation room, but no one appeared. After sitting there for an age he started to relax his tensed body and closed his eyes once again. He so needed to sleep, even just a couple of hours would be good. But his captors had other ideas and he soon found himself hauled back into what he now regarded as an interrogation room, and he had a terrible feeling quite possibly his execution chamber too.

Once again the loudspeaker crackled into life.

"Lie on the table and shift to your animal form."

A long pause.

"Shift to your animal form now"

"I don't know what you want me to do!"

"Shift to your animal form now!" The voice had suddenly developed an angry edge to it.

"Please, tell me why I'm here."

Silence.

Okay he'd had enough of this shit. They'd brought him here for a reason, and they had been feeding him and not physically torturing him, he didn't class the roughing up earlier as torture, so he reasoned they wanted him alive. And that happened to be something he could use to his advantage.

Right! Time to get someone's attention... Big time!

Grabbing the blanket Jake upended the table so one end sat on the floor, he then wedged the table up against the wall using one of the chairs by wedging it under one of the middle legs. After a lengthy struggle which almost defeated him, he managed to tear two strips off the blanket down its length and started twisting the first into a rope, tying one end to one of the uppermost legs. He then tied a running knot eighteen inches in from the other end to form a noose. He climbed onto the chair and kneeling down on it secured the other strip of blanket around his lower legs and the chair seat holding them firm. He then slipped the noose around his neck.

He looked up, gave the camera nearest him the finger, then lunging forward his weight went onto the blanket rope causing the noose to snap tight around his throat. He laid there suspended by his neck and his shins, his hands a few inches above the floor.

Unfortunately it only took what seemed like seconds before his lungs started burning and pressure built up in his throat and behind his eyes and ears. Instinctively his body started flailing wildly around, however, the noose and the table held firm despite all the thrashing about.

Too late he realized it really hadn't been such a good idea after all and tried to haul himself back up. But he couldn't pull the chair towards him as his weight pulling down on the table wedged it tight. His attempts to remove the pressure on the noose became more frantic. He tried to grab for the top of the table but his peripheral vision had already started greying out. Just before his world went black he thought he heard voices.

Jake found himself looking into a dazzling white light. Attempting to move he found he couldn't raise his upper body, he then tried moving his arms and legs but they wouldn't respond either. He closed his eyes cutting out the glare of the light, and considered his predicament.

Maybe he'd been paralyzed? That was a possibility; he could have broken his neck trying to hang himself.

Or had they simply just left him die after all?

Oh no... Dead! Bastards! The fucking bastards had left him to die!

He stopped trying to move, not so much as being resolved to his fate, more like too depressed to do anything.

Death, Jake decided sucked big time.

And what about the bright light? Weren't you meant to go into the light? Or maybe that had just been something he'd seen in a movie?

He turned his head over to his right side; at least that part of him seemed to be working. Opening his eyes again he saw the intense light had now gone, although everything still seemed very bright. Looking out of the corner of his eye, which he assumed had to be downwards, although he couldn't be a hundred percent sure, he realized he was lying on something.

A 'something' that looked suspiciously like a metal autopsy table.

Yep, definitely dead... Fuck! What a bummer!

It didn't take too long before he realized his throat and neck were killing him, and he had the headache from hell. So if he was in so much pain he couldn't be dead, right? Surely you didn't feel pain anymore? Trying to move again he managed to looked down at his arm, and realized his lack of movement wasn't down to paralysis, death or any other unpleasant affliction, but due to large padded plastic straps holding him securely to the table. As he took in the room he could see the bright light came not from some ethereal gateway into whatever laid beyond this life, if anything, but from a massive circular operating room lamp array above him. And surrounding the table were positioned a number of trolleys with what were obviously surgical instruments on top of them. He was now even more confused.

So if he wasn't dead then what was he doing in a mortuary?

As he lay there desperately trying to work out things out, somewhere to his left came a beeping noise followed by the hiss of automatic doors sliding open, then the click-clack footsteps from what sounded like two people wearing hard soled shoes, and someone else with squeaky rubber soled sneakers. They stopped on his left side, turning his head he expected to see the two masked heavies who had dragged him from room to room. To his surprise there were two regular looking guys in probably their early or mid-thirties, clean shaven with neat haircuts; one in a pinstripe suit the other in a dark gray one.

They stood silently, occasionally glancing round in the direction of the doors as if waiting for someone, a few seconds later a younger man in a white lab coat joined them. This latter arrival's appearance contrasted starkly to the other two, apart from the shaven head, Jake could see a neck tattoo peeking out just above the collar of his coat, and the large gauge circular bar through his septum looked seriously cool but less than discrete.

Another beep and the doors swooshed open again, Jake listened as a single set of footsteps approached and stopped directly behind him. Jake saw the three by the table turn to face whoever stood behind him.

After a brief pause a man behind him spoke. "Very well done indeed Mr Palmer, quite an impressive performance back there. For a brief moment there you almost had me convinced it was a serious attempt."

The voice instantly recognizable as the one he'd heard over the speaker earlier.

Jake didn't detect any malice in the guy's tone. He sounded calm, well spoken with no noticeable accent, there even seemed to be a slight hint of amusement in his voice.

"Why am I here?" Oh man, speaking hurt his throat.

"It's very simple, like you were told earlier we want you to change to your animal form."

"I don't know what you mean. What animal form. Change how?"

The mystery man moved from behind Jake's head and stood on his right side. Turning his head in order to see the man left Jake a little surprised, the guy didn't look anything like he'd expected. Not that Jake could say what he'd expected really. The guy looked to be in his fifties with grey hair neatly styled on top of a square set face. His stocky build partially disguised by the clever tailoring of an expensive looking dark blue two piece suit. He could easily have been the CEO of a large company, or a banker, certainly not a kidnapper and torturer.

The man unbuttoned his jacket, bent over and placed his head near Jake's. Now the man's voice took on a very real deep threatening tone, the slow quietness with which he spoke accenting the air of menace.

"I do not have the time, nor do I have the inclination to play any more games with you. You are a cougar shape shifter, like your father and all the male line of your family. Of which you are now the last."

Out of the blue, the guy's smell hit Jake like a sledgehammer. Wolf!

Jeez! He must have been too confused earlier or he would have picked it up sooner. Feigning ignorance any longer wouldn't get him anywhere, apart from in a world of hurt, or worse.

"Okay, so you know what I am, what do you want from me?"

"We want you to do some little jobs for us. And so I want to see what we're getting is up to the mark."

Jake thought hard, which he knew to be a dangerous thing as he frequently managed to come out with something pretty dumb when he did.

"And if I refuse?"

Yep, and today was obviously no exception to the rule.

"Oh you'll help us one way or another young man. I assume you've noticed you're in a laboratory?" He held his hand out and gestured to the room.

"Yeah I noticed all the equipment and that I'm on an autopsy table."

Suit man reached across and pulled one of the trolleys to him. Jake watched as the guy picked up various surgical instruments turning each round in his fingers seemingly studying it for a few seconds before putting it down and repeating the process with next one.

Eventually settling for a large surgical knife, he turned back to the table. He looked into Jake's eyes and a smile that only just moved the corners of his mouth upwards flickered across his face for a second. He then broke eye contact and turned his attention to the knife in his hand.

"Oh it's not an autopsy table Mr Palmer, it's a vivisection table. I assume you know what vivisection is?"

Jake nodded.

Shit! Shit! Shit! This was NOT a good place to be in.

He really didn't fancy being dissected like some frog in a school biology class. Especially whilst still breathing.

Jake saw the guy lean forward and slowly bring the knife down. He felt the cold steel press down on his sternum. Then as the knife started to run down his chest, he closed his eyes in an attempt to blank out the horror of being cut open whilst alive. He felt the incision carry on down his stomach stopping just above his navel. Surprisingly there wasn't the amount of pain he expected, then after a few seconds he felt the warmth of his blood trickling down his flanks.

Lying there, he all too easily envisaged his blood trickling off him onto the stainless steel surface of the table, collecting in a puddle before making its way to the drain hole. The thought made him feel physically sick, and his concentration started to drift as real pain began to kick in. It felt like the center of his chest and abdomen had been set on fire, but he could just about bare it. He guessed the cut hadn't been too deep, but sufficient to force him to shift quickly in order to heal it before he lost too much blood. The message came across loud and clear, this was a taster of what would be in store for him if he didn't go along with whatever they wanted of him.

Assholes!

He heard the metallic clink as the man returned the knife to the trolley. He kept his eyes tight shut; he didn't want to know what instrument the guy planned to use next. But there were no further sounds of vicious pieces of medical grade cutlery being selected. Instead he heard rubber tired wheels squeak as the trolley moved across the floor.

The voice was back. "The deal is very simple son. You work for us when we need you to, in return I will not hand you over to our research staff for them to try and find out what's special about you… while your heart's still beating and your eyes are open. Does that sound good to you?"

Jake opened his eyes, looked up at the guy and nodded.

A warm smile appeared on the man's face. Without doubt this had to be the scariest thing yet, either the guy suffered from one of those multiple personality disorders, or was an out and out evil son of a bitch.

"Good… Plus to show our appreciation, when you have completed a task to my satisfaction, we will deposit regular sums of money into a bank account for you. This should keep you living modestly but comfortable until the next time we need you. So you see you'll help us one way or the other, which way though is now up to you."

The smile then dropped away as quick as it had appeared. "One word of warning, fail too often or fail deliberately in the tasks you're given and very bad things will happen. Now, which is it to be?"

"Guess I don't have a lot of choice do I? Release me and I'll shift."

The man gestured to the table and the two younger men started unbuckling the straps holding Jake down.

As suit man started to walk away Jake turned his head and called after him.

"Can I ask just one question?"

The guy stopped and turned.

"You can, but I suspect you may not like the answer."

"What is it I will have to do for you?" inquired Jake.

47

"I could dress it up in Agency speak, make it sound more palatable, but I'll do you the courtesy of being straight. You will be required to undertake very specific targeted killings both here and in South America. In fact anywhere cougars or big cats are found in the wild."

"I can't kill anyone!" exclaimed a stunned Jake.

"You have it in you to kill son, it's what you are. But if you won't then my associates here will refasten your straps and our conversation is over."

"But I've never done anything more than shoot cans with an air gun!"

"There will be no need for a gun as you have a very special talent." The guy went on to explain, "Who would ever consider a fatal attack by a big cat as being anything other than a tragic accident? And if it makes you feel more comfortable the targets selected for your attention will be certified threats to the United States, our national security or the wellbeing of the American people. Think of it as a chance to do your patriotic duty for your country if it makes you feel better."

Not waiting for Jake to speak, he continued.

"You will need to inform anyone back in California who may wonder where you are that you will be moving back to Kansas. We will arrange for any possessions you have to be collected, any personal keepsakes will be passed on to you, the rest disposed of."

The guy's phone chirped, after reading the message he placed it back in his pocket and continued.

"Furthermore you must understand that no one can ever know of what you do or that you work for us. Failure to comply with that one simple rule will cost them their lives. Do it more than once and it will cost you yours too."

Jake could only nod his understanding, he didn't know how else to respond. He was in way, way over his head here. He hadn't even reached twenty four yet and the CIA, or some other shady government organization had recruited him as an assassin. But right at this moment in time he could see no way out of it.

"Do you understand what I have told you Mr Palmer? I want to hear you say it."

"Yes, I understand. No one can ever know."

"Good. Now shift and heal yourself. Then once you have shifted back to human, cleaned yourself up and eaten you will leave here immediately for a training facility for the next six months in order for you to acquire the very specific skills and knowledge you will need to function efficiently."

With that the man turned and left with the two others in suits, leaving just the guy in the lab coat behind who started preparing a syringe. Turning to Jake he explained he needed to take a sample of Jake's blood whilst still human, and another once he'd shifted. The lab technician told Jake to sit on the table once he'd gained full control of his animal form, so he would know when it was safe to re-enter the laboratory. The technician then added that a guard with his sidearm drawn would accompany him when he returned should Jake think of attacking.

So in return for his life not ending on a slab in some laboratory the angry young man would work for his new employers as and when they had use for his 'special talents'. In the cold light of day it didn't seem such a bad deal, he needed to unleash the rage and guilt he'd built up inside him for not being around to save his parents. Plus he told himself he'd be protecting loads of innocent people by getting rid of the bad guys.

Back then, it had been enough to keep his conscience in check, but over the ten years since it had become brutally clear that he was nothing more than a puppet, and they pulled his strings whenever they wanted. Plus he knew he would never be the avenging superhero he first imagined himself to be. Instead he'd become a professional killer, both cold and calculating in equal measure. Initially he'd needed to know the reasons his targets had been designated for discontinuation. He'd also come up with the term 'discontinuation' early on as it didn't sound as brutal as 'kill' or 'murder'. And occasionally he'd be told the reason if it had been deemed beneficial to the operation, but after a few years he didn't want to know the justifications anymore or any personal details of the target as he tried to mentally distance himself from what he done for a living.

Jake came to with a start as the long forgotten cigarette burnt his fingers. He stood and flicked the butt up into the air, the force separating the filter tip from the burning tobacco, the latter landing on the dusty asphalt parking lot just in front of him.

The sound of the gas station bell distracted him from staring absent-mindedly at the thin wisps of smoke as they curled up from the smoldering tobacco. He looked across just in time to see a whale of a station wagon wallow to a stop in front of the gas pumps, its lone male occupant levered his bulky frame out, leant against the roof and mopped his brow. The guy spoke animatedly to the man in the bib overalls as he pumped gas, while all the time wiping his forehead with what looked like a hand towel and panting like some overheated hound. Jake snorted in disgust and decided the lard ass in the sweat soaked pale blue shirt and loosened tie had the look of an agricultural merchant's salesman about him. Jake had seen his type many times before, as they visited the family's farm selling seed and fertilizer, all bought in a valiant effort to grow something profitable in the windblown soil.

And so once again, here he was, stuck in the middle of nowhere, surrounded on all sides by everything he both despised and feared. If he'd had an ounce of common sense about him he would have dumped the truck with the keys still in the ignition in one of the seedier neighborhoods in Chicago after completing his last 'job' and caught a flight down to California. But oh no, he just had to be smart and want to do the whole road trip thing.

Even then when he'd dropped off of Highway 70 down to Garden City to visit his parents and grandparents graves he didn't have the balls to go visit the small farm where he'd been raised. Instead he sat on the side of the blacktop for nearly an hour looking down the dirt road that led to it. He would probably have sat there longer too if he hadn't had felt the urgent need to drive off when he spotted a vehicle coming up the track towards him from the new buildings that stood where his childhood home had once been.

He needed to get back to the sea and proper civilization, and very, very soon too. For the last six years or so he'd been a nomad, constantly on the move, living out of flea pit motels, cheap boarding houses, and most recently his truck. In order to ground himself he needed to get back to

California, where he felt at home. He'd liked to have added 'safe' to that, but knew he'd never be truly safe anymore.

Jake reasoned it had to be a good nine or ten hour drive down to the coast south of L.A. And now the truck had a full tank of gas, the idea of making a 'balls out' run for the coast first thing in the morning started to appeal to him big time. Yep, that's what they were going to do. Well he would be anyway. He still intended to drop Billy off at the first decent town or truck stop they come to. Jake knew he'd get by a whole heap better once on his own again.

Turning he looked back into the gloomy little motel room, some inane game show played out silently on the small, old style TV. He couldn't decide which was more irritating, the fact the screen done a slow rolling vertical flip every thirty seconds, or the moronic looking contestants jumping up and down and waving their arms around in the air when they somehow managed to get a question right.

One team comprised of two girls with long bleached blond hair under white and silver novelty cowboy hats. The pair of them making a less than subtle display of their huge sweater puppies, which looked fit to burst out of their tight blouses any second. These were real deal cheerleader stereotypes as portrayed in all the best comedy movies.

Jake could just imagine it.

'Hi I'm Tiffany. And I'm Amber. And we're both from Backwater, Texas. Our only achievement in life is we once screwed the entire college football team between us after they won the league and now we'll get on our backs for any guy who'll stand us drinks all evening'.

Yep, just looking at them he reckoned their tits outnumbered their brain cells two to one.

Stepping back into the shade, he stopped half way to brush some stray cigarette ash off the mat of short blond hair that covered his broad chest. Taking in the room properly for the first time since arriving he noticed the décor comprised of almost every shade of yellow, orange and brown going. This he reckoned had been done in order to blend in with the dust to save the cleaners work. When first built maybe the place had looked okay, but he doubted if it had been decorated or remodeled many times, if at all, since.

Jake walked over to the bed, pushed the bags to one side and flopped down, hands behind his head. The temperature in the airless room had now reached that point where it felt physically heavy, sapping both strength and will. He thanked his lucky stars that Utah had pretty low humidity. Back in Kansas his pop had always referred to the hot and humid days of late summer as 'dog days'. Typical he thought for a dog to have something to do with the most oppressive few weeks of the year.

He watched the small wall mounted fan while it vainly fought a losing battle with the heat. The wire cage gently vibrated and wobbled while the stubby black rubber blades hummed tunelessly. Holding an arm up he turned his palm towards the fan, despite keeping it there for several seconds he couldn't feel any discernable air movement. Giving up, he let it flop back down onto the bed, it was no good, he had to do something.

Studying the fan again he decided on angling it a little more downwards. As he went to sit back up he stopped dead.

Urgh!

He could feel his bare back stuck to the silky-smooth fabric of the comforter which had started to lift up with him. He'd been out of a cool shower less than half an hour and he'd started sweating profusely already. This he decided was a major oversight in shape shifter design, at least in his animal form he only sweated through his paws, and grooming could help him cool down further. Grooming however had just one small downside… fur balls.

Much to his amusement over the years he'd found many a fur ball had been expelled during the shift from cat to human if he'd been in his animal form for any real length of time. The changing body naturally expelled any foreign object, even bullets. And he could attest to that one personally, having suffered the ignominy of getting shot in the butt one time after being caught in the act by an unexpectedly home early boyfriend. Managing to grab his jeans, he leapt naked out of a second floor bedroom window as he heard a somewhat upset boyfriend charging up the stairs. He'd made it all the way across the front lawn, vaulted the picket fence and was struggling to unlock his car parked in the street when a twenty-two caliber slug hit him in the right butt cheek.

It was no good; he couldn't just lie there slowly dissolving into a puddle of sweat. Grimacing, he peeled his back off the bed one shoulder blade at a time, the comforter still lifting with him. Once sat up he wiped a hand under an armpit and his fingers came away wet with warm sweat.

Yuck!

He must have been seriously wicked in a previous life to deserve all this crap. And what he'd done already in this one really didn't bode well for the next. Karma was going to be a real bitch next time round.

Billy emerged from the bathroom wearing just his black jeans and walked barefoot across the shabby mustard colored carpet. Stopping in front of the television, he inched the volume up just loud enough to hear the words without straining. He stood watching the screen for a minute then turned it down to a whisper. Moving over to the window he leant forward resting his palms on the sill and stared out at nothing in particular.

The low sun muted by the vertical blinds and window grime framed Billy's mop of freshly showered hair in a halo of gold and orange. Jake looked across and watched as larger dust particles caught in the shards of sunlight coming through the blinds seemed to still, as if frozen in time. Then as Billy moved slightly they began dancing again in a chaotic frenzy of motion.

Early evening saw the room temperature start to drop at long last; the TV chattered away softly to itself in the background while the pair of them sat about talking. Jake made sandwiches from the cold cuts and bread he'd bought in town, spreading mayo over the dry bread. They then ate the two chocolate bars he'd bought for dessert. It wasn't much, but enough to keep their bellies from complaining too much in case they didn't manage to hunt anything down later.

Once fed they sat outside their room on the curb and watched the sun now devoid of its earlier ferocity start its journey down behind the distant mountains. An ever expanding giant brush that painted everything in an orange glow that gradually turned into a vivid blood red. Overhead the big Utah sky in turn enriched itself by transforming from the pale azure blue of day into layers of purples, reds and dusky pinks. Thin strips of clouds formed and stretched out; their tops almost ink black while the undersides seemed to reflect the vivid orange of the land beneath them. Then after the last vestiges of the sun finally disappeared, the sky steadily turned into a blanket of the deepest indigo, studded by a myriad of busily twinkling distant stars. And in its center hung a huge crystal clear full moon that washed everything in its silvery white light.

As evening started to turn to night, an indefinable yearning started to grow deep inside Jake and Billy. A primitive hunger rooted deep in their kind's ancient past tore at them, unrelenting in its determination to overwhelm their self-control. Jake could see Billy becoming more and more restless by the minute, and Jake knew he too would soon start struggling to contain his own urge to run, hunt and kill.

Of course if absolutely necessary Jake could suppress the monthly need to shift to his animal form, but like most shifters it meant finding a suitably intense diversion. And there were a number of ways a shifter could distract himself, lengthy sessions of aggressive, animalistic sex being one of the best.

At the relatively tender age of twenty six Jake had been surprised to discover that a very substantial network of underground and hence illegal sadomasochistic sex clubs run by shifters existed. The club in a rundown commercial zone of downtown Washington D.C where he'd learnt all this had four of the biggest wolf shifters he'd ever seen as security, he could have sworn their muscles had their own muscles. Once inside Jake headed straight to the bar and ordered a bottle of beer mostly by sign language due to the ear drum battering volume of the music. Moving away from the bar he stood propping up a wall while the throbbing bass from the speakers thumped deep in his chest. The pounding hard house music, pulsating red lighting cut through by blue lasers and a mass of heaving semi naked bodies on the packed dance floor made the whole scene totally surreal and incredibly erotic. Not that he needed any help there, he'd been as horny as hell with anticipation before he'd even set foot in the place. His aroused state probably explained why the bouncer who'd patted him down at the door grinned and winked at him. He guessed the guy had a personal desire to check out the concealed weapon Jake had in his pants a bit more thoroughly.

Jake knew perfectly well that with his looks he wouldn't be long in finding someone, especially as he seemed to be attracting a fair amount of attention already. He was just studying the people on the dance floor, trying to decide on whom he wanted, when from behind a hand lightly rested on his shoulder, and warm breath sweet with aromatic liquor brushed across his neck. Suddenly a sharp pain made him flinch as somebody bit on his earlobe. As the teeth let go he turned to see a tall, stunningly attractive woman in her late twenties or early thirties dressed in a silver studded black leather corset and matching knee length boots, the red edging on the corset contrasting against her flawless black skin. As she moved round to face Jake, she drew a long slender finger ending in a blood red false nail along his jaw.

Within a few seconds, a slightly older powerfully built man in brown leather jeans and a ripped black mesh tank top joined her, the guy being every bit as handsome as the woman was beautiful. Jake soon discovered the pair were actually the club's owners, the man being a cougar shifter and the woman his human dominatrix girlfriend, as they chatted the pair's joint interest in Jake soon became all too clear. After a few more drinks 'on the house' they led him down into the basement to their own private room at the end of a corridor lined both sides by a series of heavy wooden doors with hotel style keycard locks. Behind each door, a 'private torture chamber' for paying clientele made up from shifters and those humans both male and female who craved the extreme side of sexual gratification.

Then there was fighting, a simple one on one stand up fight wasn't nearly enough of a diversion, certainly not against a human. But a good old fashioned bar room brawl always got the job done.

Jake had fond memories of one particular scrap in some biker bar down in Texas a few years back. Having unexpectedly met up with a lone wolf shifter, also in need of an outlet for his aggression that night, the pair decided on livening up that particular bar as it was well away from town, and would take the local sheriff a good while to rustle up sufficient deputies to be able to adequately deal with it.

After several beers and in a deliberate display of brashness, the pair put their money down on one of the pool tables. They then proceeded to hustle the two biggest and meanest looking guys in the place in the most blatantly amateur way they could. But despite numerous threats to Jake's and the wolf's wellbeing for the poorly attempted hustle, nothing happened. Only when the wolf whacked one of the bikers in the balls with his pool cue did all hell finally break loose.

After being flung clean through a window by two huge, bearded bikers, Jake burst back into the bar a few seconds later. Then spotting the pair in amongst the ruckus, launched himself at them a second time. Despite putting up a good fight, it didn't take long before he found himself flying through another already broken window. Only this time to land on top of the wolf that'd gone through the same window just moments earlier. Battered and bruised, but very happy the pair staggered off together to get in their cars and go find somewhere quiet to get completely wasted on the bottle of bourbon the wolf had in his car.

However, once Jake had started to cut himself off from society in general and other shifters in particular, he found three or four well loaded black hash joints over the course of the late evening would help knock the edge off the hunger that raged within him. He really needed to get the good times back rather than just reminisce about them…

Jake looked across at Billy, and guessing he needed to take the lead, stood up.

"Guess it's that time." He said shrugging.

Once back inside, Billy closed the door and locked it, he checked the window and made sure to close the blinds and drapes with no gaps.

"You go first." Jake gestured to the bed and sat down in the chair. Taking off his jeans and boxers Billy climbed onto the bed and curled up on his side his back facing Jake. Averting his gaze away from Billy's nakedness Jake lowered his head and closed his eyes. He'd often heard that wolves were quite relaxed about being naked in front of others, even when sexually aroused. This he'd decided had something to do with the whole pack togetherness thing. Being a solitary creature by nature, he'd never been into that sort of stuff, nor could he ever imagine doing so; your dangly bits were meant to be kept private in human form.

Sure he'd skinny dipped as a kid. He'd even flashed on the beach a countless times having accidentally dropped his towel whilst trying to get in or out of his wetsuit, but all surfers done it. It was nothing to do with some 'all boys together, look what close buds we are' thing. This led him to imagine a pack of wolf shifters running about trying to sniff each other's butts, he almost choked trying not to bust out laughing as he pictured them trying to do it in human form. And if that reinforced the notion held by a lot of wolves that cat shifters were stuck up and conceited, then tough shit.

Oh hell! He hoped Billy wouldn't try and sniff his butt when they were animals. That would be a major gross out.

Jake woke with a jolt, and realized he must have dozed off.

Idiot!

The whole point of shifting separately had been to protect the other. His eyes flashed instinctively round the room, taking it all in. Everything appeared as it should be, he simply couldn't believe how lax he'd allowed himself to get, and the episode with the deputy earlier should have made him even more alert. The TV channel had finished for the night, the screen just showing a silently waving Stars & Stripes, he stood up, walked over and switched it off.

After watching the picture shrink to a little white dot on the old style TV screen he turned to the bed and saw Billy watching him. Billy stretched, then climbed off and walked over to Jake. Not knowing why, Jake squatted down and looked into the wolf's face who fixed his unblinking gaze straight back on Jake. The wolf's pale silver-green eyes seemed to be staring right into Jake's soul leaving him feeling very exposed and vulnerable. Jake rapidly broke eye contact before he became an open book for Billy to read. Yeah okay, so he was being silly and superstitious, but no one, absolutely no one was getting in.

Jake put his hands on his knees and pushed himself back up, "Time to go."

Billy's earlier eagerness to get out and run had now turned to real excitement, causing his tail to thrash from side to side, in turn making his whole body rock. Unlocking the door Jake peered out into the moonlight, the only discernible noise came from hundreds of randy crickets chirping, each desperately trying to outdo the others in the race to attract a female. The wolf poked his head out the door and scented the air. Having established to his satisfaction they were alone Billy pushed his way out between Jake's leg and the door frame then trotted off past the last two rooms, which as luck would have it appeared empty. Not waiting for Jake, Billy turned the corner and headed off into the wooded area behind the motel. Jake switched the light off, locked the door and pocketed the key, all jobs that required the use of fingers and opposable thumbs.

After entering the wooded area behind the motel, Jake soon picked up the sound of Billy's soft but regular guiding 'yip' noises. In common with all shifters, Jake's night vision, and senses of smell and hearing were all more acute than a normal human's. After a few minutes jogging through the woods he came across Billy in a small clearing hidden within a dense patch of trees and bushes. Keen to get into his animal form Jake immediately stripped off and hid his clothes and sneakers beneath some undergrowth. As he lay down to shift, the wolf moved in closer, and adopted a defensive stance over him. For Jake the transformation normally happened while safely hidden away, but he knew the wolf wouldn't leave his side, and unlikely to fall asleep on the job.

Jake had discovered long ago that by adopting a meditative state at the start of the shift he could actually speed up the transformation progress. Closing his eyes, he started to concentrate on his breathing, making each deep breath slow, noisy and deliberate. Gradually muscles began to relax and his limbs became leaden. All the thoughts that were dashing around in his head quietened down, leaving him with just the image of his cougar.

As his mind focused on releasing his cat, he felt the familiar fluttering sensations begin in his chest then slowly spread outward to his shoulders and down to his hips, they then travelled along his limbs. Gradually his already slow breathing became shallow and he felt his heartbeat grow ever slower and fainter. Tingling sensations like pins and needles started in his fingers and feet, he then started to lose his sense of feeling as all the nerve endings in his body progressively shut down. Very soon all aware-ness slipped away, and he fell into a dream free state of unconsciousness.

As Billy maintained his guard over Jake, the human body on the ground started its transformation into something new. Fingers and thumbs gradually fused into one with the hands. Arms and legs began to shorten as they were drawn into the body, as they did they widened, eventually becoming nothing more than four swollen stumps before they too were reabsorbed. At the same time the face lost all its features before the head too became one with the body.

In less than twenty minutes, Jake had become unrecognizable as a human being, having become a large oval shaped entity, devoid of any features as the morphogenesis process to Jake's animal form reached the halfway mark. Every so often, the smooth surface of Jake's intermediate form gently undulated like waves rippling on a flat sea. Its thickened skin having taken on a ghostly bluish white hue under the light of the moon, which contrasted sharply with the web of dark colored veins that now threaded their way over the surface. Then for a few minutes, the form ceased all movement, becoming completely still.

Billy cocked his head to one side while he watched the miracle of accelerated metamorphosis taking place before his eyes. Although he'd seen shifters change many times it still fascinated him, especially as this time he knew the end result wouldn't be a wolf, but a big cat.

Then something peculiar caught Billy's eye, from deep inside the shape, several small pools of pulsating white and pale blue light seemed to flow rapidly from one place to another. Having never seen anything like it before he moved in to get a closer look, but he only saw the phe-nomenon for another few seconds before it faded away. He stood watch-ing for another few minutes, but nothing else happened. What the hell were they? He would have liked to put them down to nothing more than his eyes playing tricks on him. Caused by the moonlight where it shone through the tree canopy, but he knew what he saw, and it wasn't normal.

Gradually surface movement begun again, slowly but surely something new was starting to take shape. Small gentle waves in the skin formed, progressively getting stronger, spreading out like ripples on a still pond, precursors to the formation of limbs, a head and a tail. The wolf stood patiently waiting, occasionally scenting the air to check they were still alone, and then when satisfied everything was well returned to watching the shift.

The developing body now started to hold its shape without pulsing; a long tail had grown along with what would become the cougar's head. Four muscular legs had almost fully developed with the exception of pads, toes and claws. Gradually short, dense fur started to cover the bald skin. Once the transformation completed, the wolf moved in closer as he watched the rapid rising and falling of the chest slow and Jake's breathing start to normalize, as blood and cells became oxygen rich once more.

As he checked out the now fully formed cougar its eyes shot open and blinked a few times. Taken by surprise, Billy instinctively leapt backwards knowing only too well that upon coming round Jake would be confused and disorientated. And if feeling threatened, the animal mind that always took control for the first few minutes after waking would instinctively lash out without the human side being able to control it. Very aware that the cougar's huge front paws held some pretty fearsome claws, he kept his distance.

The cougar strained to focus its eyes, but everything appeared fuzzy and distorted, so it promptly shut them again, its brain not yet accustomed to processing feline eyesight with its color shift and vastly superior night vision. Something not helped by its brain being swamped with an unimaginable amount of information from its other animal senses that couldn't simply be switched off in order to get used to one new sense at a time.

Opening it eyes a second time; the cougar managed to maintain focus, and immediately registered another animal's eye shine in the moonlight. Unable as yet to fully understand its surroundings, and still confused it emitted a deep rumbling growl of a warning. Acutely aware of its vulnerability, and that another animal, probably another predator was close by, the cougar needed to get up, and quick. Its first attempt at standing up simply ended up with it falling over, but as the mind became more in tune with the new body it managed to stand on the second attempt. Unsteady, the cougar swayed slightly from time to time, but never once taking its big closely set eyes off the wolf as it targeted the potential threat.

Billy took a tentative step closer to the big cat, however another long low growl stopped him in his tracks. He decided his best option would be to lie down on his back and expose his belly to the cougar in a classic sign of submission, and for good measure, he'd throw in some whimpering too. Fortunately, something in the still animal controlled cougar sensed the wolf now presented no immediate threat and the growling ceased.

Gradually Jake's human mind started to take over from the basal animal instincts that protected the newly changed body. He shook his head as if somehow it would help clear things; instead it just had the effect of making his head throb wildly. He tried to cuss out loud, but the strange guttural sound that came out didn't bear the slightest resemblance to his thoughts, so he stood still trying to gather his thoughts.

After a few minutes with his human side now fully in charge, Jake slowly walked over to the prostrate Billy and sat down near him. It was the only thing he could think of doing that wouldn't be seen as potentially aggressive. He had no intention of licking the wolf or anything, as it was a well-known fact in feline circles that all mutts had cooties. Hoping he wasn't misreading Jake's actions, Billy gingerly got up, though he kept his ears flat against his head in a show of submissiveness, just in case. It was only when Jake had stood back up that Billy truly appreciated just how big and powerfully built cougars actually were. Especially compared to a scrawny thing like him.

The next couple of hours saw the two of them running through the woodland together chasing rabbits and hares. Not having the stamina of the wolf for extended periods of running Jake had to stop and rest occasionally. Though he did manage to give an adolescent grey fox a pretty good scare by pouncing over twelve feet from his downwind hiding place and landing right in front of the fox while it snuffled about in the leaf litter. The startled fox instantly jackknifed its body around and shot up the nearest tree.

It had to be just the darnedest thing Jake had ever seen, a fox up a tree. So he sat at the bottom of the tree looking up at the fox, while perched high up on a branch the fox looked down at Jake wondering why an expert tree climber like a cougar had decided to sit there just watching him. After a while Billy trotted over and sat down next to Jake, then following Jake's stare looked up to see what had the cougar so captivated.

After the pair became bored fox watching they left to carry on with their hunt. Eventually Billy spotted a mule deer and using his superior speed and agility, he effectively herded it straight into the teeth and claws of the waiting cougar, one of the nature's foremost ambush hunters. Billy felt a little sorry for the deer; it had stood no earthly chance against two apex predators with human minds, working together. But the joint hunt despite its short duration had been exhilarating. After feeding they rested for a while before starting to head back to the clearing where Jake's clothes were so Jake could shift back to human. As they walked they both just listened to the sounds of the night, taking in the rich mix of smells and generally enjoying being in their animal forms. Tonight had been everything Billy had hoped for, and so much more, plus Jake was definitely a lot more fun in his animal form.

They'd hadn't been walking for long when Billy suddenly stopped, held his head up and start air-scenting, the wolf's agitated state told Jake that Billy had picked up the scent of something that had him worried. Jake in turn lifted his head up, his mouth half open to let the incoming air flood over his scent receptors, he smelt nothing, but his sense of smell wasn't anywhere near as sensitive as the wolf's. He'd just started to look around hoping to see what had gotten Billy so anxious when three large wolves appeared on top of a low ridge to their left, their menacing black outlines silhouetted against the shafts of bright moonlight filtering down through the foliage canopy.

Jake turned to face them and scented the air again; only now could he pick up their scent. A decreased sense of smell due to a short muzzle had been the cougars' evolutionary trade-off for their increased biting power. But even with his slight olfactory limitation he could tell that all three wolves were definitely shifters, and one of them none other than the psychotic deputy from their confrontations in town and the gas station earlier.

The wolves had no doubt been trailing him and Billy from a downwind position, waiting until they had the added advantage of slightly higher ground. This was not a good situation to be in; he quickly glanced around, taking in the lay of the land, looking for anything that might aid him and Billy, and drew a blank. He knew he should be more than powerful enough to win one on one against even a large wolf such as these. However, there were three of the bastards and he was afraid for Billy who due to his slight build would stand no chance.

Catching movement to his right Jake hastily glanced across, to see Billy creeping up to him; turning his head again the cougar hissed at the approaching wolf causing Billy to stop dead in his tracks. As the cougar hissed a second time, Billy received the 'back off' message loud and clear and started slowly walking backwards. Although scared as hell, Billy wanted to fight alongside Jake; however, the big cat quite clearly wanted him to stay out of the way.

Just as Billy got himself clear the three wolves moved forward down the slight slope towards Jake, their snarling and baring of teeth clear indicators of their intent. Then halfway down the middle wolf held back leaving the other two to carry on. Seeing him stop they followed suit, the center wolf growled at them, when neither of them moved forward he lunged snapping at one of the wolves as if to attack it. Jake now realized that it had to be the deputy holding back whilst the other two were to become cannon fodder.

Jake knew that even if he won outright against the two wolves he would be totally exhausted from the fight and without doubt badly wounded. That would make him easy pickings for the deputy, who would then probably turn on Billy, that being pretty much a no contest fight.

Reluctantly resuming their advance, the two wolves carried on down the slope. Jake knew he had but one chance at this, locking his vision on his target he drove straight towards the two approaching wolves, who on recognizing the rapidly approaching danger immediately adopted defensive stances. Then right at the last second of his bounding sprint he unleashed every ounce of the immense strength in his powerful hind legs and vaulted straight over them. He'd cleared a good eighteen foot before his broad flat forehead slammed into the unsuspecting deputy's head sending the pair of them tumbling down the slope, snapping and snarling wildly at each other.

Seeing this, the other two wolves hightailed it out of harm's way before they too became embroiled in the maelstrom that was fast bearing down upon them. Once at a safe distance, they turned around and waited for the inevitable battle to commence. From his vantage point on the opposite side of the wolf and cougar Billy knew as well as the other two spectators did this would be a fight only the winner would walk away from. And if Jake lost Billy knew he too would end his short life here, ripped to pieces by the three wolves.

Now locked into a battle for their lives, the two adversaries faced off. One a bully since elementary school, driven by the need to obey the mocking, controlling voice of his former classmate that now never left his head. The other a cold, calculating, but reluctant assassin motivated by the first law of nature…

Self-preservation.

The pair circled each other like gladiators in their own woodland amphitheater, human minds commanding powerful animal bodies. Each sizing their opponent up, deciding on how best to kill them.

For Jake it would be whilst sustaining the least injuries doing it.

In Deputy Earl Miller's case he knew he had to kill in order to appease Jabbo, only then might his tormentor stop yelling in his head all the time telling him who to hurt.

Even when the bullying buddies first got together at elementary school, Jabbo would occasionally hit and taunt Miller in front of the other kids. By the time they'd reached High School life for Earl Miller had taken a downturn. Now if prevented from satisfying his need to bully by the intervention of teaching staff or other adults, Jabbo simply vented his spleen on Miller instead. Unfortunately for Earl Miller, Jabbo's frustration reached a violent peak during the summer months after they'd both left high school as he perceived the lack of prey as being all Miller's fault.

Then one hot afternoon in late August down at the old local dump, Earl Miller's beatings came to an abrupt end after he attacked a stunned Jabbo with an old kitchen knife he'd taken from his father's tool shed.

While Jabbo had stood poking a dead dog with his boot, Miller came up behind him and plunged the knife into Jabbo's back trying to stab him in the kidney. As Jabbo hollered out in pain and instinctively tried to put his hand to his back Miller pulled the blade out then immediately thrust it deep into the other side of the guy's back before yanking the knife back out again.

Bellowing and cursing the enraged Jabbo turned to face his attacker, but before he could do anything Miller's assault turned frenzied forcing him to raise his arms up in order to defend his face as Miller started slashing wildly. Then taking advantage of Jabbo's defensive stance Miller stabbed the guy in the guts. The force behind the blow buried the four inch blade up to its handle before he tore it back out. As Jabbo crashed to his knees clutching his stomach, Earl Miller hacked at one of Jabbo's ears leaving a large piece of it hanging by a thread of cartilage; Miller then stabbed the blade into Jabbo's bicep before suddenly stopping.

Jabbo's swearing and threats of earlier had now turned into a pitiful whine as crying he begged for his life. But Miller never heard Jabbo's pleas, he simply stood there, his face devoid of any expression. Then without warning, the assault started again. This time Miller lashed out with his boot kicking Jabbo hard in the shoulder, causing him to topple over and roll onto his back. Dropping to his knees Miller stabbed the knife repeatedly into Jabbo's groin almost emasculating the guy in the process, one wild off target blow sliced through the femoral artery in Jabbo's upper thigh.

Satisfied he had stabbed Jabbo in all the places his tormentor used to punch or kick him, Miller got back up and stood staring down as the still breathing Jabbo bled out. Then once Jabbo had finally stopped breathing, Miller dragged the lifeless body over to the back of the dump, where he buried it in the rubbish near to the bodies of the two out of town teenage hitchers the pair had deceptively befriended then killed and buried there the year before.

But even though Jabbo didn't beat him anymore, he now resided in Earl Miller's head, and wasn't planning to leave him alone anytime soon. Now he wanted Miller to kill both these city boys too.

Jake attacked first, springing at the wolf's head, his intention being to seize the wolf around the neck with his front claws and using his weight and strength to drag it down before inflicting the fatal crushing bite to the neck. But the wolf managed to deftly side step his lunge and in doing so succeeded in inflicting an opportunistic tearing bite at the cougars left flank. Jake attempted to blank the searing pain in his side with little success.

He needed to reposition himself in order to get to the wolf's neck which would allow him to bite down with his immensely powerful jaw muscles and snap the neck, or crush the base of the skull. But if he couldn't come in from above he'd go for the throat, clamping down on the windpipe until he'd suffocated the life out of his enemy.

Immediately deciding to go for the wolf's neck a second time, Jake's large rear claws found purchase in the myriad of roots that crisscrossed the surface of the ground under the leaf litter. He powered himself headlong towards his target. He wanted to keep the wolf on the back foot, and not give it any time to think. Besides he felt sure the wolf wasn't nowhere near bright enough to be any master tactician.

But once more his adversary managed to twist its body out of harm's way at the very last moment. Jake had severely underestimated the agility of the big wolf, a stupid schoolboy error caused by his arrogance, a mistake he'd been lucky to get away with twice, but one he wouldn't be making it a third time.

However, Jake didn't get chance to implement any new strategy. The wolf now buoyed up by what he considered to be his superior fighting skills launched his own attack. Caught off guard Jake tried to spin around so as to avoid the mouthful of teeth heading his way, but not being prepared for the suddenness of the attack, he had no chance of getting completely clear. The wolf's lunge missed Jake's throat, and instead its teeth sank into the flesh of cougar's shoulder, causing Jake to hiss loudly with the pain.

Jake considered raking the wolf with his claws, but afraid the wolf's weight would cause him to overbalance him decided otherwise. He had only one option open to him and that was to get out of the bite despite knowing only too well he'd sustain greater injury doing so.

The wolf for its part wanted more than just to hurt now, the voice in its head repeatedly demanded it kill, and then to rip the cougar apart limb from limb. And that meant biting somewhere more vital than just flesh and muscle. He needed to get to the cougar's throat. Using his weight to try and unbalance Jake, he bit down even harder and tried twisting in order to force Jake over.

Out of options, Jake in his desperation decided he needed to try and rear up, so as to be able to use his front claws, hopefully hurting the wolf enough to cause him to release the bite. As Jake toppled over, he got ready to slice at the wolf's shoulder with his front claws. But just at that moment, the wolf released its bite in order to reposition itself.

Now wholly confident of his impending victory, the deputy sought to pin Jake down in order to kill him. He'd get rid of this city boy first then he'd do the same to the other one. And this time he'd be in no trouble over these bodies and maybe he'd be left alone for a while, three in one day had to be enough even for Jabbo.

But the momentary pause in the attack while he shifted his body was a critical error of judgment on the wolf's part. Seizing his chance Jake steeled himself against the pain. He jack-knifed his lower body round so his hind quarters were directly under his adversary and drew his rear legs in as tight to his body as he could get them. As the wolf prepared to rip the flesh from Jake's throat, blood and saliva dripped from its open mouth in anticipation.

The wolf's hesitation was about to cost it dear as the four huge razor sharp claws in each of Jake's hind paws extended fully just before they thrust upwards and tore into the soft unprotected belly behind the wolf's ribcage. The power in Jake's rear legs lifted the wolf's back half up in the air as the wicked curved claws ripped through skin and flesh, cutting deep into the underlying abdominal muscles and nerves.

The wolf's eyes bulged in their sockets and immediately it started howling in agony as its rear legs gave way due to the partially severed muscles and ligaments. Twisting round Jake used the wolf's prone form as leverage to help push himself back up. The searing pain from his wounds now only served to increase his resolve to finish the wolf off. He had no intention of letting his adversary live.

He launched at the wolf one final time, his formidable teeth finding their target as his jaws clamped around his adversary's throat, crushing the windpipe whilst his canine teeth cut deep into flesh. As his mouth started to fill with the all too familiar coppery tang of blood, his powerful jaw muscles tightened their vice like grip even further as blood lust took over from reasoned thought.

The soft ground quickly absorbed the wolf's precious blood as it spilled from the wounds to its throat and belly. Its death throes became weaker and weaker as its body used up what precious little oxygen remained in its lungs, until it ceased to move any more. Despite its stillness, Jake refused to release the wolf until he was absolutely certain that all trace of life had left its body.

Finally letting go he turned towards the other two wolves and started to growl, while doing so he deliberately exposed his huge canine teeth, the wolf's blood still dripping from them. This ploy needed to work, if he stalked towards them they would know by his limp that he'd been badly injured, and he had no doubt the pair would attack together finishing him off. However, the two wolves stood their ground, knowing the first of them to attack would likely suffer the same fate as the deputy.

With the deputy dead, Billy wanted to back Jake up in case the two wolves decided to attack, so he adopted an aggressive stance and started growling. Unfortunately his plan backfired and only served to set the wolves off acting aggressively and joining in the snarling and growling match with the smaller wolf. Jake crouched, his ears back and his tail thrashing from side to side as if positioning himself for an attack. The ruse effectively brought an end the Mexican standoff, and the two wolves started backing away until they were in a position to skirt the slope, when they both turned tail and ran full pelt, hurriedly disappearing from view.

The strain of the fight, and loss of blood had left Jake badly weakened. His adrenalin swamped body needed to shift very soon in order to repair his injuries. If he didn't, he could run the very real risk of becoming too weak to start the shift, and effectively signing his own death warrant. As he turned away from the deputy's corpse towards Billy, a noise above and behind him froze him to the spot. Seeing the wolf's ears flatten back against its head, Jake knew it wasn't a good sign, whatever it was behind Jake had the wolf on edge, big time. Turning back around to see what had caused the noise and gotten Billy so anxious; Jake spotted four wolves standing on top of the ridge. Two more wolves then joined them from the left side, these he presumed were probably the two that had just run off.

Now that there were six of them, it became all too clear how it would play out. He could think of many quicker and preferable ways to die as opposed to having a pack of hick shifter wolves tear him apart. Not being in any fit state to take the fight to them, he could only stand his ground and go down fighting.

Then as he prepared himself for their attack something curious happened, the first four wolves turned on the latest pair to appear, snapping and snarling at them, forcing them to adopt submissive stances. Jake reasoned the pair were being rebuked over their cowardice and reluctance to fight him.

As Jake watched the two wolves getting chewed out, another large wolf pushed through the middle of the group and stopped. The four other wolves immediately stopped their admonishment of the other two.

Oh shit!

The new arrival had an all too familiar scent and not one associated with pleasant memories either. It was obvious to Jake now that the sheriff was the pack alpha, and Caesar had turned up in order to give the thumbs down resulting in Jake and Billy's slaughter. And it didn't take a great mind to work out the deputy lying dead at Jake's paws had been one of the sheriff's pack, and retribution for his killing would be swift, bloody and coming his way.

What a total clusterfuck!

Jake knew Billy's only hope of survival would be if all the wolves were to pick on him, leaving Billy with a slim chance to make good his escape. Being young and fast Billy stood a good chance of getting away if he managed to get a decent head start. And the only way to ensure that happened would be for Jake to go for the sheriff, thereby causing the other wolves to go for Jake in order to defend their alpha. Unfortunately there were two serious flaws with this plan. The first being Jake was in no condition to fight, with his injuries he doubted if he could even run up the slope. And secondly, Billy would need the good sense to make a run for it as soon as it all kicked off in order to save himself. But that wasn't going to happen, Jake just knew Billy would stay and try to fight.

One of the two wolves that had been with the deputy edged its way to the sheriff on its belly, only to be roughly pinned to the ground by the neck. In pain, the wolf cried piteously, but it took several seconds before the alpha wolf released its hold. As the admonished wolf tried to slink back to its position on the outside one of the others nipped it hard on the back leg, causing it to yelp again.

Then came the moment Jake had been dreading. He watched as the sheriff started down the slight slope towards him. He readied himself for the coming attack, but to Jake's amazement none of the others followed. Alone, the alpha wolf carried on downwards, his eyes never leaving Jake's. He then stopped the opposite side of the deputy's corpse, so close that Jake could even make out the gray hairs around the wolf's muzzle. The sheriff held Jake's stare for a few more seconds before slowly looking down and studying the lifeless body. Then lifting his head back, up the sheriff looked Jake square in the eyes once more.

The pair continued to eyeball each other for what seemed like an eternity. Jake felt every muscle fiber in his body burn as he held himself tensed to strike, ready to unleash what little energy he had left should the wolf attack. He knew he couldn't win this fight, but sure as hell, he'd try to do some serious damage. Maybe even enough to prevent the bastard from shifting to heal the injuries, effectively a death sentence in itself.

Then just to compound the surreal nature of what was happening the sheriff peered down at the body once more, lifted his head and gave Jake one last glance, then turned away and started walking back up the slope. Once at the top he disappeared over the ridge without stopping or looking back. The other wolves silently turned and followed their alpha, leaving behind, one dead wolf, a confused Billy, and a stunned but very relieved Jake.

That was it? He'd just killed a pack member and they simply walked away from it? What sort of screwed up crap went through these people's minds? It didn't make any sense. But sure as hell he wasn't going to complain, at least it looked like he got to fight another day.

Billy walked up to Jake and gently rubbed his head against the side of the cougar's bloodied muzzle, earning him a brief and faint purr. Jake turned and limped away, he needed to shift real soon and repair the damage wreaked upon his body during the fight before he became too weak to shift. The sight of Jake struggling to walk made Billy's heart heavy with concern, his tail drooped and he fell in behind the cougar.

Jake hadn't gone far before he decided he had to shift right away, every time he breathed in it hurt like hell suggesting he had several broken ribs as well. It had to be a good half an hour's walk back to the clearing where he'd hidden his clothes and he simply couldn't make it. He walked for a few more minutes then found a secluded spot by a large fallen tree. The strength now all but gone from his legs, he practically collapsed as he went to lay down close by the tree trunk.

Jake's shift back to human couldn't happen soon enough for Billy, he was convinced they were still in danger of some sort, he didn't know quite what, but he felt it. After a while when there had been no obvious sign of the shift beginning, Billy began worrying that Jake could have been too badly injured and weakened for the shift to even start.

Come on Jake!

He stood staring hard at the cougar as in his desperation he tried to will the process to start.

Come on... Shift damn it!

But he could do nothing to help. He just had to wait.

After what seemed like an eternity and despite his fears for the worst, Billy noticed the first signs of the change starting. And although not a record breaker by any means, the shift completed without any problems. However, once again Billy saw the transient luminosity that moved around deep within Jake's shapeless transitional form, though this time they appeared much fainter than before. Billy couldn't help but feel the weakness of whatever the lights were had something to do with Jake being badly injured.

But whatever they were, he'd never seen the phenomena in any of the wolves from his pack. Maybe it was just a cat thing. Weren't cats meant to be creatures of both light and dark? Although he wanted to know what they were, he didn't feel he could ask Jake, the guy really didn't come across as 'approachable' like that.

Once Jake's shift completed and he became reasonably compos mentis the pair of them made their way to the clearing where Jakes clothes were. Once Jake had dressed, they returned to their room where Billy jumped onto the bed and took his turn to shift.

Despite the shift having healed his internal and external wounds, Jake felt totally drained of energy. The post adrenalin rush crash had hit him hard this time and he really needed to get some decent sleep as soon as Billy had finished his shift. Jake sat down in the chair, plugged his earbuds into his cell phone then selecting his Nu Metal playlist he cranked up the volume, this time he would not fail in his protector's role by falling asleep again.

After drinking two bottles of water to stave off dehydration, the growing ache in his bladder forced him to get up and go to the bathroom. Standing in front of the toilet he propped himself against the wall with one arm while he peed, after trudging back into the bedroom he checked on Billy who was now almost fully human. Flopping back down into the chair he looked across to the window, despite still being dark outside, he knew neither of them would get long to recover, as sunrise wasn't far off.

Once the album he'd been listening to finished, he stood up, put his phone on the nightstand and checked on Billy one last time. Happy that the shift had completed and that Billy was now sleeping soundly, Jake carefully climbed onto the bed in order not to disturb the sleeping Billy and turned the nightstand lamp off. Jake laid on his back staring into the darkness for several minutes just listening to the slow rhythmic sound of Billy's breathing. It felt so strange being in bed next to someone after all this time, but no matter how much he wanted some form of comfort through human contact, he couldn't do it, he wouldn't do it. His eyes closed and he promptly fell into a fitful sleep still as much alone as he'd been since his parents' deaths.

After what seemed like the worlds shortest sleep, Billy woke and saw the sun had already become bright enough to penetrate both the blinds and the drapes softly lighting the room. He put his hands together, stretched his arms upwards and yawned deeply; lowering his arms he turned over and saw Jake fast asleep facing him. Cool, it gave him a chance to check the guy out close up so to speak. As Billy lay there looking at Jake's face, it suddenly dawned on him he was very naked and Jake fully clothed, causing an uncommon embarrassment to flare up within him. After a brief struggle, he managed to reach down, snag his boxers lying by the side of the bed, and carefully wriggle into them without waking Jake.

Having regained his modesty, he returned to studying the sleeping Jake's face. It seemed so peaceful and innocent looking; he couldn't believe this was the same person as the fearless killing machine that had fought for both their lives just a few hours earlier. It also seemed strange seeing Jake with normal hair, his Mohawk having been lost during the shift. No one had ever managed to explain to Billy's total satisfaction why facial hair didn't grow back after shifting, but body hair did, and head hair always seemed to grow a couple of inches. Why weren't you bald all over or completely hairy come to that?

As he lay there, Billy found himself struggling to fight the urge to touch Jake's face. What had got into him? He didn't even really like the guy and touching him would be just plain dumb. Then against everything his better judgment told him not to do, he gingerly reached out. His fingertips made it to within just a few inches of Jake's cheek when the guy stirred. Billy snatched his arm back so fast he was convinced he'd dislocated his shoulder. He then watched as Jake slowly opened his eyes revealing golden brown irises, the eyes blinked a couple of times, then a smile spread across Jake's face, who managed to croak a rather sleepy "Hey."

"Good morning, how do you feel?" enquired Billy.

Jake stretched his back and immediately regretted it.

"Ow! That hurts! I feel like I've just been stampeded by a herd of seriously pissed rhinoceroses, some of whom came round for a second go."

Billy chuckled, "It might not have been a bunch of rhinos you fought, but you were amazing last night, so cool and calm. Man you were fearsome!"

Jake gently sat himself up, so as not to give his head a chance to start pounding. Unfortunately it didn't work, boy he needed some aspirin. Once propped up he managed to answer. "Not sure I'd go that far, but we're both still here, so we must have done okay."

"Okay? You call that okay? I would say saving both our lives goes well beyond just okay. But if you're determined to be all coy and modest I won't inflate your ego anymore."

Billy finished the sentence by laughing, then in a serious tone he added, "You saved my life last night Jake and I don't know how I can ever thank or repay you for that."

"Aww gee shucks, weren't nothing." Jake acknowledged, grinning.

Well, Jake thought, perhaps his passenger wasn't so bad after all and maybe, just maybe he wouldn't leave him at the next town.

Spotting his cell on the nightstand Jake checked the time, almost seven fifty. Oh man, he could sleep for hours yet, but he wanted to get away from Milton as soon as he could. He swung himself off the bed, grabbed his hair clippers, toiletries, and clean clothes out of his bag then went to cut his hair and get showered. Forty minutes later, he walked back into the bedroom with his hair now starting to resemble his version of a Mohawk again. He noticed Billy had the outside door open, the slight breeze bringing fresh morning air into the room, boy that felt good.

Jake watched as Billy started towards the bathroom.

"Erm, I'd probably leave it a while longer before going in there."

"Why?" said Billy, the quizzical look on his face contorting into one of disgust as he picked up the smell.

"Uurgh, you stunk the bathroom out? That's disgusting!"

"Sorry, raw meat seems to do that to me nowadays." apologized Jake.

"Maybe you should eat more fruit and yogurt?"

"Yogurt?"

"Just saying…"

By the time Billy had braved the toxic and potentially explosive atmosphere in the bathroom, showered and dressed it was almost nine thirty.

"Right, let's get away from here." Jake swung his bag over his shoulder, "Ready?" As he turned and started for the door, Billy took hold of Jake's arm and stopped him. "We should go see if the girl from the gas station wants out from here."

Jake shook his head, "Why would she want to leave? Is this because of what happened with the deputy yesterday?"

Billy shrugged, "That's part of it."

"Don't forget this is her home," Jake continued, "and I'd guess it's all she knows. Billy you have to realize she's likely conditioned to this way of life, so I doubt if she'd want to leave, besides the deputy's dead now so he won't be hassling her anymore."

No way did he need another passenger. One was more than enough.

Billy knew the girl's wanting to stay was a real possibility.

"I still need to find out, I get this feeling like something's very wrong and it's to do with her, but I can't explain what though. At least we can offer her the chance to get away. Maybe she's got relatives somewhere else she can stay with. I just…"

He held his hands out in front of him, palms up, and shook them as if frustrated at not being able to explain himself.

" I just have this feeling something really bad is going to happen … Please Jake?"

Jake looked at the now pleading expression on Billy's face and sighed inwardly. The look was one that would tug at the heartstrings every time. How could he refuse someone whose heart was so big it cared about a total stranger's wellbeing so much? So he agreed that they would at least speak to her.

"Thank you." Billy said as he leant forward and squeezed Jake's arm.

Returning the room key to reception Jake found it deserted, he called out a number of times, but getting no answer he placed the room key on the register, turned and went back out to the truck. As they pulled up onto the gas station forecourt, Billy opened his door. "I'll go and speak to her."

Jake shook his head, "No, we'll both go, just in case the repair shop guy gives any trouble."

They walked across the forecourt and into the store. Again the complete absence of people and the store's run down condition gave an eerie, almost abandoned feel to the place. Jake put his hands on Billy's shoulders as he moved past him towards the counter and called out; getting no response Jake went round the end of the counter and disappeared through an open doorway at the back of the store. Billy waited, picking up and examining the maps and travel guides on the two rotating wire displays. Just as he decided to go find out what was taking so long, Jake reappeared.

"There's an apartment out back, but no one's there either, however one of the bedrooms definitely belongs to a girl."

It had taken Jake several minutes to work that one out, due to the lack of girly things in the room. A few old and obviously well-loved plushies and a few snapshots stuck around the edge of the dressing table mirror were the only personal items on display in the room. Only when he glanced inside an old wardrobe with its missing doors did he discover a few tired and well-worn dresses hung up. All except for a couple of pretty frocks at one end that he guessed had to be Sunday best for church.

Shaking his head, Jake explained, "I've got your bad feeling now, something really doesn't feel right here. Let's go next door to the repair shop, but if there's no one there we're leaving. I'm not hanging around here a minute longer than I have to; this whole place is starting to give me the willies."

The pair of them left the store and went across the forecourt to the repair shop. As they walked through the open doors Jake spotted the man from yesterday working under the hood of a car and strode over to him.

"Where's the girl who works here?" demanded Jake.

The guy glanced up at Jake for a moment then returned to his work.

"I politely asked you a question; could you do me the courtesy of answering."

The man straightened up but still no reply. Jake didn't have time for this bullshit.

Grabbing hold of the front of the guy's overalls Jake spun him round so their faces were almost touching.

"Where's... the... girl?" Jake growled, his patience now all but run out.

Jake inhaled the guy's scent, hoping to smell fear on him, but he smelt nothing, and he was human too, not a shifter. Jake looked into the guy's eyes and saw in them the reason why he wasn't afraid. They were completely devoid of emotion; the guy was nothing more than an empty shell.

"Last time. We want to speak to her. Where is she?"

All of a sudden a fleeting color shift lasting a few seconds appeared in Jake's vision, an all too frequently experienced warning for him to calm down. His cat's temper had the shortest of fuses which affected him in human form as well. And its fiery feline nature had begun pushing hard to get out and vent itself on someone or something. As the man tried to push himself away from Jake's hold, Jake responded by tightening his grip even further. Now something burned in the guy's eyes. Jake sensed a real deep anger.

Without warning, the guy snapped at Jake, "Why do you think you got away last night? You went and done their job for them."

How did the guy know what had gone on last night? Not being a shifter he shouldn't be aware of what had gone on, besides Jake would have remembered the guy's scent if he'd have been there.

"What do you mean, done their job for them?" asked Jake.

A tear formed in the corner of one of the man's eyes and rolled down his grimy cheek past the corner of his taught mouth. As a second tear from the other eye swiftly followed, the guy's head swiveled to the left slightly as he looked over towards the workbench.

Looking in the same direction as the mechanic, Jake spotted the twelve gauge shotgun lying on the bench.

Seeing that Jake had noticed it the guy turned his head back and sighed.

"It wasn't really meant for you two; though earlier I planned on shooting any of your kind who came through that there door."

Looking back at the guy, the wretched expression on the man's face helped subdue Jake's anger a little.

"You gotta help me out here fella," insisted Jake. "I don't understand what's going on."

Billy came up behind Jake and stood by him in an effort to lend him some moral support.

The mechanic continued, "When my wife called us in for dinner last night, Stacey-Leanne never showed up which was unusual as she always helps her momma out at dinner time laying up the table. So I went out to look for her, and that's when I found her out back behind the old pump shed, just lying there, dead. Her eyes were still open, just staring up at nothing."

The guy physically shuddered as the memory of the previous evening replayed in his mind. Jake released his hold on the guy's coveralls, then after a few seconds, the guy carried on with his story.

"Her clothes were all messed up and torn, and there were bruises round her throat. When I called the sheriff's office Deputy Miller answered. He drove over, and said he reckoned you two had done it, and that he'd get some more deputies and go arrest you. I said I'd fetch my gun and we'd go get you. But he said he it was police business and I couldn't get involved, and he'd deal with it.

Then I kinda got to thinking that if you'd done it why was you still here? And something about the way he acted made me kinda suspicious. The more I thought about it, the more convinced I became he was lying about you two being to blame. A while after he left Sheriff Hutton came by wanting to know why Miller had come out here, I showed him Stacey-Leanne as Miller told me to leave her and not touch anything as they'd need the evidence to get you executed. Then after making some calls Sheriff told me that he reckoned it had been Miller who'd done it and not you boys. Then he called the funeral home for them to come collect Stacey-Leanne."

The guy sobbed, and then sniffed hard to stop his nose running.

"That son of a fucking bitch messed with my little girl then killed her. So for doing what you did I guess I owe you some show of gratitude."

"The deputy that was here yesterday? You're saying he raped and killed her?" Jake suddenly regretted his choice of words and sounding so uncaring.

The guy nodded, "Sheriff said he'd sort it, told me it was a 'pack issue'."

It was Billy's turn to get confused now, "What do you mean pack?"

The guy gave him a withering look before answering, "Don't play dumb with me kid. I know what you two are, and I know about the local pack, that's run by Sheriff Hutton."

A human knowing about a pack or a shape shifter wasn't unheard of, Billy knew that obviously a wife would know about her husband being a shifter, He'd heard guys talking back at the ranch about the CIA and FBI apparently knowing about shifters. Then there were humans with special connections to a pack that were also trusted with the knowledge. Billy guessed the gas station guy to be one of the latter.

"How do you know about the pack? Why would they tell you these things?" demanded Billy, now needing to know about the guy's connection to the pack.

"Nancy my wife who runs the motel, well her sister is married to one of them, not that we ever knew what he was to start with. Anyways, he got hurt real bad one evening a good few years back by some machinery out on their farm and Nancy who'd been there visiting her sister helped tend his wounds. That's when she saw him do the 'changing thing' to heal himself. After that, Sheriff Hutton came round with several men and explained that the things Nancy had seen needed to be kept secret at all costs. And that there'd be serious consequences for me, Nancy and Stacey-Leanne if we ever let on."

Jake slowly shook his head, "If I'd had known what he'd done last night, I'd have made the bastard suffer."

The guy looked at Jake, pressed his palms into his eyes and wiped them, leaving a dark oily smear across one of his cheeks.

"There's been enough killing and suffering here. Just go, and leave us be with our grieving."

Hearing a noise behind them, they turned round to see Sheriff Hutton and another deputy standing in the doorway, their silhouettes clearly showing the pump action shotguns they both held.

The sheriff spoke first, "There'll be no need for the gun Roy. Don't be putting Nancy through having to mourn at another funeral."

The unquestionable tone of authority in the sheriff's voice come through loud and clear. The 'command voice' as Billy called it was obviously something all Alphas possessed, and one he'd heard way too many times since his mom died.

Even though the gas station guy wasn't a wolf, he fell in line with the order, and stood with his head lowered in deference. Billy too felt compelled to become servile. Damn it, the guy wasn't even his Alpha, in fact he didn't have a pack leader anymore, but power just seemed to roll off the guy. Billy turned to look at Jake who stood there impassively; he couldn't sense anything from him in terms of whether it affected him or not, but somehow he had a feeling that even if it had Jake wouldn't show it.

The deputy, pushed between Jake and the mechanic, picked the shotgun up, broke it and took the shells out. As he walked back to the sheriff, Jake picked up the deputy's scent, another of the wolves from last night.

Jake turned to the sheriff, "Look I know you probably don't reckon you owe us anything considering, but it would be nice to get some explanation of what the fuck's going on here."

Sheriff Hutton nodded. "Yeah, well I guess that's only fair son. The wolf you killed last night wasn't just one of my deputies; he happened to be my nephew and one of my betas. I'd suspected he'd been hankering after young Stacey-Leanne for a good while now, but until last night when it seems he forced his unwanted attentions upon her, it had never been anything too concerning. Maybe the full moon drove him to do such a wicked thing, maybe it was something else, only the Good Lord knows the answer to that."

"Something else?" inquired Jake.

"For a good while now folks round here been saying they've seen him going about talking to himself. Even been seen punching himself in the head," the deputy chipped in almost cheerily.

The sheriff gave him a withering look, "Yeah well that's all by the bye now, no sense in bringing these things up anymore."

The deputy apologized to the sheriff for his lack of discretion.

The sheriff continued, "Going by the bruises on her I reckon the poor little mite must have put up a good struggle while he... Yeah, well. Now whether he killed her to keep her from telling, or whether it was an accident we'll never know. But obviously he needed to find a patsy to take the rap for what he'd done, and you two were perfect for it."

He slowly shook his head, before continuing, "He phoned two of the pack, spun them a line about how he'd found her dead with her panties down round her ankles, and that your scents were all over her. He then told them they had to go out with him looking for the pair of you, with supposed orders from me to kill and not capture."

Billy having managed to shake himself free of the alpha's hold over him, looked quizzically at the sheriff. "He done all that without you authorizing it?"

The sheriff's expression mirrored his astonishment that Billy should even have to ask such a question. "You're a wolf son; you should know all about pack rules and loyalty. Being a beta the others would have accepted without question his word that I'd sanctioned it. End of day only thing that mattered to him was silencing the pair of you and for that he waited 'til you become animal so you weren't going to be able to shout your innocence. Then with you dead no one could question his story, or so he thought. When he and the other two turned up at the motel, you'd already headed off into the woods. So they shifted and tracked you down."

The sheriff sighed, "But, what he didn't know was I'd had someone keeping an eye on the two of you all the time, so I knew you were still in your room when he said you'd killed her."

"You had someone spying on us?" Billy couldn't believe they'd been under surveillance.

"I wanted to make sure you weren't going anywhere, or doing anything I didn't want you to. So when I heard about what he'd claimed had happened I knew it to be a complete crock of shit. Then when I saw Stacey-Leanne's body I could only smell him on her, confirming what I suspected. And that's pretty much all you need to know."

Billy nodded his thanks, but Jake wasn't done.

"You bastard, you fucking used us! You let me do your dirty work for you, 'cos you didn't want to kill a member of your family."

The sheriff rounded on Jake instantly, the authority instantly snapping back into his voice. He jabbed a fat index finger at Jake's face.

"Look boy, I'll never have any qualms in doing whatever I think is best for the pack and the townsfolk. Now you two get going and don't ever be coming back this way. You've got no further business here. And trust me; this is not a good place for the pair of you to be just now."

The sheriff's thinly veiled threat had not been lost on Jake. He knew everything had possible had to be done in order to prevent outsiders from finding out about the pack. And Jake had no doubts whatsoever that Sheriff Hutton wouldn't hesitate for a second to arrange for him and Billy to end up in a shallow grave out in the desert somewhere.

On the other hand, Jake knew the sheriff would be fully aware that he and Billy needed to maintain their shadowy existence too, and as such were just as vulnerable, a fact that would ensure their total silence. The other reason Jake reckoned they were walking away from it all instead of getting a bullet in the back of the head each was that despite what Sheriff Hutton said earlier, maybe he did consider he owed them some debt of thanks for saving him from having to kill his own nephew.

Billy and Jake started to walk out to their truck, only for the sheriff to stop Jake by grabbing his arm on the way past. "Shame you're not a wolf son, you'd make some Alpha a pretty fine Beta."

Jake shrugged, and acknowledged the compliment with a brief half smile.

They stepped outside into the warm, bright sunshine. Once in the pickup Jake grabbed his shades off the sun visor and fired up the engine.

"Right, let's get outta of here!"

Billy looked at Jake, "You'll get no argument from me on that one."

They pulled off the forecourt and out onto the road, every turn of the wheels felt good as it put more distance between them and Milton.

Four miles further on they re-joined the highway and headed west to eventually join up with Interstate I-15.

The three hour drive down to the Arizona state line seemed to take forever, resulting in a subdued atmosphere. But thirty minutes after having crossed the state line into Arizona they left it and entered Nevada, being two states away from Milton it felt as if they could finally think of the place as a bad memory and start to relax.

A grinning Billy produced a 'Triple A' map of California from down by his feet, "I kinda 'found' this in the gas station store."

He unfolded the map and held it up.

"So... Where to then? I'll navigate."

Jake chuckled, "Hey, you do know the I-15 takes us straight through Las Vegas first don't you?"

ARIZONA SPIRITS

"Have you done this before?" Billy enquired trying to look over Jake's shoulder.

Jake laughed, "What lose money? Yeah I graduated high school with a diploma in it."

Billy shoulder bumped Jake just hard enough to make him sidestep so as to maintain his balance and not spill his drink.

"Sillyhead, you know what I mean. Gambling!"

Jake lowered his head, turned and looked sideways at Billy, then wiggling his eyebrows he smirked for a few seconds. Then as quick as the smile had appeared his face reverted to its usual blank expression and he turned his attention back to the roulette table.

Damn!

Billy so wanted these all too brief flashes of candidness to last longer, it showed that deep down Jake had a light side to him and could be fun to be with. But the guy seemed insistent in maintaining a certain distance and remoteness, something that Billy knew had more behind it than just his solitary feline nature.

This Billy decided worried him, well worried probably wasn't the right word, more like it troubled him, but in a way he couldn't put his finger on. He didn't think Jake was some crazed axe murderer or anything bad like that, more like there had been some serious hurting in his past that the guy constantly struggled to keep suppressed, and somehow he'd managed to lock the real Jake away with it. But Billy decided he had more than enough baggage of his own at the moment to be going around criticizing others.

Billy rejoined the world as he heard Jake's voice above the background noise,

"Chips please."

He watched as Jake placed two fifties on the table. The croupier, a girl in her early or mid-twenties with wavy, blond hair that tumbled over the shoulders of her raspberry red shirt drew the bills towards her. Then in one well practiced fluid movement spread them apart then back together again. After poking the bills through a slot in the table, she selected two stacks each of ten pale green chips. Glancing back up at Jake she smiled more warmly than Billy thought entirely necessary then pushed the chips across the table.

Whoa! A hundred bucks, gone, just like that.

Okay, obviously for Vegas it was a drop in the ocean compared to what some people gambled, but to Billy a hundred dollars happened to be a heck of a lot.

But the chips did look cool, and when Jake picked up a stack of them and dropped them into his other hand they really did make that dull chinking noise you always hear in the movies.

Hanging with Jake kind of made Billy feel of proud of the guy, Jake had a worldly knowledge about everything, something Billy knew he lacked big time.

So far his life had consisted of...

Ha! Life. What a joke.

To date everything he'd ever done, or more correctly, ever been allowed to do, had been regulated by his father and centered round the pack. This meant that his father or a 'chaperone' always supervised what little contact he'd had over the years with the world outside the sprawling ranch he lived on. And as no one ever volunteered for the job, his father always ended up having to assign the role to someone who then typically made no secret of the fact they resented having to 'babysit the brat'.

But this wasn't the time or the place to wallow in self-pity; he'd left the pack and his father far behind now, hopefully soon to become nothing more than a dim memory. Besides, he was in Las Vegas, on 'The Strip' and planned to enjoy every single second of it.

When they'd driven down Las Vegas Boulevard earlier that day he felt his head had been in imminent danger of falling off as he continually swiveled it from left to right and back again trying to take everything in. It wasn't just the Eiffel Tower, the replica New York skyline, fairy-tale castles and the massive glass pyramid that mesmerized him. It was the scale of the buildings he found unbelievable; sure he'd expected 'big', but some of the casinos and their adjacent hotel complexes just seemed to go on forever, encompassing several blocks.

Then when they came back in the evening to visit a casino the whole place had become even more magical as millions upon millions of twinkling colored lights wrapped everything in webs of vivid shimmering colors. Sure he'd seen it on television, but nothing could have prepared him for the sheer magic that was Vegas up close and personal at night.

Billy reminded a somewhat bemused Jake of a kid with his nose pressed up against the glass of a candy store window. Every few seconds a 'Wow!', or an 'Awesome!' or an 'Oh man!' came from across the cab. All interspersed with lots of 'Jake, Jake, look at that!'

Once inside the casino a totally awestruck Billy just stood, turning round and round trying to take in the brash décor with its mismatch of imitation art deco and tasteless styles that spanned the past three or four decades. The vast sea of gaudy red, green and yellow patterned carpet he stood on seemed to go on forever no matter which direction he looked. Looking up his eyes widened at the sight of enormous chandeliers that hung from the high vaulted ceilings like vast upside down fountains that spewed out sparkling glass beads instead of water.

And everywhere he looked there were people, hundreds of them; short ones, fat ones, the tall, the skinny, young and old, all moving backwards and forwards, just like waves on the carpet sea. There were those with happy faces that Billy imagined were just out to have some fun like him and Jake, and then there were those with blank or drawn expressions. He reckoned those ones were the hard core gamblers who'd lost their money and were off back to their hotel rooms or wherever they'd come from, to brood over their losses with a bottle of cheap whiskey, if they could still afford one.

But the thing that really struck Billy was the incredible noise. One monstrous cacophony of sounds remorselessly battered his sensitive hearing. Most of it seemed to be coming from row upon row of slot machines all lined up like a modern day version of the Terracotta Army warriors in China. A few were classic slots that used long chrome handles with a brightly colored ball on the end to set the reels spinning and clunking, but the majority were modern ones that had buttons and screens. However, they had one thing in common, they all contributed to a mind numbing, tuneless chorus of clunks, beeps and high pitched, tinny sounding digital medleys interspaced every so often by the 'ching, ching, ching' sound as one of them paid out into their coin tray.

And every electronic warrior had a human opponent sat in front of it. Hypnotized by its relentlessly spinning reels or brightly colored display; they were compelled to keep feeding it money. Then once a machine had consumed all their money, it released its prey, only to replace them with another willing victim clutching their plastic cup of coins before the red vinyl seat even had time to cool. Billy decided that if aliens ever wanted to take over the world, all they would have do in order to conquer the human race would be to transform into slot machines.

Turning back to the roulette table he watched as Jake placed a number of bets and lost each time bar one. After a quick '*Humph!*' Jake took hold of Billy's hand and lifted it up.

"Here you go, let's see if your luck's in, 'cos mines definitely not at the moment."

Billy watched as Jake dropped the remaining chips into his hand.

"But I don't know how to play," he protested, "and it's your money."
Ignoring Billy's objections Jake gestured at the roulette table.

"Okay, let's start simple then, red or black are one to one odds, same for odd or even numbers, which means if you win you get your stake money back plus the same again. So what you reckon then? Put a chip on your choice of red or black, or odd or even."

Looking at the chips in his hand, and with some hesitancy Billy put one of his chips on red. He watched fascinated as the croupier fired the ball onto the spinning roulette wheel, trying in vain to follow it as it went round and round. His anticipation grew as the ball started chattering as it hopped and skipped over the wheel's pockets before dropping into red sixteen. The croupier placed another green chip on his original one.

Jake nodded towards the table, "Those are yours, you need to pick them up or they will think you want the bet to stay on for the next spin."

Billy picked his chips up and dropped them into his other hand just to listen to them chink, then he beamed at Jake, his excitement barely contained, "Ten bucks! Oh yes, I rock!" His excitement faded slightly as he noticed Jake wasn't looking at him but appeared to be staring past him over his shoulder into the mid distance.

He shook Jake's shirt sleeve, "Hey I won ten bucks!" he said excitedly.

"Sorry, just looking at something."

Billy turned round and looked across the room to see what Jake had been watching, but couldn't see anything of special interest happening so dismissed it.

Taking a sip of his drink Jake looked at the chips in Billy's hand, smiled, then said, "Well we're not millionaires yet, and actually you won five dollars, the other five were your stake back. Now let's see if you can win us enough for a decent dinner."

"Oh, no pressure then?"

"None at all Mr Thompson." Jake cheerily replied.

After having some more betting options explained to him, Billy had several more small wins but more loses. Then it dawned on him that he had just placed his last chip on the table. Billy looked despondent when the croupier raked his chip away having lost his last bet.

"I've lost all your money." he said dejectedly.

Jake just grinned, "It's the enjoyment from playing that's important; the fun's not just in the winning, if we actually win anything it's a bonus. Besides I've still got some betting money left, let's go play a little Blackjack."

As they waited by a blackjack table for a seat to become free, Billy caught himself standing slightly behind and to one side of the guy. Oh no! Surely he wasn't going all omega and submissive on Jake? He'd hoped he'd left that sort of behavior behind him after leaving the pack. He tried to put it out of his mind by deciding it had been nothing more than an old ingrained habit done without thinking, nothing else. He then stepped forward so he stood alongside Jake. Besides, he felt sure that being a cat Jake wouldn't have spotted the subservient mannerism.

After a while a man and woman left the table, Jake sat down and bought two hundred dollars' worth of chips from the dealer. After placing two five dollar chips in the betting circle, the dealer dealt Jake his cards. A jack and a ten, Jake waved the palm of his hand across his cards. Billy watched intently as the dealer dealt cards to the other players then eventually turned his own cards over. He then added some chips to the ones Jake had bet with.

"You won?"

"Yep, dealer got seventeen to my twenty, table rules says he has to stick on seventeen."

Over the next hour Jake's stack of chips went through a steady cycle of going up and down as his luck swung back and forth.

Billy so loved the way Jake knew just what he was doing and generally acted super cool; it reminded him of those casino scenes in the James Bond movies. He looked Jake up and down and contemplated what the guy would look like in a tux with his blonde Mohawk and decided the guy would look pretty damned sexy, in a sort of punky, unconventional way, a real head turner.

Whilst Jake played, Billy took in the others sat at the table, and decided it was a shame Jake's coolness didn't rub off onto a few of the other players, especially the young woman sat next to Jake who seemed to shriek with excitement every time the dealer dealt her a card, a matter not helped by her being egged on by her equally excitable girlfriends. His feeling of irritation with the woman turned to instant dislike when she started laying her hand on Jake's bare forearm and flirting with him.

Eventually the green eyed monster in Billy took over and he leant into what had now become a very small space between Jake and the woman. He put his hand on Jake's shoulder in a move he hoped would emphasize some sort of closeness between them.

"Hey, fancy another drink?"

The woman glared at him and removed her hand from Jake's arm.

Jake passed his glass to Billy. "Ooh yeah, I'll have a JD and Coke."

Billy turned to walk away, but just couldn't help himself; he sneered at the woman.

Yeah, mine! So back off… Bitch!

Feeling very smug, he headed off to the bar.

Oh my God! Had he just become possessive of Jake? Oh wow!

Feeling possessive about someone was definitely a new emotion, and he thought he kind of liked it. But the thrill of the moment quickly evaporated with the realization that the attraction was very much one sided. Still, if he could only get to be good friends with Jake he'd happily settle for that.

As Billy returned with their drinks he noticed Jake looking over at him. The thought struck him that Jake had been waiting for him to come back. However, as Billy drew closer it became apparent that once again Jake had been looking past him at something. Billy jiggled Jake's glass at him then handed the drink over, only then did Jake's attention return to the table. Billy turned round and looked across the floor towards the bar but still could only see a forest of faces. He turned back to the table somewhat perplexed; still at least the woman who'd kept flirting with

Jake had gone, replaced by some older guy in a cream suit and hair so shiny and pure black he'd have bet anything the dude was wearing a rug.

After another half hour or so, Jake declared his intention to quit and had his chips colored up. He pushed a chip across the table towards the dealer and thanked him.

"How much you win?" enquired Billy excitedly.

"After tipping the dealer, sixty five bucks up and definitely time to call it quits. Dinner?"

"Ooh yes!"

"C'mon then." said Jake downing the rest of his drink, "Let's cash these chips in at the cage and go find us some big fat juicy steaks."

"Mmm... Just gotta love being a carnivore." Billy opened his mouth and showed his teeth and mock growled.

Jake smirked, "My, what big teeth you have Mr Wolf!"

Billy felt so tempted to give the response 'All the better for eating you up with'. But thought better of it, just in case Jake took it the wrong way.

Once outside Jake spoke to one of the valet parking attendants for directions to a 'decent but not too expensive' steak restaurant.

As they hit the sidewalk Jake grabbed hold of Billy's upper arm, "This way."

"Why down here?" Billy asked, "The guy said the restaurant's that way."

Billy tried turning and pointing back the other way, but wasn't strong enough to stop Jake hauling him off.

"Trust me, you'll see, I have my reasons, and stop looking back."

They walked down the street, then after a couple of blocks Jake dived into a service road where after a few feet he grabbed Billy again and pulled him over against a wall so they were hidden in the shadows alongside a huge dumpster.

"Jake! What are we doing here? It smells like something's died in...."

"Shhh! Quiet!" Jake hissed, and raised a finger to his lips, suppressing Billy's protest.

It didn't take long before an elongated shadow appeared past the end of the dumpster. As the figure it belonged to came into view Jake pounced and dragged the individual back into the shadows with him and Billy.

"What are you playing at? You planning to rob us?" Demanded Jake.

"No! Nothing like that, I swear." Spluttered the guy.

"Yeah right, you've been following and scoping us out all evening. Maybe I should just snap your frickin' neck and leave you in this dumpster."

Jake now had both hands gripping the front of guy's denim jacket just below the collar and had lifted him up so the guy's sneakers were actually off the ground.

What the...? Billy was confused as hell.

He hadn't spotted anyone watching them, when did Jake notice it?

Oh hang on, that's what he'd been looking at earlier, Jake must have spotted the guy when they were at the roulette table, and again when they were playing blackjack. How come Jake was so perceptive to things like that?

Billy gave up trying to figure it out, he hadn't the faintest clue as to what had just gone down, but as Jake seemed to, that was just fine with him.

However, he started getting a little concerned for the guy Jake had by the throat. He put his hand on Jake's shoulder.

"Um, maybe you should put him down so he can speak, I'm not sure he can breathe like that."

Having thought about it for a few seconds, Jake lowered the guy so his feet touched the ground once more and released his strangle hold, but one big hand still held onto the jacket. Billy could now see the guy's face better. Not very old; He guessed him to be probably same age as himself, and decidedly very scared. Billy actually felt a little sorry for him as he didn't look like a robber, not that Billy had ever seen one, apart from on TV cop shows.

"Honestly, I'm no thief; I needed to make sure you were who I thought you were."

Jake barked, "You know us from somewhere? Have we met?"

"No, but I've seen you before."

"That doesn't make any fucking sense. Now once more, where do you know us from?"

Any more elusive answers and Jake would start to get seriously pissed.

The guy sighed, "In a vision quest, to help me find you. I'm Daniel Harris, but everyone calls me Daniel Redfox."

The guy gingerly held out his hand.

Jake let go of the jacket, but refused to shake the offered hand, which dropped back down again. Instead, Jake studied the face taking in the high cheek bones, dark straight shoulder length hair and the Roman nose. Hmm, definitely American Indian heritage.

Daniel started to explain that his maternal grandfather Albert Simmons was a 'singer', one of the most revered and respected members of the Navajo community he lived in, and he had sent Daniel out to find the two of them.

"He says the people of our settlement desperately need your help and asked me to bring you to the reservation so he and some of the other elders can speak with you."

Jake racked his brain, but couldn't think of any elderly Navajo he knew or had met.

"More to the point how does he know us?"

"Through a vision quest." Replied Daniel.

"Hmm, vision quests seem very popular in your family. Why does he want to see us?"

"I don't know exactly, but he said to give you this and you would realize the truth in my words."

Daniel unbuttoned one of his jacket pockets and handed Jake a piece of folded paper tied with some sort of yarn. Jake opened it up, his eyes briefly widened.

"Jake, what's wrong, what is it?"

Billy craned his neck trying to see.

Daniel looked at Jake, "I'm guessing it means something to you?"

Jake snorted, "Nope means nothing to me." And promptly tried gave it back. When Daniel refused to take it, Jake screwed it up and threw it on the ground.

"Jake. What is it?" enquired Billy.

"It's nothing Billy, it's just some dumb drawing. C'mon, let's go, I'm hungry."

As Billy went to pick up the piece of crumpled paper Jake attempted to kick it under the dumpster, but Billy anticipating Jake's move quickly stepped in the way and as Jake miskicked Billy reached round Jake's leg and snagged the paper. Straightening back up he unfolded it and saw what Jake had tried to keep from him. Although highly stylized, the faces of a mountain lion and a wolf were unmistakable.

Leaning over Billy whispered into Jake's ear so quietly only Jake could hear.

"Maybe there's something in this Jake, I mean it's a hell of a coincidence. You gotta admit that much."

Turning back, Billy offered the painting to Daniel who held his hands up at the gesture and shook his head going on to explain that he couldn't have it back as his grandfather had forbidden him to see it, and the temptation to look would be too great. Billy shrugged, folded it up and tucked it in one of his jacket pockets.

Convinced the images had to be more than just mere coincidence, Billy's curiosity had been aroused, he wanted to know more. "Come on Jake, maybe we should find out what these people want, it could be important."

"Look Billy, I don't need to go out to find trouble, okay? It finds me easily enough. Like the last thirty six hours, yeah?"

Billy carried on his protest. "It wouldn't hurt to go speak to them, especially if they really do need our help."

"You go see them then. The way things go in my life, maybe it would be the best and safest thing for you if we went our own ways now."

"No!" snapped Billy.

No way would he let Jake run off like a scared jack rabbit, not that he could ever envisage Jake being scared of anything.

"If you have problems, we'll face them together, we done alright together yesterday."

"You really don't get it do you? Bad shit happens to me all the time. I don't need to encourage it!"

"I don't care! I'm not leaving." Billy had never won an argument in his life, but he was determined to have the last word in this one. He suddenly became aware of the pain in his hands, where he'd been fisting them so hard his nails had dug into his palms.

"Fine, just don't say I never warned you."

"Fine… I won't!"

Sensing victory Billy opened his eyes wide, wrapped his arms across his stomach and smiled, "Can we go eat now? I'm SO hungry."

Jake who had again been instantly disarmed by the tactic sighed deeply. He turned to Daniel and prodding him in the chest asked if he'd eaten yet, Daniel shook his head, too scared to answer in case he said the wrong thing.

"Okay, Daniel Redfox, I'm gonna take a chance and buy you dinner too, on the condition you explain what this is all about. Okay?"

A much relived young Navajo nodded enthusiastically.

As they walked to the restaurant, Billy introduced himself to Daniel and the two exchanged general pleasantries while Jake walked on a few steps ahead.

"Is he always like this?" whispered Daniel hoping Jake wouldn't hear.

"Oh what, the 'bad tempered and snarly' thing you mean? Yeah pretty much so, but don't let that fool you, he's really a nice guy."

Billy didn't want to admit he'd only met the guy less than two days ago; it didn't seem the appropriate place or time.

Over dinner they listened as Daniel explained some of the bad things that had been happening to his people. He went on to tell them about a skinwalker that had been said to be causing it all, and then there were the two young men from his settlement who defied their parents by going out to look for it and who never came back.

Jake glanced pensively at Billy then turned back to Daniel.

"Let me get this straight. A skinwalker is a man who turns into an animal?"

"Yes, an evil spirit."

"I thought they were werewolves?"

"It's not a joke, skinwalkers are very real to my people, they're part of our folklore."

Jake apologized and said he hadn't meant be disrespectful about Daniel's people's traditions. But added in mitigation that the whole idea of people turning into animals was a bit 'out there'.

"My grandfather also gave me this for you," he stuck his hand in his jeans pocket and put a wad of bills on the table in front of Jake. "There's eighty dollars there for gas."

"Eighty bucks? How far you reckon on going?"

"Arizona, to the Navajo Nation."

"You're kidding, that's gotta be at least a six hour drive from here."

"Ooh, Arizona, I've never seen the Grand Canyon before." Said Billy grinning from ear to ear.

"It's not that far from where we live. I could show you if you like Billy, be your guide." Suggested Daniel.

"Aww man, that'd be awesome." Enthused Billy, his smile now almost as wide as the canyon itself.

Jake's head hit the table with a theatrical thud, rattling the plates and causing neighboring diners to turn and stare.

"Why me? Why me?" Jake groaned, much to both Billy and Daniel's amusement. Billy rubbed his back, "Never mind, I'm sure you'll have a good time too."

Jake sat back up. "Okay, I know when I'm beat. We'll go. And Daniel, I figure I owe you an apology for threatening to break your neck earlier."

This time Jake offered his hand in friendship, a gesture that Daniel readily accepted. As the three of them walked out the restaurant Jake turned to Daniel, and asked whereabouts he was staying.

"In my truck."

"I don't think so. You can sleep on the floor in our hotel room."

"The trucks fine, it's no prob..."

The dismissive wave of Jake's hand cut Daniel off mid-sentence.

"It's a twin room so there's enough space to squeeze you in, and you'll be quite safe, there's no skin walkers or monsters lurking in the closets."

Billy tried to suppress a laugh, but having only succeeded in converting it into a loud snort he hurriedly turned his head away.

Daniel attempted one last protest, but quickly gave up as he could see he wouldn't win the argument.

Jake smirked, and then added that if they were both good boys, he'd buy them breakfast in the morning.

Billy smiled to himself. *So... If I'm a good boy tonight I get breakfast. If only I had the chance to be a bad boy, I wonder what I'd get then?*

No! Why did he keep having these kinds of thoughts about Jake?

As Jake explained the whereabouts of their motel to Daniel, it turned out Daniel had parked up on a lot only two blocks further on. Once they reached the motel, Jake gave Daniel their room number, who then went off to bring his truck back so he could get his sleeping roll.

Once Daniel had walked off down the block Billy turned to Jake.

"So a guy that changes into an animal is a 'bit out there' eh? Mr Cougar?"

"It's probably just superstitious nonsense, or more likely it's some guy in a Donnie Darko scary bunny costume." Jake hesitated for a second then continued. "But… There's always the outside chance it's a renegade shifter who needs sorting out."

"So we're going to help them then?"

Jake shook his head, "Now do you see what I mean about trouble always finding me?"

All three woke to the alarm on Jake's cell which made that awful buzzing, beeping noise that cheap digital alarm clocks make before the snooze button gets smacked.

Billy groaned, "Dammit, couldn't you have chosen something a bit more tuneful?" After what seemed an age of the noise drilling into his head like some deranged hornet, the buzzing stopped.

Just as he pulled the pillow over his head, in case it started again, he caught sight of Jake sat up in his bed looking far too pleased with himself and declaring it to be a lovely day outside. The growl that came from under Billy's pillow only seemed to bolster Jake's cheerfulness. If this sort of thing made Jake happy in the morning, then Billy would quite happily settle for the quiet and brooding Jake. He didn't 'do' mornings, and especially not early ones.

After taking turns to shower and get changed, the three of them left the room, Billy and Daniel headed to the trucks, while Jake dropped the key card off to reception. This time noting thankfully the receptionists were two very polite young women in dark blue and mauve uniforms, their white and gold name badges declaring them to be Kimberly and Angela. He decided this to be a major step up from some old, sour, bouffant haired, small town dragon. Just the thought of the still all too raw memory of Milton made him shudder as a chill ran down his spine.

Yep, there was definitely something to be said in favor of motel chains Jake decided, especially ones with personable staff and big bowls of complimentary hard candy on the counter. Scooping up a handful of brightly colored candy he walked away from the desk to waves and a cheery chorus of 'Have a nice day.'

As he neared the doors, his sensitive hearing picked up stifled giggles behind him and the whispered "Oh my god, he was cute, did you see the size of his arms?"

"I know, what about his ass? Talk about being able to crack walnuts between the cheeks."

Another bout of muffled giggling followed.

Still smiling, Jake grabbed his Oakley's from their resting place hung over the neck of his tee shirt, put them on, and headed outside to find the others.

Sat in a downtown diner recommended by the two hotel receptionists, the three travelers ate their breakfasts. Jake looked up at Daniel and waggled his fork at him in order to get his attention, while the piece of link sausage on the fork dripped a large dollop of tomato ketchup onto the table.

"So, if we leave straight after we've finished here, how long to get to where you live?"

"A good seven hours, maybe more, I'm pretty sure neither of our trucks is gonna make it in record time. I called my grandfather last night and told him we would be leaving for the Rez this morning."

After a butt numbing eight hours that included gas, bathroom and food stops, they reached the small Navajo settlement of about thirty houses and trailers that Daniel called home late afternoon. Once out of the trucks, Daniel took the lead and led them over to a small group of older men sitting around talking and gestured to one.

"This is my grandfather, Albert Simmons."

The old man stood and looked them up and down, then nodded slowly and gave the pair of them a 'knowing' smile. Both Billy and Jake got the spooky impression that they were exactly as the old man had been expecting them to be.

Jake offered his hand.

"It's a pleasure to make your acquaintance sir, I'm Jake Palmer," then gesturing to his side, "and this is Billy Thompson."

The old man shook their hands then beckoned for them to follow him. He briefly stopped to whisper something in another man's ear who nodded in return then walked briskly away.

Billy looked at Daniel who shook his head, "I can't come with you; the meeting is only between the two of you and some of the elders."

They followed the old man to a mud and wood hogan beyond the edge of the collection of trailer homes and small adobe or cinder block houses that comprised the settlement. Albert lifted the patterned blanket covering the doorway, upon entering the round hut Albert gestured to where Billy and Jake should sit. Albert busied himself lighting a fire in the center of the floor, and as the flames grew and the fire took hold they watched as a number of other, mostly older men entered and sat down.

After a while some of the group of started chanting while Albert held a bunch of twigs in the fire, then shook the flames out, he proceeded to waft the smoke around the hogan and at the people in it. When the chanting stopped Albert turned to Jake and Billy and explained that the smoke from the flat cedar purified everything and would attract the Holy Ones so that they would know Jake and Billy had arrived.

The old man sat down and lowered his head, then after a minute or so of what appeared to be contemplation he looked back up and spoke.

"Our people are in great fear and danger. A skinwalker has taken to drive us from our land and homes. Two of our young men went out to hunt it almost two weeks ago, they have never returned to us. After four nights of keeping vigil and with no word from them we decided to ask the Holy Ones for their help and they guided us to you."

He gestured to Jake and Billy.

Billy looked at Albert, unsure at first as to whether he should speak, "A skinwalker?"

"Yes, like you." He pointed at Billy, "But not grey wolf, like you."

He then turned and pointed at Jake, "Or mountain lion like you. He is coyote."

Billy looked at Jake, "Dude, I think the cat's out the bag so to speak."

Jake nodded in agreement.

Albert went on to describe the things that had been happening over the past few months, a lot of it repeating what Daniel had told them the previous evening. That several of their horses and dogs had been viciously attacked and killed, or been left to die a lingering death from some unknown sickness caused by their wounds. Three people had been injured in separate auto wrecks. Two houses and their local store had been badly damaged by fires, and a number of young children stricken with night terrors. Albert added that there were probably a good number of adults affected too, but none would openly admit to such a thing. And of course there were the two missing young men.

As there seemed little point in trying to hide what they were anymore, Billy attempted to explain that shapeshifters didn't possess any magical or mystical powers, just the ability to change at will between their two forms. He laughed inwardly at the last part, as if that wouldn't be seriously freaky to a normal human.

Albert shook his head and pointed towards the door. "There are many things in this world we can see. But there are other things, both good and evil that do not permit man to see them unless they so wish. The skinwalker has been seen by more than one person, each of those who had wrecks say they saw it too just before they crashed, or that it caused them to wreck."

Billy asked if anyone could tell them what they've witnessed.

One of the other men stood up; even in the flickering light of the flames the telltale signs of a number of fresh scars and scratches on his face were clear to see. The man then proceeded to tell Billy and Jake about his encounter with the 'skinwalker'.

"All I can tell you is that what caused me to wreck my car was not human. It appeared in the road on the bend that's before the fork by the three rocks. Shocked by what I saw I instinctively swerved to miss it, lost control and hit one of the rocks. As I sat there as it jumped onto the hood and tore the shattered windshield out. It then crouched down and leant into the car staring straight at me with hate filled eyes that burned red with fire. Then it jumped down, and ran off into the night."

Billy asked if it had definitely been a coyote that he'd seen.

The man glared briefly at Billy, offended that the truth of his story had been brought into question.

"It was a skinwalker, I know what I saw. It had the body of a man, but had animal hair over some of its skin, with claws for hands and the hind legs of an animal. Its face that of both man and animal together, with long drawn out jaws and large teeth."

Noting the look on the guy's face and his tone Billy apologized. "I'm sorry. I didn't mean to cause offense."

The man nodded his acceptance of Billy's apology and sat back down.

Billy decided this was no shifter, just some guy wearing a Halloween mask with red LED eyes. But a little face to face time with a snarly wolf and a grumpy cougar should make the asshole think twice before coming back.

After a considered pause Albert finally spoke.

"What you have been told is the same for everyone who has seen the skinwalker. Tonight after eating you must sleep in here," He pointed at Jake, "And tomorrow night you must go on a vision quest to give you the sight. The third night you rest, and on the fourth you must begin your hunt."

A very puzzled Jake looked at Albert, "But what I don't understand is why choose us?"

The old man shivered and pulled a blanket over his hunched shoulders. "We didn't choose you, the Holy Ones did. They told us to seek out the mountain lion that walks with the wolf. Then they told Daniel where and when to find you."

One of the other men then addressed Jake and Billy.

"Back in the great past, in the time of the creation of the Navajo, First Man and First Woman had a daughter they called Asdzáá Nádlee-hé which means 'Changing Woman', and it is from her all the Navajo clans are descended. It was she who gave the mountain lion to the first Navajo people as their guardian. Our name for the mountain lion is Náshdóítsoh, which means 'walking silently among the rocks'. The wolf, who is called Ma'iitsoh she gave to the animals as their protector."

Albert studied Jake's face before continuing. "Now you see why you are very special to us. You are our protectors and the only ones who can kill the skinwalker and save our people. Now come, you must eat, before returning here to sleep."

After their meal Billy and Jake walked back to the hogan and sat in silence watching the fire.

Eventually Billy spoke, "Have you ever heard of a coyote shifter?"

Jake shook his head, "No. I mean I've only ever come across wolves and cougars, but you've gotta ask yourself are we only types of shifter?"

He poked the fire with a stick, causing a flare of bright sparks to briefly soar upwards before vanishing. "You know the thing that puzzles me about all of this is the description; it sounds more human than animal."

Billy agreed, "Yeah plus the size thing, coyotes are small, like forty, fifty pounds, and you can't lose or gain weight changing forms. Plus how scary could a fifty pound coyote get?"

"You're right," concurred Jake, "This isn't a monster we're looking for, my money's on it being some guy dressed up to look scary. There's just way too much hocus-pocus going on here."

A puzzled look then fell across Jake's face.

Billy looked at him, "What's up?"

"I just realized that Albert said they asked their spirit guides or whatever for help four days after the two boys disappeared, and the spirits put *both* our names forward."

"Yeah, and?"

"And… If you do the math my young Padawan, that was almost a week before we first met."

"Oh crap!"

"Exactly! This whole thing is starting to give me the willies, and it's the second time I've had that feeling in the past couple of days. Plus I haven't even been on this vision quest thing yet. Who knows what's going to happen to me after drinking a load of magic cactus juice."

"Magic cactus juice?" enquired Billy, thinking he'd misheard.

"Yeah, it's called peyote, and basically it contains mescaline, a hallucinogenic drug."

"How'd you know all these things?" asked a bemused Billy.

"Discovery Channel of course!"

The next morning after breakfast, they walked around with Daniel and some of his friends. Billy turned to Daniel. "Do you know why we're here?"

Daniel shook his head and explained they'd only been told that Billy and Jake had come to help. And that the elders had said no more except that Daniel and his friends were to ask no questions, or go near the hogan. The other young men with Daniel looked serious and nodded in agreement.

Jake decided they should have a drive around the area and familiarize themselves with it in daylight. So in the afternoon they took off in their pickup, complete with an old Winchester 88 rifle that had belonged to Daniel's father. Daniel had been adamant they took it 'just in case' after Jake insisted on him and Billy going out alone.

After a couple of hours driving around Jake stopped the truck and after stretching their legs they sat leaning back against an outcrop of rock admiring the spectacular scenery.

"There is something pretty magical about this place I have to admit." Jake gestured towards the stunning landscape stretching endlessly out in front of them, "It's a feeling of tranquility, a kind of 'oneness' with nature I guess."

Billy had to agree; the area definitely had 'something special' about it.

As they sat there, Billy's sensitive hearing picked up the faint sound of an engine causing him to turn round.

"Someone's coming."

Billy then pointed to a vehicle tearing along a dirt track towards them.

Jake turned to see the approaching black shape and the dust cloud that followed in its wake, "Hmm, I reckoned we'd have company sooner or later."

Once again Billy attempted to get his mind around the fact that Jake had anticipated this happening. They weren't sitting here just to have a rest; Jake had actually been waiting for someone to show up.

Now if he was honest, Jake doing all this knowing what was going to happen shit had started to get to him a little freaked out. Jake leant over and squeezed Billy's knee as he stood up. The ripple of excitement that tore through Billy and went straight to his groin distracting him from his thoughts.

"Whatever happens, just stay back and let me do all the talking, okay?"

Getting up Billy brushed the dust off the seat of his jeans then turned and watched as Jake walked a few paces from the rocks and stopped, he leant the Winchester against a lone chunk of rock a couple of feet from his right side. The position of the rifle behind the rock effectively hid it from the view of anyone approaching them, but left it close enough to grab in an instant.

A black Chevy Tahoe with dark tinted windows slewed to a halt thirty feet away, throwing up a shower of dirt and stones.

As the two occupants got out, the driver said something to the passenger in some deep southern state accent. The passenger then pulled the peak of his ball cap down and leant his back against the truck as the driver walked up to Jake.

Not expecting the exchange to open with introductions and hand-shakes, Jake spoke first, "You know, nobody likes a showboat."

Ignoring Jake's sarcasm the man spoke slowly, his southern drawl again evident. "There ain't nothing here that concerns you… Leave now, before you get hurt."

Whatever he was, the guy definitely wasn't human! Though Jake had never come across a scent like it before. Could this be the smell of coyote? Sure wasn't like any coyote Jake had ever smelt, but there again even in animal form, shifters didn't smell the exact same as their normal animal counterparts. No, a coyote shifter simply wasn't possible; he had to be some sort of wolf.

"We're here at the invitation of some friends, and we'll leave when we're ready," retorted Jake, as flatly as he could manage.

The shifter wagged a finger at Jake, "You obviously have yourself a hearing problem there boy."

Okay, now Jake was pissed, he'd been called 'boy' or 'son' way too many times the past few days, and he had no intentions of taking it from someone the same age as him. Jake stepped right up to the guy and straight into his personal space.

"So it appears do you."

Leaning forward until his face stopped just inches away from Jake's, the guy swiveled his sunglasses up onto his close cropped ginger hair and snarled. "Don't push it kitty cat, I don't like turning on our own kind."

"Neither do I… Especially twice in one week." Countered Jake.

If Jake's remark had been meant to faze the other guy, Billy decided it had failed dismally, but then again Jake didn't seem to be rattled in the slightest, and neither of them gave off any smell of fear. Billy continued to mentally compare the pair of them, and wondered if they started slugging it out who would win.

They weren't too dissimilar in size, and although the shifter probably had a good two inches over Jake's six foot, but nowhere near as stocky, and maybe a lean one ninety pounds or so. But his arms and chest muscles under his tight fitting black tank top all looked sharply defined, like those of a boxer or athlete.

Yep, this was definitely testosterone fuelled posturing at its best, real 'mines bigger than yours' shit.

The guy straightened back up and laughed, "I've only come across a couple of cat shapeshifters before and they were just as ballsy as you, didn't help them any though."

Jake tilted his head over in an exaggerated leaning movement to look past his adversary and at the logo on the side of the truck.

"Might have guessed you had a corporate sponsor. Let me guess, these people are in the way and *you* have a *very* special talent that makes scaring them off easy. How am I doing so far?"

"I enjoy my work, what can I say?"

"So whatever it is your owners are into was it worth the lives of the two young guys from the settlement?" Jake demanded.

"No one owns me!" The skinwalker spat in reply, his face flushing red with anger.

Billy smirked; Jake's probing had just found a chink in the guy's armor.

"If that's really true, how about you prove you're your own man and tell me where the bodies are, so their families can bury them properly."

The shifter lowered his sunglasses.

"Try Perching Crow Mine, think I might have overheard someone say they saw buzzards circling there."

He jabbed Jake in the chest with a finger.

"I've done you a favor; now do yourselves a big fucking favor and leave. From now on in, you get in my way and you two won't live long enough to be able to regret it."

Turning on his heel, the guy stormed off back to his SUV. Approaching it he aggressively gestured and shouted at the other man, as it pulled away all four tires kicked up dirt and stones as they tore at the ground under the excessive use of the throttle.

Jake picked up the rifle.

"Hmm, I think that went pretty well. Now, I need a beer and a cigarette, and not necessarily in that order. C'mon, let's get back and we can tell Albert where the bodies may be."

Billy followed Jake back to the truck. His admiration for the guy had just gone up yet another couple of notches.

Jake could see both sadness and relief in the old man's eyes at the news. Albert clasped both his hands around Jake's hand and thanked him.

"I will tell their families so they may go and bring them home. Then we must start to prepare for the vision quest ceremony."

Early evening found Jake sat on a folded blanket on the floor in the hogan starving hungry. After their return, he found out that the ceremony dictated he could not eat anything until after it had finished. This left Billy having to deal with an increasingly irritable Jake.

Dusk had fallen when Albert and a number of other men all wearing ceremonial dress came into the hogan, they informed Billy that he would have to stay with Daniel as it was not permitted for him to be present for the ceremony, but he would have to come back to sleep in the hogan afterwards. Billy decided getting sent away actually wasn't so bad as it meant everyone else would have to deal with Mr Grumpy instead, as he left the hogan he met up with Daniel outside and the pair walked off to spend the evening at Daniel and his mother's house.

After having sat down, Albert handed Jake a knee length shirt and a pair of moccasins and explained that Jake needed be dressed correctly or the spirits would not come. As Jake changed clothes Albert described the ceremony and the sort of things that might happen to him once the peyote took effect.

"You have to be able to leave everything of this world behind you in order to free yourself." He explained.

Albert put his hand on Jake's shoulder and looked him in the eyes.

"When you come back to us, you will never be quite the same again; the change in you will become apparent over time. You will not understand all the things you see and hear tonight. It will take time for these things to become clear. This is why tomorrow you must start to reflect on what you have experienced."

One of the men passed a small wooden bowl to Albert, who in turn offered it to Jake. "Now... drink."

Taking the bowl, Jake swallowed a mouthful of the vile bitter liquid, gagged, and nearly brought it straight back up again. He struggled to keep it down, and with much encouragement over the course of the next ten minutes or so managed to drink it all. However, his stomach was far from happy and after half an hour it could take no more. At the sound of the first heave, someone pushed a large plastic bowl in front of Jake, who promptly threw up in it. Maintaining a tight hold on the bowl he continued to intermittently chuck up for several minutes. Then after an all too brief respite, it started all over again.

He hated being sick and sat there feeling like death warmed up. No wonder they didn't want him eat earlier, it would have been a complete waste of good food. He then started to become aware of the smell of puke, the bowl had to go or he'd start barfing all over again. As he went to move the bowl, someone took it from him and a damp cloth thrust into his hand, he wiped his mouth then looked up.

Another small wooden bowl appeared in front of him, he shook his head. No way, he couldn't do any more of the stuff, he pushed it away. Again, someone offered the bowl, this time with the explanation that it contained just a little water to rinse his mouth out with. Jake grabbed it, after swirling it around his mouth and spitting it back out, he passed the bowl back. As he started to relax a little, he realized everything seemed normal and definitely not at all trippy, maybe with all the puking there wasn't enough left in him to have any effect.

As his stomach started to calm down, he found himself feeling a little more comfortable. Someone placed a blanket over his shoulders; in response he clasped it to him. Closing his eyes he felt the warmth of the fire tingling on his face and gradually became aware of people chanting and drumming. Opening his eyes he stared into the fire.

He sat there and wondered how, if at all, the peyote would affect him. Not being a normal human being the effects could be unpredictable, maybe it would turn him crazy. No, probably not. Maybe it wouldn't have any effect at all, which meant he'd tortured his poor stomach for nothing.

The addition of more wood to the fire caused it to crack and pop, a shower of sparks rushed upwards, watching them Jake tilted his head back and saw how the flickering flames lit the roof of the hogan. Pools of orange light danced across the roof, seemingly chasing each other into the shadows.

Nope, nothing was happening, still, he decided he should go along with what they wanted, as he didn't want to offend anyone, and besides they wouldn't be any the wiser.

As he lowered his head back down and stared into the flames the deep melodic tones of the rhythmic drumming and chanting crept into his head rolling through his consciousness like night sea fog invading the streets of a seaside town. It swirled around, searching out the dark recesses of his subconscious mind. The deeper it pervaded his brain, the more absorbed he became in the flames, their orange and yellow tops reached upwards, flickering and stuttering as the new wood crackled and popped. Further down in the fire white hot sprites formed fleetingly before vanishing back into the base of the flames. Each time they returned, they increased in number and appeared for longer before fashioning themselves into what appeared to be some animated figure. Jake stared hard trying to make out what it could be. Then he realized, it was an animal, a cougar!

It promptly disappeared back into the fire only for the sprites to appear and reform again, now there were two animals. A wolf had joined the cougar. Jake stared, mesmerized. He continued to watch as the two figures leapt and danced on their hind legs through the flames in time with the drumming. Then they merged together and another, much larger figure started to form, this time a man's face stared out of the fire straight at him.

Jake didn't recognize the face but the man had a goatee beard and looked quite old. But one thing was for sure, he didn't look happy. All of a sudden the face transformed into that of a roaring dragon before it too melted away back into the flames. With nothing in the flames anymore to hold his attention Jake's head lolled down and he saw bright green and yellow plant roots coming out of his shirt sleeves where his wrists should have been. The roots burrowed their way into the ground by his crossed legs. Or rather they would have if he'd had any legs. Where his legs were a short time ago, there were now dozens of cigarettes all standing on end gently waving back and forth like corn ears in a light breeze. The thin wisps of pale grey smoke from them twisted upwards and joined to form tiny brightly colored humming birds that after separating from the smoke flew upwards before they too turned back into smoke as they continued their journey up to the roof. Jake sat there captivated by what he saw, and accepted it all as being perfectly normal.

Lifting his head back up to look at the roof he could see the shadows cast by the firelight cycle through red to green to blue, moving his head also caused the colors to change. He felt his head and shoulders involuntarily moving in circles, when he made himself stop he felt a cool breeze on his face. As he closed his eyes, the feeling grew more intense; almost as if the wind had become stronger, then it changed direction and grew icy cold as it blew across the back of his head making his neck hairs stand on end.

He opened his eyes; the fire had vanished. In fact everything had gone, the hogan, everyone in it, the settlement, even the land and the sky had disappeared. Instead, only an absolute, unfathomable darkness existed. As Jake strained to see into it a large cat flanked by two jackals with eyes the color of hot coals emerged out of the dark and stalked towards him. As they drew closer the jackals' bodies started to fade as a swirling steel gray mist appeared and enveloped them. As the fog diffused back into the gloom, it took the jackals with it leaving just the cat, which noticing the jackals were no longer with it stopped.

Jake attempted to make out the type of cat; it was heavily built and had dense markings on its fur. Then before he could decide, its head transformed into that of a jackal before the inky blackness closed in and swallowed it too. Staring into space he became aware of the chanting and drumming once more. As he listened, the sounds started to change, as they took on the form of voices, distant and indistinct at first but little by little becoming clearer. He closed his eyes in order to concentrate on what the voices were saying.

Gradually the voices quietened to little more than a whisper, he then heard a woman speak to him, calling him by his name, her voice calming and gentle. Then Jake realized it was his Navajo name she spoke, not his regular name.

Náshdóítsoh… Náshdóítsoh…

There were many other words too, not ones known to him, but somehow he understood everything the woman said.

When Albert saw Jake's head drop he knew the spirits were talking to him and he went back to focusing on his prayer chant. All of a sudden one of the other men in the hogan gasped and dropped his prayer fan; a couple of the others stopped chanting. Albert looked up at them in time to see the stunned expressions etching onto their faces; he then turned to see what could have caused such reactions.

Even he fleetingly hesitated in his chant as he stared at Jake who now sat with his chin almost touching his chest, his body surrounded by a shimmering gold aura that radiated out from his very core and looked as if should be bright enough to bath the hogan in a soft yellow light. In all his long years Albert had never seen anything like it; truly, this had to be a sign that the original guardians sent to protect the Navajo had taken control of Jake's spirit. Today was indeed a very special day in his life.

As the aura started to fade away Albert saw Jake's head lift and his eyes sluggishly open as he became once again transfixed by the flames in the fire. This state lasted for almost another hour as the peyote gradually let his mind be, slowly returning him to his own world.

Jake felt woozy, like someone had snuck in and filled his head with cotton balls, and his eyes were sore and dry from the heat of the fire. The gentle murmuring of voices had replaced the drumming and chanting of earlier. He tried to make some sense of the events earlier, but couldn't concentrate.

Summoned from Daniel's house Billy entered the hogan and seeing Jake lying on a blanket bed knelt down in front of him. Billy gently put his hand on Jake's shoulder but before he could shake him Jake's eyes blinked open.

"Oh sorry, I didn't mean to wake you." Billy apologized.

"It's okay, I wasn't asleep."

"Do you want some food? Apparently some soup's been made for you."

Jake shook his head and instantly regretted it, he groaned and closed his eyes again.

"Maybe later eh?" Jake murmured.

"Okay, no problem, I'll fetch some when you're ready." Billy pointed towards one of the low benches. "Can I sit over there? I promise I'll be quiet and not bother you."

Jake thought about answering, but deciding it would probably make his head pound again, he settled instead for affirmative grunting noises.

He lay there desperately trying to make some sort of sense of what he'd experienced. Eventually Jake decided it wasn't happening and keeping his eyes tightly closed, slowly sat up. Okay, keeping the eyes closed had definitely been a good thing, as the thumping headache or giddiness he'd expected hadn't happened. When he eventually decided it should be safe to open his eyes he found both Billy and Albert sitting opposite him, watching intently.

"I'll have that soup now if it's still on offer?"

"Yes sir!"

Billy jumped up, bowed gracefully and then still grinning widely left the hogan. Albert passed Jake a beaker of water.

"It will do you good to eat. You must keep your strength up for what is to come. What the Holy Ones have shown you isn't just for now, or for the fight to come. It also relates to your destiny and your purpose in this life."

"Yes, I think I understand, but I'm really not sure how to make sense of what I saw."

The old man nodded, "That will come in time, it is the one reason that today you must take time to think about the things you have been shown and told."

The two of them sat in silence while Jake again tried to get his head round everything. This stopped with Billy's arrival.

"I have your food order Sir." He handed the bowl and spoon to Jake, who started scooping the hearty soup into his mouth as fast as he could swallow.

He looked up then felt bad as he was the only one eating. Albert and Billy both said not to be concerned, as they'd already eaten.

Putting the empty bowl down Jake said, "So that's the end of the ceremony then?"

"Yes." replied Albert, "This is a time to rejoice as the Holy Ones have allowed you to come back into this world from your vision quest. When everything is over and the skinwalker is dead then we will celebrate. But now you must both sleep."

Before long Jake started to doze off, the ceremony having left him physically and mentally drained. Jake woke several times during the night, each occasion after some particularly vivid dream. Billy woke just as the sunrise broke and seeing Jake's bed empty went outside where he found him leant up against the hogan deep in thought.

"You okay?" Billy asked.

"Yeah, it's just I keep having these really weird dreams; I think maybe they're visions, but I can't get my head around them. It's just getting to me a bit I guess."

"Aren't dreams meant to be the brain's way of dealing with all the things that have gone on in the day?" asked Billy.

"Now who's been watching the Discovery Channel?"

Billy had something he needed to say, and he was fast running out of time.

"I'm coming with you when you go to kick the coyote's butt, and I'm not taking no for an answer."

Billy folded his arms and put on what he hoped was his sternest look. When Jake started smiling he guessed the look hadn't come across as serious as he had hoped.

"I think that's how it's meant to be." said Jake, "You and me fighting whatever this thing is together. So I was hoping you'd be up for it, didn't really fancy doing it alone, but wasn't going to ask you straight out."

Billy felt somewhat relieved but also a little disappointed; he had a whole speech worked out in his head ready to counter all the objections he expected Jake to put in his way.

Albert remained steadfast in his belief that both Jake and Billy had to be fully rested before facing the skinwalker the following day. And although they had left the hogan during the day to socialize, shower and eat, come dusk they were ushered back inside where they would again be under the protection of the Holy Ones for the night. And of course the two guys with pump action shotguns outside the door, plus Jake had Daniel's Winchester rifle hidden under the blankets that made up his bed.

After breakfast on the fourth day they went out in the pickup with Daniel in the cab riding shotgun, and two of his friends in the back. Jake had initially wanted to scope out the area with Billy to get directions and distances fixed in his mind. However, Daniel and his friends were insistent that they come along and help in the hunt for the skinwalker, and provide protection for Jake and Billy. Convinced they wouldn't meet up with the guy, Jake agreed to let them tag along.

By noon Jake decided they'd got everything they needed from their reconnaissance mission and they headed back to the settlement for lunch. They then spent the rest of the afternoon sitting about relaxing and chatting with Daniel and his friends. After their early evening meal Albert ushered the pair back to the hogan.

The next few hours went by with very little said between the two of them. For the fiftieth time since Albert left them Jake checked the time on his cell phone, it had just turned nine pm.

He turned to Billy, then managing a brief smile proclaimed. "Showtime."

The bravado Billy had been feeling earlier during the day had all but evaporated over the last couple of hours. He now doubted that what little courage he had left would be enough to carry him through, as he was terrified of what could happen. The memory of Jake's bloody fight in the woods with the wolf less than a week ago still all too fresh in his mind.

Spotting the apprehension in Billy's face Jake shuffled across the floor and put a reassuring hand on Billy's shoulder.

"It'll be fine; there are two of us against that jerkwad we met the other day. So he's a shifter, big deal, the guy's full of piss and wind."

"Yeah, guess you're right."

"I am, trust me. It'll be fine. We'll send him away with his tail between his legs."

They both stripped off and lay on their blankets. This time they could both shift together without having to worry as they knew that Albert and two of the others were outside guarding the hogan.

Something special was going to happen tonight, Daniel had been convinced of that all day, and he'd be damned if he was going to miss out on it.

He turned the kitchen light off and sneaked out the backdoor of his mother's house. Then crouching low made his way towards the hogan, as he reached the remains of an old trailer home by the side of the path he dived under its chassis. Carefully he wriggled his way to the other end and settled himself into a position where he had a good view of the hogan with no chance of him being spotted.

He didn't know how long he'd lain there, but he'd become chilled to the bone and one of his arms had gone to sleep. Careful so as not to make any sound, he extracted his numb arm from under him. He'd just started to get some feeling back in his fingers when he spotted his grandfather and the other two guards get up. From his vantage point he watched as the old man lifted the up the blanket that covered the entrance.

Daniel's eyebrows shot up as his eyes widened in surprise, and he only just managed to stop himself from gasping out loud as first a cougar then a wolf walked out of the hogan and stood by his grandfather. Albert reached down and placed a hand on each of their heads. Daniel could hear his grandfather speaking to the animals but couldn't make out the words it then dawned on him that the old man was talking to them in Navajo.

Straightening back up Albert took his hands off the animal's heads before the pair padded off into the darkness. Suddenly the wolf stopped in its tracks, turned its head and looked straight at the abandoned trailer home. Daniel's heart skipped a beat; he was close enough to see the fire outside the hogan glinting in the wolf's eyes. It raised its head sniffing the air, before turning round and trotting off after the cougar. Now

Daniel knew why all the secrecy, Billy and Jake were good skinwalkers brought here by the Holy People to kill the evil skinwalker. It all made sense now, kind of.

Albert let the other two men walk on ahead back along the path to the settlement. Daniel saw his grandfather approaching and held his breath so as not to make even the slightest sound. He listened as soft footsteps in the gravelly dessert soil approached then stopped.

"Daniel Redfox, I will make us both hot chocolate, you must be cold from lying there for so long."

The old man smiled at the muffled 'Yes Sir' and shook his head. He waited until his grandson joined him and put his arm around Daniels shoulders.

"We have many things to talk about and do. Tell your mother you will stay with me tonight and tomorrow."

Sat on the floor in front of Albert, Daniel sipped his hot chocolate.

"So Jake and Billy are real skinwalkers then Grandfather. I mean they're good ones aren't they?"

"Not skinwalkers, they are guardians of the Navajo, brought to us by the Holy Ones.

"But they've gone to kill the skinwalker though?"

The old man took a sip of his drink and nodded.

"As they're both so much bigger than a coyote it will be easy for them won't it?"

Albert shook his head, "It is different to them, not animal or human like them. This is something born of an old and very malevolent evil, something that should not be here."

Daniel looked down into his mug and thought for a while before looking back up at his grandfather, "They will beat it though, won't they?"

Albert considered his answer for a few seconds, "We must trust in the Holy Ones, they sent the wolf and the mountain lion to us and Jake is…"

The old man's voice trailed off, there were things that had to stay unsaid, and his belief that Jake had within him some sort of connection to the Holy Ones was one of those things.

Looking back down at Daniel he carried on, "The bond between the two of them is very powerful it will help give them strength."

"Bond?"

"There is a very close bond between them. They are destined to be together."

"You mean like a couple, or a Batman and Robin thing?"

Albert put his hand on Daniel's head and smiled, "I do not know what form it will take, at the moment only the Holy Ones know such things, and I suspect that neither Jake nor Billy know themselves yet."

But Albert knew that alone would not be nearly enough. He hoped that the Spirits would give them the strength and wisdom they needed not just to win, but for both of them to survive the impending battle."

For several hours Billy and Jake walked and trotted around trying to cover the greatest area in an effort to spread their scent about in an effort to attract the attention of the coyote, skinwalker or whatever. Jake made sure they rested every so often so as to not exhaust themselves. Eventually they ended up back at the top of the deep gully where they'd first met the shifter and waited.

They kept completely still and silent during their vigil, all their senses on full alert. After they had sat there some considerable time, Jake decided he would give it a while longer before returning to the hogan to shift. He wanted to get back well before the morning sun broke the horizon so as not to be seen and alarm anyone in the settlement.

Suddenly Billy got up and cocked his head first to one side then the other. Jake watched as the wolf's ears flicked and swiveled as Billy strained to pick up some obviously distant sound. Then Jake heard it, although initially faint, the regular thud, thud, thud of something two legged with a long stride running their way grew louder by the second. Just as Jake stood, the footfall abruptly stopped and the desert's silence enveloped them once more. Both Jake and Billy repeatedly sniffed the air in a desperate attempt to get the scent. Nothing, it had to be approaching downwind of them. Billy stared out into the dark, something really wasn't right, why he couldn't see it.

Neither he nor Jake saw or sensed its arrival until it appeared less than thirty feet away from them.

And there it stood...

Billy reckoned it had to be well over six foot six, taller than when in its human form. What skin wasn't covered by random patches of matted, straggly hair, seemed dark and looked marbled in appearance, though the moonlight made it impossible for him to make out the color of the skin or the hair. The creature's narrow head with its long muzzle, tall pointed ears and close set eyes looked almost Doberman like, but much, much bigger. Its bald tail appeared substantially thicker near the body and looked almost scaly, reminding Billy a bit of a rat.

One thing was for sure though... It was definitely no coyote.

He could see now where Daniel's people got the Hell Hound burning red eye thing from. The creature's eyes seemed to have an orangey glow to them. Billy wanted to put it down to them simply reflecting an unusually high amount of the light back with the blood vessels giving the red color. But he wasn't doing a good job of convincing himself.

Fuck! Right there in front of him stood the monster everyone had always told him only existed in the movies. Maybe they'd have to fight it Hollywood style with silver bullets in the Winchester, a gallon of holy water and a few wooden stakes thrown in just for good measure.

Slowly Billy moved away from Jake, his teeth bared but not snarling, he decided to follow Jake's lead and keep the menace low key. He kept moving sideways hoping to distract the creature by making it think he would try to outflank it. But the creature's eyes only flashed his way fleetingly before they locked back onto Jake again.

Once Billy had moved about twenty feet out to the side he stopped and looked back at Jake. Geez, if the size of those huge canines now on full display didn't make the skinwalker crap itself then the guy, thing, or whatever the hell it was had a serious death wish.

However, he felt compelled to take that back when he saw the size of the claws attached to the skinwalker's huge hands. Slowly it moved forward on sturdy legs that somehow gave the impression of moving all wrong. It took Billy a few seconds to realize they were a cross between human legs and canine hind legs making it bipedal, but he suspected it could also leap or even run on all fours when it needed to. For crying out loud, the thing was a total freak of nature.

The creature stepped forward several paces before stopping again now less than twenty feet away. Still maintaining eye contact with Jake it leant its whole upper body forward and snarled, revealing a mouthful of dagger like teeth, while saliva dripped liberally from its lower jaw.

Worse still, Billy concluded that his distraction ploy had failed, the creature had taken no notice of him whatsoever, its gaze remained unfalteringly fixed on Jake, who for his part stood motionless, his unblinking stare locked onto the skinwalker's eyes.

Sheer terror froze Billy to the spot when without any warning the creature dropped onto all fours and lunged at Jake, whose powerful rear legs responded instantly to the not unexpected attack by instantly releasing all their pent up energy, sending him near vertically up into the air. The cougar's ultra-flexible spine allowed his whole body to twist with amazing agility for such a stocky frame as he easily cleared the mass of cruel looking teeth and claws headed his way.

Jake landed and spun round at the same instant as the beast, now the face off started all over again. The skinwalker started snarling and snapping its jaws in an obvious attempt to intimidate and leave Jake wondering as to when it would strike next. However, Jake didn't have to wait long, the follow up attack came almost instantly, this time though the creature anticipated Jake's evasive reaction and its front claws latched firmly onto the cougar midair bringing Jake down on his back with the skinwalker landing on top of him. The weight of the skinwalker hitting Jake knocked the wind clean out of him, the air leaving his body so fast it made a whooshing sound in his head.

The creature's claws held tight as its teeth sank into the fleshy part of Jake's shoulder. Although it held the bite, for some reason it didn't attempt to bite deep or to tear, though Jake still hissed loudly with the pain. Then without any warning, the creature let go and swiftly stood off several paces.

Never taking his eyes off the skinwalker Jake got up. Fuck! The bastard was toying with him. As he watched, it seemed to be sneering.

It was! It was actually trying to laugh at him.

Jake knew he had to attack now in order to try to cover the extent of his injuries. The only downside to this plan being the skinwalker would no doubt be prepared for him to do just that.

Jake drove at his enemy, who anticipating the attack met Jake in mid-air. They both crashed to the ground, Jake landing on his injured shoulder. The shifter tried to seize hold of Jake's neck in its jaws but this time Jake managed to twist himself out of the way just in time and the creature merely ended up with a mouthful of desert.

It spat the dirt out of its mouth and leaning forward at Jake voiced its rage and frustration. However, the sound it emitted wasn't like anything Jake expected, being more akin to a scream than a roar. To Jake it sounded similar to the cry a vixen fox makes trying to attract a mate.

So could it be a fox? No, that would be less likely than it being a coyote would. It had to be a wolf with something gone very badly wrong in its genetic makeup, some sort of freaky genetic throwback. Jake decided that whilst in human form it probably had a very small dick too. Shame he couldn't tell it that just to piss it off some more.

Still enraged the creature launched at Jake once more, its speed and agility almost catching him out. This time however Jake's rear legs found purchase against a half buried rock and he leapt up twisting midair in order to get onto the shifter's shoulders with the aim of wrapping his powerful front legs around its neck before delivering the killer bite to its spine where it joined the back of the skull.

But before he could do anything, the shifter dropped down causing Jake to go sailing over the top and losing the chance to grasp the creature's neck. Jake heard the creature's high pitched shriek as Jake's talon like front claws tore into its flesh in a desperate attempt to hold on.

The second Jake landed he twisted around, his muscles tensing as he readied himself to strike, but the shifter had matched his speed and had already positioned itself in order to strike. As they both lunged at each other Jake's vision started to blur and he came over all unsteady, he hit the ground not knowing where he was. As he struggled to get back up, he suddenly felt both teeth and claws sink into his flesh, the intense pain momentarily focusing his attention.

Still grasping Jake in its jaws the creature drove towards the edge of the gully. Fighting the fog developing in his mind Jake grasped what it was attempting to do. His claws scrabbled at the loose dessert soil in a desperate attempt to prevent the inevitable. The creature in turn dug its claws in as it made one last concerted push.

The glowing red eyes were the last thing Jake saw before he plunged nearly thirty feet down to the bottom of the dry gully, bouncing off the side on the way and ended up stunned and bleeding on the gully floor. What was happening to him? He felt nauseous, giddy and weak when he should just be feeling pain.

Then he realized, the creature's saliva had to be poisonous like that of the Komodo dragon, and the toxins in the saliva were now coursing through his blood stream. That's why it didn't bite deeply or rip at the flesh, it knew this would happen. And it had to be the reason why the Navajo's animals had become sick or died, their blood had been poisoned.

Oh man! He was fucked. Big time.

Billy watched as the skinwalker raised itself up to full height and let out what he assumed to be some sort of victory howl. He simply wouldn't let Jake's death be for nothing, he had to take Jake's place. And despite knowing that attacking the creature would probably be futile, he was determined to fight until the very last drop of strength left his body.

He tore at full speed towards the creature but the distance meant he didn't have the element of surprise he needed. The skinwalker turned to face the charging wolf, then at the last second it sidestepped and struck Billy with a backhand blow sending him spinning through the air, the wolf letting out a yelp as he hit the ground.

Standing back up, Billy shook his head clear and once more hurled himself at the creature, his claws dug into the ground as he raced across the gritty desert sand to confront his adversary. Again, the creature lashed out and caught Billy, this time vicious claws tore into flesh as the blow sent Billy flying some distance from the creature causing him to land hard against an outcrop of rock. The resulting pain was excruciating, as Billy lay there white and yellow lights flashed across in his vision.

Without warning, a white hot fury tore through him, blinkering his reasoning and wrestling control of his body away from him. Before the overwhelming rage took him over completely he realized he'd experienced this phenomenon once before, when he'd deliberately stopped himself from shifting during a full moon and as a result completely destroyed his room in the ranch house, and everything in it. Now, beyond pain; he had no thought for his own life, and the power within him that had taken over only wanted to kill and destroy the enemy. Billy had all his senses, but it felt as if he was merely an observer, as he couldn't seem to restrain the raging forces within.

The creature stood on the edge of the gully looking down. For a third time Billy launched himself at the shifter, almost upon it he watched in astonishment as the creature leapt off the edge of the gully down to where Jake lay. Billy resisted the urge to throw himself off the edge after the creature and instead skidded to a halt. He immediately turned and sprinted along the top of the gully to where the previous day he'd seen a pathway down to the bottom, his overwhelming need to attack and kill not diminished.

At the bottom of the gully Jake lay on his side, his remaining strength leaving him fast. He knew he was dying and he could do nothing about it except lay there and wait for the end to come. He told himself t wasn't so bad really, his life was pretty shitty anyway, and this seemed the right way to end it. Going out in a blaze of glory as they say.

A feeling of calm settled over him and he closed his eyes, but instead of the darkness taking him as he expected, he saw a point of faint yellow light that steadily grew bigger and brighter as it seemed to approach him.

Then as the light behind his eyelids seemed to fill his head it shrank, transforming into the face of the cougar that had been on the piece of paper Daniel showed him back in Vegas. The cougar's face then became the face of a young man wearing a shiny black helmet.

"I am Naayéé' Neizghání, the Monster Slayer, elder of the twin sons of Asdzáá Nádleehé, Changing Woman, the mother of the earth and creator of the Navajo people. Náshdóítsoh, you were summoned by my mother to protect the Navajo. I can give you no weapon here in your world, but my brother and I can give you strength. Now get up and fight Náshdóítsoh. Slay your monster as we slew ours."

Jake's eyes flew open, and he instinctively looked up. As he did, he saw the skinwalker look down over the gully edge high above him, then it launched itself off the top. A surge of raw primal energy tore through Jake like a bolt of lightning. Instantly both his hind legs rammed against a large rock then using the extraordinary new energy feeding into them, he powered himself out of harm's way.

Mid-decent the shifter saw the blur of Jake's movement and attempted to turn its body in an effort to reach him but the maneuver was ill judged and the creature screamed out as it hit a jagged rock outcrop hard, bounced off and landed awkwardly.

Jake had already positioned himself for an immediate attack against the skinwalker. However, instead of going for the creature something made him hold back, he then watched as it attempted to stand upright on its hind legs, but as it tried, it fell back onto all fours emitting a cry of pain. As it took a step forward its left hind leg gave way. Instead of attacking Jake decided to wait in order to see how bad its injuries actually were.

It limped again as it tried to put weight on that leg.

Yes! The asshole had obviously broken or dislocated something when it hit the rock. An injury that bad would require it to shift in order to heal the damage.

So preoccupied with attempting to stand and conceal the extent of its injuries, the skinwalker failed to notice the wolf bearing down on it, until the snarling Billy hurled himself at its head. He missed biting into the back of the creature's neck as it dipped its head at the last second. Instead, his jaws clamped hard together on one of its large pointed ears. Cartwheeling over the creature's head Billy landed in a heap with the torn off ear still firmly grasped between his teeth.

The skinwalker once more shrieked in pain and instinctively tried to hold a front paw up to its head causing it to momentarily lose its balance. Even though unable to stand on two legs or run, it still presented a formidable enemy with vicious claws and a poisonous bite and Jake knew to be extremely wary of it.

Only now had Billy became aware the cougar was still very much alive and kicking and obviously ready to carry on the fight. Both Jake and Billy then started approaching the creature from opposite sides. As it endeavored to ready itself for the impending attack, it hobbled and stumbled as once again it tried to put weight onto its injured leg.

Jake knew that wherever his new strength had come from it wouldn't last long, he had to attack, but Billy beat him to it. Fury still surging through the young wolf's body and mind he charged at the creature then turned at the last moment hitting it full pelt in the good hip with his shoulder. All of his and the creature's weight went onto the injured rear leg, which crumpled underneath it, and it fell over onto its hind quarters.

Now with the skinwalker on the ground, a deep seated primitive instinct took Jake over as he saw his chance to go for the kill. He lunged at the creature's throat his huge front legs and paws gripping around its neck forcing its head down onto the ground. Trying desperately to defend itself, the creature brought one of its semi human hands up and the claws sliced at Jake's back leaving deep gouges in Jake's flesh. Seeing this Billy threw himself at the creature's forearm and clamped his jaws onto it just below the wrist preventing it from lashing out again.

As Jake's jaws fastened around the skinwalker's throat, his four huge canine teeth sliced deep into the unprotected flesh. Sensing its impending fate the creature desperately tried to bite at Jake but the cougar's wide head was wedged under the skinwalker's lower jaw and effectively blocked the attack. Jake now having bitten down as hard as his powerful jaws would allow, let go with his front legs then twisted his body crocodile style. A huge chunk of the creature's flesh came away in his mouth. A strange hollow gasp came from the skinwalker's throat, the bite having torn deep into its windpipe and the surrounding tissue.

Spitting out the bitter tasting flesh, Jake quickly pushed himself backwards out of harm's way. Seeing Jake back off, Billy let go of the skinwalker's arm, and scooted away. As the writhing creature attempted to lift itself up, Jake saw the thick jet of arterial spray spewing out from its neck, as its still pounding heart rapidly drained the body of blood. It crashed back onto its side unable to stand; then tried once more, but the feeble attempt came to nothing. As its head fell back, a hand with the claws still extended pitifully sliced at thin air.

They watched its forearm drop to the ground as the creature's remaining life slipped away. Its dying breaths now gurgled through the gaping wound as blood started to fill its lungs. It made one final stuttering struggle to breathe. Then as the last breath left its body with an empty sigh, its front limbs trembled briefly, and it was all over.

The pair of them stood there staring at the body, half expecting it to get up. But after a couple of minutes when it became obvious it wasn't going to turn into a zombie Billy gently nudged Jake with his nose and started to walk off, Jake followed and they took the rough sloping path up to the top of the gully. Two thirds of the way up Jake staggered, nearly plunging back down. Billy heard the noise and looking round saw Jake struggling, he ran back down and somehow managed to squeeze around the outside of Jake, once behind him he lowered his head and pushed against the cougar's rump helping to prevent him faltering again.

Once they'd reached the top of the gully Jake knew he had to keep going, he had to get back to the hogan and the medicine men, very aware that if he collapsed now it would be game over and he wouldn't get up again.

With the skinwalker dead, whatever had taken Billy over for those few short minutes had buried itself back deep in his mind somewhere, returning full control of his body to him. His sole concern now being to get Jake back to the safety of the settlement. He walked close alongside Jake occasionally running in circles around him making excited yipping noises trying to encourage the cougar to keep going. But Jake's body was tiring fast, the mysterious energy that had surged through him only a short while ago had all gone, leaving him reliant on willpower alone in order to keep going. While all the time the skinwalker's poison in his blood stream spread ever deeper. He tried desperately to blank out the burning pain that racked his entire body, and doggedly carried on, but he could tell his pace was getting slower almost by the step.

After what seemed like an eternity of walking, Billy spotted a pin-point of light coming from the settlement.

Oh please Jake it's not too far now, please make it... Please!

Billy could only will Jake on now, but despite his best efforts the cougar soon stumbled again, only this time Jake couldn't stop his legs buckling underneath him and the big cat collapsed heavily onto his side. Billy dashed over to him. He had to do something! Lowering his head, he tried nudging the cougar with the top of his muzzle, but it didn't move. He then kept still so he could tell if the cougar was still breathing. He sighed with relief when he saw the chest gently rising and falling, though each breath seemed slower and more labored than the previous.

He knew he had no time to shift; instead he ran the last half a mile or so to the hogan as fast as he could and howled. Albert, Daniel and three of the other elders ran over to him. Billy began barking then turned and started to walk away, only to stop and look back at the men.

"Grandfather, what's wrong with Billy?"

"I think we are to follow him; something must have happened to Jake. Daniel, get one of the big blankets from the hogan. Go quickly now!"

They followed the wolf until it stopped by the motionless body of the cougar. Daniel ran over to it, and placed his hand on its chest.

"He's breathing but it's very shallow and it's all stuttery."

Daniel held his hand up, and looked at the palm, the moonlight making the blood on it look black, he turned his palm towards his grand-father, "And he's bleeding." he added. Albert signaled to the others and the five of them gently picked Jake up and placed him on the blanket, they then carried him back to the settlement and laid Jake, still on the blanket, onto the ground in the hogan.

Albert looked down at Billy, "Do you need somewhere to change back?"

Billy went over to his pile of clothes, barked and wagged his tail, he couldn't think of anything else to do.

Albert pointed, "Daniel, take his clothes, go to my house and let Billy change there."

Billy and Daniel ran to Albert's small cinderblock house on the edge of the settlement just across from where Daniel lived with his mother. Once inside Billy lay down on the bedroom floor and tried to get the shift to start as fast as he could, not caring if Daniel saw or not. His concern for Jake overrode all common sense, and all the caution instilled into him since he been old enough to know about his heritage simply thrown to the wind.

Daniel couldn't believe his eyes as the grey wolf on the floor started its gradual transformation to human form. He stood rooted to the spot, partly in total disbelief, partly in fear. But after a while his anxiety eased as fascination and wonderment took over. Not taking his eyes off what just a short while ago had been a wolf; he climbed onto the bed and sat cross legged completely spellbound by what was happening on the floor in front of him. He looked down at an unrecognizable, gently pulsating shape, with no limbs, tail or head. Then slowly a human shape started to take form, at one stage he thought it looked a little like one of those mannequins you see undressed in store windows when they change the display, bald and lacking definition. In another twenty minutes the shape had become fully human again and recognizable as Billy.

Coming to with a start Billy sat bolt upright gasping for air, he felt weak and disoriented after his record breaking time to complete a shift.

"Are you alright?" Asked a concerned Daniel.

Turning to face the voice Billy stared quizzically at Daniel, his instinct told him he wasn't in any imminent danger, although as yet he hadn't understood anything the guy had said. Then little by little, things slowly started to click back into place as Billy recognized Daniel. He didn't know where he was, but he felt safe, and that would do for now, the rest would come back to him soon enough. After a few more minutes his vocal chords started to work, at first they were only capable of making peculiar sounds, but soon Billy managed to form croaky words.

"Billy, are you okay?" Daniel asked again.

"I'm fine, I think. How are you?"

"Err, I'm not sure yet Dude. That was like pretty intense!"

Billy tried to get up, but his arms came over all shaky and he promptly fell straight back down on his butt, Daniel jumped off the bed and helped Billy get up and sit on the edge of the bed. Billy's head pounded, plus he had the vilest taste in his mouth; he really didn't want to think too much about it, but if he didn't barf everywhere, he'd be surprised.

Billy turned to Daniel, "I really need a drink of water to get this taste out my mouth, then I have to get dressed and go to Jake."

Daniel jumped off the bed, went to the kitchen and came back with a bottle of water which Billy proceeded to gulp down in one. Most shifters Billy knew from his pack days complained of dehydration to some degree after shifting, but for some reason he'd always suffered more than most.

After the pair of them had managed to get Billy dressed, he went to stand again, but his legs were still too weak after the fast shift to support him unaided.

"You need to sleep Billy, you must rest." insisted Daniel.

"I'll sleep when I know Jake's okay, not 'til then. Help me up, I've got to get to him."

Daniel knew if he didn't help the guy, Billy would crawl to the hogan on all fours if he had to. Billy put his arm round Daniel's shoulder for support and the two of them slowly made their way to the hogan.

"Billy, we can't go in!" Daniel protested, "The singers are gathered to perform a healing ceremony."

"Yeah right!"

Billy had no intentions of leaving Jake alone one minute longer just to fit in with somebody's superstitions, however well-intentioned they were. Letting go of Daniel, he held onto the rough timber door frame with one hand and yanked the blanket aside.

One of elders hearing the commotion outside moved to the entrance just in time to grab Billy as his legs buckled under him and he fell through the doorway. As the man held Billy up he looked to Albert for guidance, once Albert had nodded his consent, the man half guided, half carried Billy to a small low bench where he sat him down.

Looking around Billy saw Jake on the blanket still in his cougar form, his body now covered in leaves. Beside Jake, Albert was knelt down creating a sand painting while two of the others rhythmically chanted. The man who'd helped Billy to the seat sat down next to him and quietly explained that they must perform a 'sing', that being the part of the healing ceremony where they summoned the Holy Ones to help heal Jake.

Tears now freely streamed down Billy's face as he pleaded, "You gotta hurry, I know he's dying, I can feel it."

The elder went on to explain that everything had to be in strict accordance with their traditions, and that if the songs and prayers were not performed exactly right the Holy Spirits would not come from their homes in the four sacred mountains. Another of the men draped a blanket around Billy's head and shoulders, clutching the blanket to him, Billy sat in total silence and watched as the ceremony progressed.

Waking with a start; Billy looked up to see Albert kneeling down in front of him, the guy's hand gently shaking his shoulder.

"You must talk to him now." Albert explained letting go of Billy, "Let him hear your voice, tell him all the things he must know in order for him to want to remain here. These are things he must hear from you, things only you can tell him."

"What things? I don't know what you want me to say?" Billy stammered.

"There are words that need to be said, words that come from here." Albert reached out and his middle three fingertips touched Billy's chest over his heart.

The action left Billy stunned. What did Albert think his feelings for Jake were? Sure he liked the guy, admired him even, and he wouldn't deny he lusted after him a little too. And despite Jake being grouchy at times, he was a pretty cool guy to hang with. But Billy most definitely didn't love the guy if that's what Albert had been intimating at. He wiped the tears from his eyes again on his hoodie sleeve, and then sniffing hard, wiped his nose on the sleeve.

So, hang on, why had he been crying since first seeing Jake lying there? And why did the thought of Jake dying leave him feeling so empty inside and sick to the pit of his stomach? He'd only know Jake for a few days, surely this wasn't how you were meant to feel about an almost total stranger, was it? To be honest he didn't have a clue how he should feel, as he'd never been in this sort of situation before. Sure, he'd fretted some over the badly injured Jake after the fight with the deputy, but that had been nothing more than a natural concern for someone who'd just saved his life, nothing more. And of course, the whole, almost getting killed thing in Milton had brought them closer together, that sort of thing did that.

But he didn't love Jake, not possible, no sir.

Aargh! He didn't know what to think, talk about being confused. He knew for certain he hadn't felt love for anyone since his mother died, and although he'd loved his father back then, over time he'd grown to despise the man and everything he stood for. Billy just wasn't sure he knew what love felt like anymore, or if he ever would again.

As Billy looked across at Jake lying on the floor of the hogan, the feeling of impending loss sucker punched him causing him to start sobbing again. The pain in Billy's chest as he tried to gulp air down in between sobs was physical and real enough, as was the cause. Typical! Only he could start falling for a straight guy, and one who could die any minute at that. But none of that really mattered right now; the only thing of any real importance now was getting Jake well again.

Kneeling down he gently stroked the fur along the top of Jake's muzzle, up between his closed eyes and then between the cougar's ears. Tears from eyes red and puffy from crying ran down Billy's cheeks once more and fell onto Jake's face sinking into the soft fur. In between sobs and sniffing he quietly spoke to Jake telling him how much he was needed here and not give up on his life. He talked about California, and that everything would be okay once they got there. He then told Jake that he had to live as they made such a good team together, they were like four legged superheroes and one day someone would write a comic book or maybe even make a movie about them. But he couldn't tell him anything else, he was still too unsure of himself, his emotions and just about everything concerning the two of them.

After a while Albert put his hand on Billy's shoulder, "You must leave him now and rest properly yourself."

Billy looked up at Albert through a haze of salty tears, "I should stay with him."

The old man shook his head. "You must eat in order to keep your strength up; we will stay and watch over him now."

Albert's soft voice although calming, had that authoritative edge to it, similar to a pack alpha's, though it didn't demand obedience, it just sort of gently made you want to go along with what the guy said. Billy leant over, kissed the cougar on the forehead then got up and walked outside, the bright sunlight causing him to squint and shade his eyes.

Albert put his head through the hogan doorway and told Daniel to take Billy to Joe Mather's house where food had been prepared. As they walked Daniel explained it had gone one in the afternoon and they were going to get some lunch. Billy shook his head, claiming he didn't feel hungry and that he really needed to get back to Jake. This being despite the fact his stomach had been growling loud enough to be heard two states over for a good while.

Daniel knew he needed to find a way to get Billy to the table and eat, so he told him their customs forbade Joe and his wife from eating until their guests had started. Okay, as lies went it was a whopper, but he reckoned on Billy not knowing that, plus he reckoned the guy would be too respectful go against what he understood to be a tribal custom. The ruse worked, and Billy agreed to have some food.

Arriving at the house Billy gladly took up the offer of a shower first. He looked down in the shower and watched as the hot water washed dirt and who knew what else off him and down the drain. It took two thorough washes before he felt clean and rid of anything to do with the skinwalker.

Once sat at the table, Joe's wife Marcie brought out food and drink for the two of them. Billy toyed with the food on his plate, Daniel touched his arm. "You must eat to keep your strength up."

"I'm sorry. I can't eat knowing Jake could die, I should be with him."

Eventually after a lot of gentle coaxing and a little arm twisting from Daniel and Marcie, Billy ate a little and drank a full bottle of water.

Just as he pushed his plate away, Albert and two other men entered the room, at which point Marcie made her excuses and left.

"His breathing is a little stronger and steadier. Do you know when he will change?" asked Albert, adding. "We must start the Windway ceremony so that the Wind People can come to him. And we believe he must be human before the ceremony can take place."

Billy shrugged, "It's difficult to say, we need a certain amount of strength and energy to start the shift as we heal our physical wounds too. He also needs the will to start the shift, but only his body will know if it has the strength to complete a shift, if it hasn't the shift won't start, even if he wants it to."

Albert looked down at Billy, his concern showing in his eyes.

"Billy, you need to understand he may have problems healing. The skinwalker has bitten him, and we believe Jake's blood to be poisoned. We have put herb poultices onto all his wounds to help draw the poison out, but you must talk to him again, you must persuade him to become human. Only when he is reborn can the Wind People come to him and make the Holy Wind blow through him again."

"Holy Wind?" asked Billy.

"The Holy Wind is a spirit that exists everywhere" Albert explained. He opened his arms and gestured around him, "And in which all living things play their part, the trees, us, animals and insects. It is the very essence of life itself as it is the giver of life. However, if Jake does not want to stay with us, the Holy Ones can do nothing for him and he will leave us and pass on to the spirit world. That is the way of things."

Billy tried to protest that Jake wouldn't be able to hear him, but Albert insisted that he would. And so once again, Billy made his way to the hogan, this time he lay down on a blanket alongside Jake facing him and chatted away, telling him of all the good things they could do together when they got to California. Every so often he pleaded with him to shift, so that he could start healing.

After several hours there was still no change, Jake just lay there, his breathing strained and noisy. Billy started crying again, his sobbing loud and open, he didn't care who saw or heard him anymore. He knew he was close to losing Jake, getting up he put his face to Jake's ear.

"I love you Jake, I know you don't feel the same way about me, but that doesn't matter. I'm just not sure that I can deal with life if you don't come back. Please change for me Jake. I need you, I need your strength."

He didn't know what else he had left to say. Billy kissed Jake's forehead and sat back watching the slight rise and fall of the leaves covering Jake, as the cougar seemingly fought for every faltering breath he took. Finally, Billy allowed himself to realize it was just a matter of time now until the cougar gave up the fight and let its life quietly slip away.

As he sat with his head in his hands he noticed one of the leaves covering Jake tumble to the floor, followed a few seconds later by another, several more then fell away as the cougar's struggling body finally attempted to make the transformation to human.

It had to be the slowest shift Billy had ever seen, but he put that down to lack of strength and the poison coursing through the cougar's veins. And the strange luminescence that he'd witnessed before now so dim he struggled to see it. After nearly four hours Billy left the hogan and went up to the group of elders sitting outside.

"You can start your ceremony now, he's human again."

Despite some initial protests, Billy went with Daniel to his house to have more food and to sleep. Billy was so utterly exhausted that the second his head hit the pillow on Daniel's bed he fell into a fitful sleep. And despite the nightmares that racked his slumber, he slept through for twelve hours straight. Next morning whilst Billy and Daniel ate a very late breakfast, Albert came into the kitchen and sat down with them. Billy looked into the man's eyes, and his fork fell from his hand, clattering onto his plate. Once again, he knew his world was about ready to collapse around him.

Albert explained that Jake's condition had changed, but not for the better. Since they'd started the ceremony Jake had been slowly weakening; and they couldn't get him to drink water or to take some broth.

"Without food and especially water, he will continue to get weaker and weaker until his body is too frail to recover from the poison.

Billy couldn't understand why there were still problems with Jake recovering; the shift should have cleared the poison from his body. He'd never known any injuries that hadn't been cured from a shift; if you could complete the shift your injuries were healed it was that simple. Without saying a word he got up and left the table, as he walked out of the room Daniel went to get up. Albert put his hand on top of Daniel's shoulder preventing him from rising and shook his head.

"He needs to be alone with Jake now."

"Jake's not going to make it is he grandfather?"

"I suspect he used up the last of this strength changing back to human, and his mind is losing the will to stay with us. I fear now it is just a matter of time."

"Is there nothing you can do for him? What about a doctor?"

"It is in the hands of the Holy Ones, only they can help him now, and then only if he truly wants to stay here."

Sat on the ground, Billy cradled Jake's head in his lap, his skin was cold and clammy, his breathing rapid and shallow. Billy held onto Jake's shoulders and managed to maneuver him into a sitting position so Jake rested up against him between his legs. Picking up the small plastic beaker, Billy scooped some water up in it and held it to Jake's dry and cracked lips.

"C'mon, drink for me Jake, just a little sip."

He poured some of the water into Jake's mouth, who instantly choked on it. Panicking, Billy dropped the beaker on the ground terrified he'd just killed Jake; then seeing him still breathing he started to calm down. Billy sighed with relief, okay maybe that had been trying to get too much in his mouth; he'd do it slower this time.

He picked the beaker back up, wiped it clean on his tee shirt, refilled it and repeated the process; but once again Jake coughed the water out without taking any down.

Billy didn't think he had any tears left in him to cry. Never since his mom died had he felt so desperately unhappy, his chest hurt him again.

"Jake, drink for me. I can't take any more, you're killing us both."

He tried a third time, then a fourth, each time the same results.

"Damn it Jake! Just drink the fucking water! I'm not gonna let you die, you ornery bastard!"

Holy Hell, he hated himself so much now, the guy was dying and all he could do in his frustration was to cuss at him.

He took a deep breath and thought hard, he had to do something.

Okay… new approach needed, Billy carefully leant over so as not to lose hold of Jake and managed to grab the tee shirt from the pile of Jake's clothes, and after much struggling and biting he eventually ripped one of the sleeves off. He dipped the cloth in the beaker then adjusting his position he managed to get Jake's head back a little against his shoulder and squeezing the cloth slowly dripped water into Jake's mouth letting it run down over his parched tongue.

No choking.

Way to go!

He rewetted the cloth and had several more goes. It was going to work! Next time he risk squeezing the cloth a little harder, he watched Jake's throat move.

Yes! He actually swallowed that time.

Billy carried on attempting to make Jake get used to swallowing; each time being rewarded by the sight of Jake's Adam's apple moving. Putting the cloth down and making encouraging noises he lifted Jake's head back up, and then tilted the beaker very, very slowly. Only the merest trickle came out, but this time Jake instinctively swallowed with no choking.

After drinking half a beaker of water, Jake's head lolled forward and he became deadweight in Billy's arms. Cradling Jake's head as you would a baby's, Billy laid the sleeping Jake back down covering him with a blanket. As Billy sat there resting, his own physical and mental strengths depleted, he noticed Jake's eyelids begin rapidly fluttering as he entered REM sleep. He hoped Jake would have a good dream and not a nightmare.

"Is that all you can do? Just lie there wallowing in self-pity?"

The man's voice didn't seem to come from any one point like it should have done, but instead it seemed to come from all around Jake. However, when he looked round he could see no one there, no hogan either, or settlement, no people, no Billy... No nothing. He looked down and his body instantly tensed up, there wasn't even any ground under his feet.

Instead of familiar surroundings there existed only darkness, a bit like when he'd been on his vision quest but this time the blackness seemed so deep and impenetrable it gave the impression of being almost solid. He stuck his arm out, and watched in horror as his hand disappeared from view, instantly he snatched his arm back, relieved to find his hand still attached to his wrist. His instincts told him that something was out there, he had no idea what, but he knew it wouldn't be healthy for him to find out.

He heard the man's voice again, only much quieter this time, distant, as if in conversation with other people, Jake could just make out the others whispering.

"Who are you?" Jake asked, trying not to sound too pitiful, "Are you the Holy People?"

"You have a destiny to fulfill. And that won't happen if you just give up and die."

Jake tried the place the accent, but couldn't, definitely not American, it sounded kind of British, not Scottish though, one of his parent's neighbors had been Scottish and it wasn't that, it didn't sound Irish either.

"What destiny?"

"Yours!" The voice said incredulously.

"Who are you?"

After it became clear he wouldn't be getting an answer, Jake continued, "I don't have a destiny. I decide what happens. The future's what I make it."

Okay that was complete BS, he didn't decide where his life went anymore, others' decided that for him. Still some voice in a dream wouldn't know that.

A deep sigh followed, followed by muttering in some strange foreign tongue. Then the voice scolded, "You fur bags always think yourselves so clever. Oh yes! You know all the answers. Well you don't. Whether you want it to or not there will soon come a wrong that needs to be righted. That is your destiny."

"Haven't I done enough already?" Jake complained wearily.

He thought of the skinwalker and the deputy, plus all the others he'd 'discontinued' for his employers. He'd had more than enough of righting other people's wrongs; he just wanted to be selfish now and do things for himself.

"I don't know, what you have done?" asked the voice sarcastically.

"I've killed people."

"We've all done that. What makes you so special?"

"Who are you? What do you want with me? Why won't you show yourself?"

Once more Jake's questions drew only silence.

Just as Jake started to get pissed about the continual refusal to answer his questions, a small hissing jet of blue and yellow flame appeared in front of him level with his face. After a few seconds of staring at it the flame started to grow, within a few seconds it had become the size of a baseball, a few more and it had reached the size of a basketball. As it became bigger and bigger by the second it started changing shape. He then realized that despite the flame growing in size almost exponentially, it didn't seem to be getting any closer, and he couldn't feel any heat coming from it.

Just when Jake started wondering how much bigger the flames would get they started to die down leaving a white hot form that smoked profusely as it rapidly cooled down hiding whatever it had become. As the smoke finally cleared, Jake could see it had solidified into what looked like a metal sculpture of an enormous dragon's head. Most of the thick, heavy scales that covered it were the color of forged steel, but there were others a rich bronze in color that together formed intricate patterns that Jake had seen the like of before but couldn't place them to start with. Then it dawned on him, the patterns were Celtic.

Jake started and gasped instinctively as double reptilian eyelids under huge horned brow ridges shot open to reveal a pair of vivid yellow eyes, each nearly as big as a football.

Oh hell! It wasn't any sculpture. It was the real McCoy. A real, living, breathing dragon!

No! It wasn't possible. Dragons weren't real; this had to be some sort of hallucination.

But real or not Jake found himself held spellbound by the eyes, unable to do anything but stare into them. Each of the huge orbs contained a dark convex slit that ran from top to bottom. As the eyes drew him in he felt sure their yellow surfaces were moving, swirling around like fog caught in a light breeze.

Leaning in towards Jake the dragon's mouth opened just enough to reveal two rows of huge dagger like teeth. Something distinctly unpleasant oozed out between the lower teeth and over its lips, as it dripped off the massive lower jaw it caught fire, the flaming droplets falling down into the black void. Jake gagged at the acrid, sulfurous stench of the dragon's foul breath. Then its eyes and mouth closed and the head retreated into the blackness, leaving Jake alone once more.

"Was that you?" Jake inquired after a while, not being too sure what he was meant to have made from what he'd just seen, or more likely imagined.

"I have awoken him." Announced the voice.

"Who?"

"The dragon! Do you not pay attention? Or are you but a simple fool?"

"I…"

"Oh never mind. Now eat, drink, and heal. Time is short, and a great darkness lies ahead of you."

"What do you mean 'A great darkness'?" Jake was becoming more confused by the second.

"Pain. Misery. Death! The end of things! The beginning of things too. Now… Awake!"

With his heart pounding in his chest, Jake woke with a cry, startling the dozing Billy. Carefully helping his patient back up Billy first wiped the sweat from Jake's face and chest with the remnants of Jake's tee shirt then managed to get a whole beaker of water down him before gently letting him back down to sleep again.

Having heard the cry, Albert and two other elders entered the hogan.

Billy looked up, "I've managed to get him to drink two beakers of water."

Albert put his hand on Billy's shoulder, "You have done very well, we shall take care of him now while we carry on with the ceremony. You must go eat, Daniel is outside waiting for you."

Not bothering to argue this time Billy got up and walked to the entrance where he stood watching Jake for several seconds before going outside.

After eating Billy and Daniel walked back to the hogan, where one of the elders stood guarding the doorway. Not being allowed back in, the pair sat outside talking. Some while later one of the other elders came out and walked over to Billy, "He woke and drunk some more water, that is a very good sign."

"Can I see him now?" Half pleaded Billy.

The man explained that Jake had fallen asleep again straight after drinking, and that they were still performing the ceremony, but when it finished and Jake woke up properly then Billy could be with him. Daniel and a somewhat dejected Billy were ushered away with instructions that it was time for them to sleep too. Taking pity on Billy the man called after them and added that he expected Jake would wake properly the next day and Billy needed to be in a fit state to look after him. Needing no further encouragement than that to go and get some sleep Billy left at speed with Daniel in tow.

Jake thought he could smell burning pine cones and a number of other unidentifiable things on fire.

Urgh! He felt crap.

Thinking about it, he decided this could actually be a good sign; because if he were dead there would be no pain, no feeling like shit, and definitely no burning pine trees.

But he knew one thing for certain, his throat felt dryer than a popcorn fart, making swallowing almost impossible. Also some asshole inside his head kept pounding away like crazy with a sledgehammer, and just to top it all he probably didn't have a single muscle or joint in his body that didn't ache like hell. All he could think to do was lie perfectly still and hope it would eventually all go away. Ha! Fat chance.

As more parts of him reported in, he realized he could feel his weight on his back. And that could only mean one thing; he was human again, as the rounded cougar back forced you to lie on your side. Gradually he became aware of the sound of voices, he tried to talk, but his parched throat and mouth only managed some unintelligible rasping noise, causing him to have a coughing fit that really, really hurt his head.

"Jake, Jake... You're awake!"

Billy practically flew off the low bench throwing himself on the ground next to Jake and hugging him. Jake turned his head and opened his eyes snapping them tight shut again as the light stung, causing his eyes to weep. Opening them very slowly a second time he eventually managed to focus on Billy's face and saw the guy's tears flowing unashamedly.

Albert and Billy together helped Jake up into a sitting position, his back supported against one of the low benches. Albert held a beaker of water to Jake's lips and told him to slowly sip. Once empty someone took the beaker from him to be refilled and Billy wrapped his arms around Jake once more.

"Could we leave crushing the poor cougar for a little while yet?" he croaked.

Billy instantly let go, "Oh sorry. It's just that it's been so long and everyone's been worried sick. You just wouldn't believe what's been happening. I really thought that…"

Billy realized he was babbling and smiled sheepishly. "Oh man! I was so scared I'd lost you."

"Ha, no chance of that." Jake reassured Billy, "Only the good die young, and I feel I'll be around for a while yet. Is there any chance I can have my clothes, I'd like to get dressed, I'm feeling a mite exposed here with just a blanket over my lap."

Billy picked up Jake's clothes and brought them to him.

Jake decided the one off humiliation of needing to be helped into his boxers and jeans outweighed the embarrassment of having to sit there naked under his blanket.

"And what exactly happened to my tee shirt?"

Putting his hand inside he waggled his fingers through the jagged hole that had once been a sleeve.

"Well… You were being obstinate and wouldn't drink and I needed something to drip water into your mouth, so I tore the sleeve off."

"Ah, I see. I take it that's when I got called an ornery bastard?"

The stunned look on Billy's face quickly turned to one of acute embarrassment.

"Oh! You heard that?"

"I heard lots of things."

Jake felt his chapped lips sting as he smiled.

"Really? Like what?" Billy's ear tips and cheeks grew redder by the second.

"Like lots of things, so how about some of this food I kept hearing I had to eat? Also I'd like another tee shirt, ideally one with two arms."

"Yes sir!"

As Billy ran out to get the food and a tee shirt from the truck, Albert passed Jake the plastic beaker back.

"You must drink plenty of water."

As Jake started to gulp the water down, Albert put his hand on Jake's forearm and gently pushed it down, "Drink slowly, just small mouthfuls or you will choke."

Jake looked at the old man in front of him. "I have a feeling I owe you my life, but I'm having a job finding the right words, 'thank you' just doesn't seem to cover it."

"In that case how do I thank you for saving my people from the skin-walker? Besides, I only played a small part. The Holy Ones saw to bring you back safely to us. And of course a certain other person who would only leave your side when forced to. Without him you surely would not be here now."

"It seemed so weird," Jake went on, "Like I knew of a lot of what was happening around me, but at the same time I was somewhere else, there were these…"

Albert held his hand up, "Your time with the Holy Ones is for you and you alone to know. But at some point you will have to share those things you are hiding inside with Billy."

Share things? Yeah like that was ever going to happen, he'd not been the sharing, caring kind for a long time. Jake nodded at Albert, his expression feigning understanding, albeit in an effort to try move the conversation on rather than in agreement. But the look on the old man's face made it clear he hadn't finished yet.

Jake now hoped a brief explanation would suffice and finally put the matter to bed. "It's just not that easy for me to open up. I've been a loner since my parent's death, and I guess I'm afraid all the bad stuff in my life will affect anyone who's close to me."

Albert nodded, "The Holy Spirits allowed me to see some of where your pain comes from, so there is no need to explain it to me. Like I said, in time you will need to talk to Billy about things, which should help ease the heavy burden you force yourself to carry. But you must open your heart, for both your sakes."

Any other time and place Jake would have killed this sort of conversation stone dead before it had a chance to get going, but he figured he owed Albert big time. And he couldn't deny the fact Billy had stayed with him through everything, the guy having fought so hard to keep him alive. But why did Albert seem so keen on him and Billy staying together? Why did everything in his crappy life always have to be so difficult?

And what about Billy's declaration of love? After considering it for a few seconds Jake decided to put it down to Billy's emotional state whilst trying to encourage Jake to get well, or at worse it had been nothing more than a momentary display of late onset teenage infatuation. So nothing needing doing there. End of day Billy was just too naïve and inexperienced in life to know how he felt.

Although Jake hated to admit it, it had been so long since he himself felt anything other than animosity for anyone, he wasn't sure he'd recognize real love even if it jumped up and bit him on his Johnson. Thinking about it he'd been 'bitten' there a good few times over the years and none of those occasions had anything to do with love. But he sure as hell wasn't ready to explain his 'other' life; the less Billy knew about that the safer he'd be. The consequences of telling anyone as fresh in his mind now as when they'd first told him whilst strapped to the autopsy table. Jake made up his mind to play it by ear, and see where things went, and if necessary discourage any attempt at Billy getting 'too close'.

Jake put away all thoughts of what to say for another time and place as Billy entered the hogan and sat down opposite Jake. It was so obvious the guy wanted to look after him, and Jake wouldn't deny Billy that. In all honesty, he really wasn't in much of a condition to do otherwise just now.

"The sausages look nice I'll have one of them first."

Billy passed a still warm link sausage to Jake, and sat there beaming, holding onto the plate, ready for the next request. Jake smiled inwardly at the sight of Billy sat there happily waiting on him, it was without doubt a very endearing quality.

Billy reached into his hoodie pocket and pulled out a can, then popping the ring he handed it to Jake, "I've got you a soda, I tried to get an energy drink, but no one had one."

Albert stood up and patted Jake on the shoulder.

"I have to leave you now, we are going to collect the body of the skin walker then drive it a long way from here, burn it and bury what's left. It must never be found."

Jake nodded his approval at the plan, and then looked up. "I'm sorry I refused to believe what you and your people told us. It was just plain arrogant of me not being prepared to believe that a mutant shapeshifter could exist."

The old man smiled, "And thanks to you, it's now a case of did exist."

Jake nodded then said. "A good friend once told me, 'You're safe from the bogey man all the time he's confined to your nightmares. It's when you meet him while your awake, that's when the really bad shit happens'."

"Your friend is very wise indeed."

"Was… He was, very wise."

Albert squeezed Jake's shoulder then walked away, as he went to go through the door to leave Jake called out to him. "Albert, does your culture have dragons in it?"

Albert looked at him quizzically, "Dragons?"

"Yeah, I've seen dragons twice now in my dreams."

"Snakes yes, but no dragons."

"Oh these were most definitely dragons."

"No dragons." Albert repeated shaking his head as he quickly turned back to the door and left the hogan muttering to himself in Navajo.

"Sooo… What sort of things did you hear?" An apprehensive sounding Billy asked.

Turning his attention back to Billy, Jake could see the guy looked embarrassed. It was obvious Billy wasn't entirely sure he wanted to hear the answer.

"Most of what went on came across pretty garbled and didn't always make sense." Jake explained in reply.

An uneasy smile briefly appeared on Billy's face as he started to realize he might not have to explain anything embarrassing.

"Oh… Oh I see."

With his mind in such turmoil, it took Billy a good while before he realized Jake was talking. Not sure how much he'd missed, he felt too embarrassed to ask Jake to repeat it for fear of offending the guy.

"So bearing that in mind, everything's going to be fine now." Jake announced, sincerely hoping it would all be fine. Quite how he'd deal with disappearing for days on end when jobs came along he hadn't worked yet. That was a bridge he'd have to cross when and if the time come.

"How can you say that after what you just went through?" Asked a stunned Billy.

"Easy, the bad guy's dead, I'm on the mend, and everything is right with the world. So there's nothing to worry about anymore is there?"

Before Billy could think of an answer, Jake leant forward and patted him on the head.

"Good! That's all settled then. Now, let me have the rest of that food"

It wasn't until an increasingly restless and tetchy Jake had spent the best part of a week building his strength back up that Albert declared him fit enough to drive down to California. The pair spent their last night on the Reservation sat around a fire with their new found friends eating and celebrating the victory over the skin walker. They listened whilst the medicine men told great stories of Navajo history and their mythology. Dances were performed, with Billy getting a big cheer as he tried hoop dancing with Daniel's cousins Travis and Shania.

After breakfast the next morning Daniel said he had something he wanted to show them before they left, and having loaded them into Albert's truck, Daniel proceeded to drive across the reservation. Well over an hour later he made them ride the last ten or so miles with their eyes closed. The truck came to a halt and they got out. Still having to keep their eyes tight shut Daniel held Billy's and Jake's hands and led the pair of them the last few hundred yards to their destination.

"Okay, we're here." He let go of their hands, "You can open your eyes now."

Billy just managed an "OH WOW!" before wonderment overwhelmed him.

Jake looked across at Billy and saw the expression of absolute awe on his face. "I was going to call it breathtaking, but I'm not sure that truly does it justice, I think I'll have to go for 'WOW!' too."

From their vantage point standing near the edge, Daniel pointed down into the magnificent vastness of the Grand Canyon, "It's over a mile deep in places and 18 miles across at its widest point."

He watched somewhat bemused as Jake and Billy stared silently trying to take in the majesty of the striated red, rocky walls that plunged down into the green of the Colorado River in the bottom.

"Maybe next time you visit we'll go down into the canyon itself and camp."

Daniel's face suddenly took on a worried look. "You are coming see us again aren't you. Say you're not going to forget us?"

Jake turned and put his arm round the back of Daniels neck and gently pulled him in between him and Billy, who proceeded to put his arm around Daniels shoulders too.

"Of course we're coming back, how could we ever forget our time here, and all the amazing friends we've made?" Billy reassured Daniel.

Raising his arms up Daniel put them around his two new friend's waists. "I love you guys, and when I'm a father my sons will be called Jacob and William and you will be their uncles."

Billy grinned from ear to ear. Him an adopted uncle? Now that had to be the coolest thing ever.

The farewells back at the settlement although not tearful were heart-felt, and everyone would feel a sense of loss with their leaving.

Billy hugged Daniel, "We promised we'd come back to visit and we will, I swear."

Jake stood with Albert and the other elders shaking hands.

Albert clasped Jake's hand tight between both of his. "There's a Navajo saying that *'Something lives only as long as the last person who remembers it'.* So all the time there are Navajo to tell and pass on the story about the time the Holy Ones called on the cougar and the wolf that walk together to save the Navajo from the evil coyote skinwalker you will be remembered."

Opening Jake's hand Albert put a small hide bag into his palm and closed Jake's fingers around it.

"Do not open it yet."

Catching sight of something being put into Jake's hand a curious Billy came over to see what Jake had been given. Albert then proceeded to put a bag into his hand too, again with instructions not to open it.

Albert then stepped back and with a smile announced. "Now you can both look."

Pulling the draw string on his bag open Jake emptied the contents into his hand. There sat a small figurine of a cougar carved from a yellow-ish brown stone complete with two tiny turquoise eyes.

Billy followed suit, and opening his bag took out a small wolf, the deep dusky red of the stone highlighting its blue eyes.

Albert smiled broadly, "Those are fetishes, keep them with you always. Now… Have a safe journey."

"Yeah, we'll keep in touch and let you know when we'll visit, not sure when it will be yet though." Replied Jake.

"We will see you in the spring, when the Bluebonnet finishes flowering." Albert assured him.

"Okay Albert, in the spring then."

The two men both laughed, and hugged.

After one last round of handshaking and back patting they carefully placed all the gifts they'd been given into the pickup and with both of them waving out the windows headed off across the reservation. When they reached the junction of the highway Jake stopped the truck, turned round on the seat and looked out of the back window.

"What's up, something the matter with the truck?" Billy thought there must be a problem with the pickup.

"Nothing's wrong with the truck… It's just that I have a strange feeling."

"What sort of feeling? A bad one?"

"I dunno, it's nothing. It's just me being stupid I guess. I think all that's happened here over the last week or so has left me a bit jittery that's all."

Turning back round, Jake put the truck into gear and pulled out onto the highway.

It wasn't 'nothing' though.

He had a hunch, a premonition; call it what you like, that one or both of them wouldn't be coming back this way. He felt himself shiver inside.

Something about him had changed in his time on the Rez. His only problem being he didn't know what.

CALIFORNIA CALLING

As Jake wriggled his heels deeper into the pale yellow sand, the warm dry grains on the surface tickled as they ran down between his toes. Propping himself up on his hands he leant his head back and closed his eyes. He felt the sun's late morning heat prickling his cheeks as its strengthening glare shone yellow-white through his eyelids. Breathing in deeply, he filled his lungs to capacity then held the breath for an arbitrary count of five. After a long slow exhale he attempted to tune out the everyday noises around him and concentrate solely on the slow rhythmic roar of the surf crashing onto the beach.

He tried a second time, then a third. After several more unsuccessful attempts he realized his Zen moment simply wasn't happening, he could still hear traffic and the general buzz of everyday life all around him.

Okay, so the positive thoughts still weren't coming easy, truth be told they weren't coming at all. But the upside had to be that finally he was back in California, sat on one of his favorite beaches under the early September sun.

Mind you there were times earlier on he thought he'd never make it here.

No! Just shut up Jake, you're here now, you're happy, everything is cool, so stop thinking that shit.

But his stupid brain couldn't let go of the past that easily. He knew it would keep bringing everything bad back, over and over, just to torment him.

If only there was a way to simply wipe everything he didn't want from his memory, like you could with a computer. However, he just couldn't stop dredging up all the bad stuff from his past, and the more he tried to lock it away, the easier things seemed to break through. And it always ended the same, with him giving in and letting the bad memories swamp him and drown whatever little happiness he had going for him. And he knew it was about to happen once again.

For almost ten years now it had sucked to be him, big time. Sure he knew shit hadn't happened to him on a daily basis or anything like that. But after the first four or five years he'd decided that everybody's best interests would be served especially his, if he just kept himself to himself. That way he'd be less likely to find trouble, which just left it up to trouble to find him, something it had always succeeded in doing with alarming ease and regularity.

Initially he justified his withdrawal from society with the almost believable 'cats are solitary creatures' justification. But over time it started to develop into a full blown obsessive disorder as his 'employers' continued to coerce him into doing their dirty work for them. It wasn't as if they even bothered trying to justify what they wanted done any more.

And to make matters worse he'd become very good at what he did, he'd thought a few times about screwing up, but he knew they wouldn't tolerate failure and especially deliberate failure. Then to compound his misery after every so called 'executive action' they'd transfer funds into a bank account for him, and to his eternal shame he'd become dependent on the money, and boy did they know how to exploit it. Up to now they'd never even had to threaten him with the vivisection table again.

He tried to convince himself that the more detached from society he became, the easier it would become not only to avoid those with the power to make him to carry out these things, but also to disconnect

himself from the reality of what he'd done and would have do again and again. However, deep down he knew this constituted a piss poor coping mechanism, as they would always find him when they had use for him. Hell his credit card trail had to be easy enough to follow, let alone the fact they provided his cell phone and paid the bill. Not that he ever called anyone; his address book being emptier than a politician's promise.

Once in a foul temper, he'd smashed the original phone they'd given him and threw it into a dumpster. Less than seventy two hours later in a town some four hundred miles away three heavy set guys in trademark dark suits and ski masks let themselves into his hotel room in the middle of the night and presented him with a new phone. He knew the beating was coming the second they told him they'd help him remember to take better care of this one.

While two of the men held Jake down on the bed, the third forced a gag into Jake's mouth preventing him from screaming out, before yanking the cap off a syringe and injecting something that felt like liquid fire as it went into a vein in Jake's arm. As an indescribable pain ripped through Jake's body with alarming speed, his back arched high off the bed as every muscle in his body went completely rigid for a few seconds while the veins on his neck and forehead stood out like plastic tubes under the skin and his eyes bulged in their sockets. Then as the muscles suddenly relaxed, he began thrashing around in agony. With that, all three of the men sat on him pinning to the bed while the acute reaction to the drug passed.

Then the beating started.

Once the men had left, he lay on the bed sobbing for a good six hours unable to shift. Whatever they'd injected him with had obviously been formulated to prolong his suffering by temporarily preventing him from shifting. Eventually he managed to shift so as to repair the eye socket that in all likelihood had been fractured, the broken arm, several dislocated fingers and a couple of cracked ribs. Baseball bats were such versatile things.

After that there were no more fits of pique, instead self-service checkouts and credit card gas pumps had become his saviors, which meant he now really only had to interact with people in order to buy food, cigarettes and to book into motels. Eventually he'd even stopped going into diners and fast food restaurants, preferring instead to go late night shopping in supermarkets for TV dinners, which he'd eat cold in his truck in the parking lot, or in his motel room if it had a microwave oven. For some strange reason he couldn't keep the food down if he sat and ate it cold at a table.

As his psychosis deepened, his self-imposed isolation became an instrument for trying to atone for past deeds, and to attempt to ease the guilt that racked his conscience. He eventually started to believe that by punishing himself in such a way, he could somehow make reparation, and at the same time protect others from himself. Eventually the mania took him over completely, and his pain turned inwards, he became self-loathing, while all the time his grip on reality became evermore tenuous.

And when his psychological self-flagellation stopped being sufficient, he decided his punishment had to be physical, only then could he drive the bad feelings away. So now some nights he'd find himself sat naked on the floor of motel showers, shivering under the spray of cold water on his back.

Resting the underside of his forearm on his drawn up knees he'd methodically draw his survival knife along his arm from elbow to wrist. Behind the moving blade tip the thin red line of the fresh cut would swell as dark blood oozed from the wound until the surface tension could hold it no longer, when it would spill down the sides of his arm through the dense blonde hair.

Concentration became everything, the pain had to be consistent and the cut had to be straight and true. If at any point it wavered, or the pain eased off, he felt compelled to stop and start a new cut.

Once a successful cut had been achieved, he'd lay the knife down on the floor by his right hip with obsessive precision, and sit there mesmerized by the patterns created by his blood as it ran off the underside of his arm onto his legs then trickled down the inside of his thigh. The tendrils of dispersing blood carried by the flow of water spread out across the tray.

By the time they'd reached the drain the water in the tray had taken on a pinkish, translucent appearance.

He'd then wait until the wound started to heal and the blood stopped flowing before rinsing all the blood off himself and the shower tray. Before drying himself he'd pat dry the wound with paper towels or toilet tissue so as not to get blood on the motel towels. Once dried he'd flush the paper down the toilet, then bandage the arm, it being essential not to leave any trace of blood in the room or on the bed. It was his guilt, his pain, and it wasn't for others to see or know about. This was his own private despair and no one else was allowed in.

And so one cold night just outside St Louis as he drove along Interstate 70 in the pouring rain, Jake's mind could finally take it no more, and he found himself standing on the edge, looking down into the murky abyss of full blown insanity. Yanking the wheel hard over, he tore off the freeway and down an off ramp. He had no idea where he was heading to, but he'd know when he got there. He had to rid himself of his demons once and for all.

Father Andrew Buchanan finished putting the last of the vestments away and came out of the sacristy to find a blond haired young man soaked to the skin, sat on the alter steps slowly rocking backwards and forwards. The priest walked over to him and looked down; he certainly wasn't one of his regular flock, or even anyone he'd seen around, as the Mohawk style haircut though somewhat bedraggled was most distinctive. As the priest watched his visitor sway he spotted the silver and black snub nosed revolver cradled in the guy's lap. But something told Father Andrew this wasn't someone intent on committing a crime, but a deeply troubled soul in need of salvation.

Discreetly crossing himself he took a deep breath. "Would you mind if I sat down with you my son and have a short rest? I have been on my feet all day and I am exhausted."

After a few seconds Jake stopped rocking, glanced up briefly and dipped his head once before he started swaying again.

As the elderly priest lowered himself down, he groaned as his sixty eight year old knees and back creaked in protest at the uncalled for strain made upon them.

"I'd forgotten just how far down these steps were, I fear that I may need to ask for a little help to get back up again."

Jake carried on with his rocking, his gaze firmly fixed on the dark patterned tiled floor at the bottom of the steps.

As he'd elicited no reply so far, Father Andrew introduced himself and his church then started chatting away about his day, none of it at all important of course, just general small talk. He presumed the guy to be listening to him, and every so often allowed the occasional pause to see if he was ready to join in the distinctly one sided conversation. It took a good twenty minutes for the priest to learn Jake's name, and almost a further thirty minutes before he managed to persuade him to hand the gun over.

"If you wish I can take your confession Jacob."

Now for the first time Jake spoke. "I'm not Catholic Father. Truth be told, I'm not even sure you could call me a believer."

"All the same my son, you decided to come into a house of God, so you must have believed something here could help you in your time of need."

Jake shrugged, he hadn't thought of it like that.

"I guess."

"Well, as you're not a member of our club Jake I can listen, I can even offer you counsel, but I cannot take your confession or give you absolution, for that you must confess to God, and to God alone."

Jake sat up straight and turned to the priest, the tears streaming down his face.

"I would like to talk." His stomach then growled loudly in protest at being pretty much ignored for the past few days.

"I'm guessing that it's been some little time since you ate last. Now… As it's Thursday that means its beef stew tonight, Mrs Batley my house-keeper is a good woman but I'm afraid she is nothing if not predictable.

And as she always makes far too much for me to eat, you are more than welcome to share dinner with me."

"Well I…"

"Good," Father Andrew butted in denying Jake the chance to finish. He held his arm out, "Now Jacob, if you would be so kind?"

Jake stood up and gently helped the priest to his feet.

"If I could also beg a strong arm to help support me for a few minutes it would be very much appreciated." The priest chuckled, "Just until the feeling returns to my legs."

Having blessed himself and locked the church doors, Father Andrew led Jake the short distance to the rectory. Walking through the large house they came to a large, but homely kitchen with a long pine table partly covered with a red and white checked plastic tablecloth. Taking pride of place in the center a seriously old Yogi Bear cookie jar, to one side of it sat one of those red plastic tomatoes that diners' use to hold tomato ketchup, the ones with green plastic leaves and a spout that is always covered in brown, dried on ketchup. On the other side a pair of chipped ceramic popcorn bucket shaped salt and pepper shakers.

Once they'd finished eating, Jake insisted on clearing the table, he then followed the priest through to the living room. After showing Jake to a chair, Father Andrew went to a circular table on which sat a on a silver tray containing three square cut glass decanters and a number of glasses. Turning to Jake he offered his guest a drink which Jake politely declined. After pouring himself a well-deserved large brandy Father Andrew sat down in a time worn dark green leather wing backed chair that faced Jake's matching chair. The priest took a sip of the warming spirit then encouraged Jake to explain what troubled him.

Jake told the priest about the things his security service masters had forced him into doing, missing out how he'd done the killing, explaining about being a shapeshifter was definitely for another time. On more than one occasion he caught the priest's eyes widening at what he heard.

Jake looked straight at the priest who was trying unsuccessfully to hide his shock, "Father, when you look in dark places you find dark things. And trust me, I have been in some very dark places."

"We are but mere men Jacob, we all lose our way at times."

"I know Father, but trust me when I say I've never been a willing participant."

The priest lowered his head slightly and as if praying clasped his hands in front of his face. He pressed his lips to his forefingers then looked back up at Jake. "In the bible, Samuel tells us that: 'The Lord does not look at the things man looks at. Man looks at outward appearance, but the Lord looks at the heart.' I think what I'm trying to tell you Jacob is that while I sense there is much good in you; God knows the goodness that resides in your heart."

Jake stood up, "Thank you for taking the time to listen Father, but I should go now, it's getting late, and it's unfair of me to keep you from your bed. But may I come back and talk to you again? There's something else I'd like to get off my chest."

Father Andrew eased himself up out of the chair and put his hand on Jake's shoulder.

"Of course you can my son. Come to the church tomorrow evening just after eight."

The next evening after the two of them had sat in the church talking for a short while, Jake went silent.

"What is it Jacob? You have been doing so well exorcizing your ghosts."

Jake glanced across into the priest's kindly eyes.

"There's something I need to tell you Father. Something that I hope will go some way to explaining why I have no control over the things I'm forced to do."

He then fell silent again.

"I sense whatever this is, it's a burden that troubles you greatly, if you wish to share it with me then please do so."

"It's not exactly a burden Father; it's something I have no control over, it is part of me and who I am. The problem is I know you won't believe me, but if necessary I can prove it to you. However, you can't ever repeat what I tell you, if it were to become known in certain quarters it would most likely cost me my life."

The priest gestured for Jake to carry on. After taking a deep breath Jake explained what he was, the basics of shape shifting and why he couldn't refuse to do the things demanded of him. A dark look came over the priest's face, and he put his hand up for Jake to stop.

Jake stood up, "I guess I should have known you wouldn't believe me, I can't say I blame you either Father, I pretty much doubt I'd believe it if some stranger told me that. But I need to prove to you what I've said is the truth, so I'll come back tonight at ten thirty in my animal form and wait near the small side door; I promise I won't harm you."

Thumping his chest over his heart, Jake explained to the priest. "I really am a good person in here, I'm not evil, the spawn of Satan, or anything like that. I just need you to see that what I've told you is the truth."

With that he walked past the priest and out of the church.

Jake flicked his long tail from side to side as he kept an eye on the side door from his vantage point sat behind a wooden bench seat near the back of the adjoining graveyard. He'd thought for a long time now that there just had to be a way to wear a wrist watch whilst in his animal form; it would come in real handy at times like these.

Eventually a light came on and shone out from the small arched window of the sacristy. Taking a final look around and scenting the air, Jake decided the coast was clear, he then stalked silently over to a large tombstone just along from the sacristy door. Before he had chance to sit, he heard the grating of iron bolts being drawn back, and the click, clunk as a large key turned in a heavy lock. Then slowly the door opened.

He scented the air again, he couldn't detect anyone the graveyard, but his sense of smell wasn't acute enough to pick up the presence of anyone else in the church. He'd have to chance it; slowly he walked round the tombstone so that the pool of yellow light that spilt out onto the path through the open door illuminated him. At the priest's startled gasp he instantly stopped and sat down much harder and quicker than he'd planned.

Ow!

Convinced he'd just squashed and bruised his balls, and being in his animal form he couldn't hold them or rub them better. Not that he'd ever consider rubbing them or licking them in front of a priest whatever the circumstances.

Father Andrew stood in the doorway and stared wide eyed at the cougar,

"Is that truly you Jacob?"

A lengthy pause ensued, before the priest carried on, "I guess I'm being foolish thinking you would answer me. But I need some sort of signal, a sign so that I can be sure that's you."

Jake thought hard for a moment then thumped the path three times with his left paw then three times with his right. As signs of reassurance went it rated about as lame as it got, but at such short notice it was the best he could come up with. A thought suddenly hit him; maybe he should try learning to tap dance in his animal form, or even do an Irish jig. Now that would be impressive.

Father Andrew gave a short chortle.

"I'm venturing that's one each for the Father, the Son and the Holy Ghost, or rather I hope it is."

Jake snickered inwardly too, that hadn't been his plan at all, but as the guy seemed reassured, it was all good.

The priest walked slowly over to Jake who stayed as motionless as any waxworks dummy. Standing in front of the cougar the priest gingerly reached out with a trembling hand and laid it upon Jake's head, causing the big cat to start purring. After petting him for a minute, the priest ran his hand down over Jake's ear making it flick in response to the touch. As he took his hand away Jake's rough tongue licked his palm. Jake looked up, and could see tears running down the man's face.

"Oh, forgive me my son, I am so, so sorry for not believing in you. You are truly one of our Lord's great miracles."

With that Jake briefly nuzzled against the priest's leg, then stood up, turned and silently padded off into the darkness.

The next afternoon Jake found Father Andrew putting out hymnals, and picking up a pile proceeded to give a helping hand. For the first few rows of pews neither mentioned anything about the previous night. When they'd finished putting out the books the priest broke the silence.

"I am sorry I doubted you Jacob, but I'm sure you understand my skepticism about your story."

"But obviously not unconvinced enough to stop you checking though eh Father?"

Jake smirked and winked.

"Touché Jacob. And I must say that although I have beheld some wondrous sights in my time on God's good earth, what I witnessed last night topped them all."

"I really wasn't sure of how you'd react, I was scared you'd run back into the church and not come out again until I'd left the county, if not the state."

The old priest chuckled, "I'd be less than truthful if I said I hadn't been tempted to initially. But tell me Jacob, have you always been this way, even as a child?"

"Shape shifters are born the way they are, it's not like the Hollywood werewolf films where you can be turned into one by getting bitten. And like I said we can change shape at will, not just under a full moon."

"How did you cope during your childhood, surely that must have been a difficult time for you?"

"You can't shift until your body stops growing, for us this is usually late teens to early twenties, though some start shifting earlier, and obviously there are others who are late developers. Same as for non-shifters I guess. It's all in the genes as they say."

Smiling, the priest reached out and clasped Jake's hand. "I sense that you're a good deal happier in yourself than when we first met."

"Yeah, I think you could say I've turned a corner."

"Praise be to the Lord, I am truly pleased for you."

"Anyhow," said Jake, "I really came to say two things. The first is thanks for everything you've done. Without you I'm convinced I wouldn't be here now, if you know what I mean. I know it's really clichéd and corny but you really did save my life the other night, and that is a debt I'll never be able to repay. And the second is to say it's probably time I moved on."

"Are you sure you won't stay with us Jacob? It's not a bad place to put roots down in, and I'm sure you could find decent employment here or maybe over in St Louis. Plus there's plenty of forest in the conservation areas for the four legged Jacob to explore and run round in."

Jake smiled and sighed, "I can't say I'm not tempted, but I won't if it's all the same. I just want to realize one dream in my life, and go back to living by the sea in California."

Father Andrew pressed his lips together and nodded. "Then I wish you well for your journey, and offer thanks to the Lord that you have at last found some peace."

"I think I have father, but I know it's going to be a long fight to get back to my old self again. But thank you again for everything, I just wish there was some other way I could repay your kindness, just saying thanks doesn't feel enough."

"You are more than welcome my son. By the way, do you want your gun back? It's in my study; we can go get it if you want."

Jake thought for a few seconds.

"I guess I should, save you having to get rid of it. Plus you never can tell who's out there; it's a big bad world as they say."

As they walked across to the rectory, Jake noted the priest appeared somewhat frail today.

"Are you okay Father, do you need a hand?"

"That is very kind of you Jacob, I'm just feeling a little tired and delicate today."

"I hope not because of last night?"

"No, not at all. Now please don't worry yourself, I'll be fine. And besides, what happened last night is a memory I shall treasure all my days."

Following Father Andrew into the study, Jake walked over to one of the dark wood bookcases that lined all the walls, their shelves filled with an eclectic mix of old books, he looked at the names on the spines, Shakespeare, Voltaire, Dumas. These were interspersed every so often with stacks of obviously well-read paperbacks. Again in these he saw several names he recognized, Hemmingway, Robert Ludlum, Tom Clancy, Patricia Cornwell, even a Dr. Seuss. He turned away from the books and saw Father Andrew standing behind a huge old mahogany desk also covered in numerous stacks of books and papers, save for the area that had been cleared in front of the burgundy leather captain's chair for the completely out of place fire truck red laptop computer.

Father Andrew unlocked the upper right hand desk drawer, then gingerly removed the gun and held it out to Jake in the palm of his hand, as if he were offering sugar cubes to a horse. Walking over to the desk, Jake took the gun from the priest and pocketed it.

"Well...Thanks once again for everything Father. Like I said, I just wish there were some way I could pay you back for all you've done for me."

The priest took hold of Jake's hand.

"All I would ask from you in return is that you always remember one thing Jake, and that is 'no man is an island'. That is something I think you will need to remind yourself of every now and then."

Jake nodded his intention to comply with the request.

"However, there is one more little thing you could do for me."

"Just name it Father."

"Well if you're ever passing this way again stop by, I would dearly love to see how you are doing."

"If I'm ever in the neighborhood I promise I'll call in."

Jake then turned and waving back walked out the house to his truck.

And so, thanks to the compassion and kindness of a complete stranger, Jake found himself back on the I-70 on route to his beloved California. It didn't take long before he'd left the urban sprawl of the outskirts of St Louis behind, and the Missouri countryside sun baked from the long summer opened out in front of him. This had to be a whole world better than ending up sticking a gun barrel in his mouth and pulling the trigger. Which no doubt would have ended up with his corpse being kept in a numbered refrigerated drawer in some nameless grey government building once the autopsy tests revealed the anomalies in his blood.

Jake was happy.

He had a full tank of gas, two and a half packs of cigarettes, and he was wearing sunglasses.

Okay, so it wasn't a full blown Blues Brothers moment, but it would most definitely do.

Yep, today was a good day.

"Hello?"

Billy leant over snapping his fingers in front of Jake's face. "Anybody home?"

Jake came to. "Oh, sorry, miles away."

"You do that a whole bunch you know."

"Yeah, sorry."

Sensing a potential lecture looming or worse still, questioning about the matter, Jake heaved himself upright and dusted the sand from his hands.

"So how about we go hire a couple of surf boards?"

He jerked his thumb over his shoulder towards a surf shack a little way down the beach front street.

"Oh no way! I don't know how to surf, and besides I've only ever really swum in a pool."

Jake kept forgetting that before they arrived in Southern California almost a week ago Billy had never seen the coast, been in the sea or even smelt the heady mix of salt air and seaweed brought in on the spray off the surf. And the look of awe on the guy's face when he first spotted the expanse of the Pacific Ocean had been priceless. It had also been the first time since they'd left the Navajo Nation Billy had been lost for words and not constantly babbling on about something or other. And as much as he had started to get used to Billy's company over the past few weeks, there were times when a 'mute' button on the guy would come in handy.

Smiling, Jake countered Billy's excuse, "You've been swimming almost every day we've been here."

"Yeah, but they weren't much more than a paddle."

"Looked more like a doggy paddle to me, or maybe even a wolf paddle."

Jake held his hands up and making clawing motions impersonated a dog paddling, once he'd managed to stop laughing, he pursed his lips and howled.

At that Billy grabbed his water bottle, popped the sports cap on it and squirted Jake, resulting in Jake retaliating and the pair of them chasing each other round in a full on water fight.

Once the bottles were empty and they'd both caught their breath, Jake returned to the subject of surfing.

"Don't worry, it'll be fine, this is an ideal beginner's beach, it has easy spilling waves, see?"

He pointed out to where the surf broke, "We can even get you some proper schooling."

"Easy waves eh? Really? I don't know Jake, I'm not sure I'm a strong enough swimmer, maybe we should leave it."

"You're fine; I've watched you swim, not the most powerful granted, but good enough. Besides I'll be with you, and whoever teaches you as well."

With that Jake declared the matter settled, leaving Billy shaking his head out of resignation. If he'd learnt one thing about Jake it was that when the guy made his mind up over something no amount of protest could sway him.

"You keep paying for everything and that makes me feel uncomfortable, like I'm dependent on you." Billy protested. "I need to get a job so I can start paying my way."

"If I didn't want to pay for things I wouldn't, and anyway it's for both of us, I need to get back to surfing again. And besides, you can make it up to me by carrying on working when I retire at say, ooh I dunno... forty? Then you can support me while I take it easy."

It suddenly dawned on Billy that he didn't know what Jake done for a living, the guy seemed to have money, so maybe his folks had money. Or it could be the guy spent the winter months working in order to be able to bum around all summer, which seemed the more likely.

Once Jake had finished making a drama out of rubbing his bicep after Billy's dead arm punch, they picked up their stuff, walked to the parking lot and dumped most of it except their towels into the pickup's lock box then walked back along the beachfront street and into the surf store. Jake explained they wanted to hire spring suits and boards and that Billy needed some tuition. After chatting to the store owner and discovering someone was free to tutor Billy, Jake paid and they went out back to change.

Billy knew he'd been told to watch Jake in order so he would learn how to put a wetsuit on, but he simply couldn't help ogling as Jake fought first to get his huge thighs, then his broad shoulders in his suit. The effort Billy decided had most definitely been worth it, as the suit bulged nicely in all the right places. He silently reprimanded himself for wanting to sneak up behind Jake and grope his butt. He really needed to stop fantasizing about the guy, but times like this made it difficult.

Once Jake had zipped his wetsuit up, Billy started to put his on and surprised himself by struggling less than he'd expected, and especially by not falling over or losing his towel. Once they were back in the store, the owner pointed at the door to the street, outside they could see a tall girl in a pale blue and grey spring suit with tangled salt and sun bleached blonde hair holding three surf boards.

Introducing herself as Hannah, the boys shook hands and presented themselves in return, Jake went on to explain that Billy was the one who needed the tuition.

"That's cool," she replied, "I'll have you in the water and catching waves in no time. So, what do you know about surfing?"

Billy pointed at the boards declaring, "Those are surf boards," then to the sea, "and that's wet and tastes yucky."

Hannah laughed, "Yucky eh? Okay, surfing 101 it is then."

The guys grabbed their boards from her and the trio headed down to the beach.

Hannah started describing the sea and what to look for when surfing, pointing at the surf she explained that the spilling waves on this particular stretch of beach were the best for novices.

Billy said he'd heard that before somewhere and gave a faux glare Jake's way.

Hannah turned round and looked in the direction of the stare just in time to see Jake pretending to surf with his arms out, obviously sending up her student. Having just been caught out, Jake immediately dropped his arms and attempted to feign innocence.

She wagged her finger at him in mock reprimand. "No distracting my pupil. In fact, how about you give us a quick demonstration?" She jerked her thumb over her shoulder gesturing to the surf.

Jake knew he'd had just had his bluff called.

"Ah, I'll just go sit over here and keep quiet then."

"Oh no mister, I think you should go out so I can show Billy all the things 'not to do', unless you'd like to join us in the beginners lesson?"

Jake's eyebrows shot up, "I'm not a kook!" he spluttered.

Smirking, Billy stuck his tongue out as Jake picked up his board and stomped off towards the surf still grumbling about not being a beginner and needing lessons.

"Does he always mutter like that?" enquired Hannah.

"Pretty much yeah. Na, I'm kidding, he's great… for the most part."

While Hannah briefly explained some key surfing terms and that 'kook' was surfer slang for a newbie, Jake waded out into the sea, pushing his board by the tail. Then giving it one last shove he laid on it and started paddling. He'd got some way out when he flipped over and disappeared under a larger wave then popped back up on the other side.

Shaking her head, Hannah laughed.

"Hmm, I think someone's showing off for you now. That's called a turtle roll and helps gets you under bigger waves when you're on a longer or fat nosed board. It's so you don't get washed back so far."

After a couple more minutes paddling Jake sat up astride his board, looked back to the beach, waved then turned to face out to sea.

"He's keeping an eye on the waves, so he can catch one that looks like its big enough to pick him up and bring him in."

They carried on watching as Jake gently bobbed up and down as waves passed under him, then spotting a suitable wave heading his way he turned and headed the surfboard towards the beach. Stroking hard he got the board moving, then paddling he caught the wave and the board rose up.

Hannah pointed out towards Jake.

"Watch, he's gonna pop up any second now."

Jake pushed himself up as smoothly as he could; knowing full well Hannah would be watching to see if he cheated by coming to his knees first. And he sure didn't fancy joining Billy for lessons.

Once back on the beach he walked up to Hannah and Billy and stood in front of them puffing.

Hannah grinned, "Not bad. Not bad at all. You popped up pretty quick and clean, though your stance isn't wide enough, that's what's giving you your balance issues, and your center of gravity is too high. But apart from that…"

Jake looked at Billy and wiggled his eyebrows, "And that's how we roll. Your turn now."

A look of dread shot across Billy's face.

"Oh no. Not yet!" said Hannah, "He's got a whole lot to learn before he's going anywhere."

After a further half hour of tuition and practicing with the board safely sat on the sand Hannah announced the time had come for Billy to hit the water and to learn to ride in prone to start with. The three of them paddled out and waited for waves, the first few times Billy tried he ended up pearling or sliding off, but gradually things started to click into place.

Then just as he felt he'd started getting the hang of it, Hannah called over to him saying that they just had time to get one more wave in. Billy caught his wave and rode it in, this time ending the ride himself as he neared the beach. After grabbing his board and running up the beach he stood looking out to sea at the other two. Hannah and Jake sat on their boards as they waited. Billy watched as almost simultaneously they both turned and went for the same wave. Hannah popped first, followed a second or so later by Jake, the two rode the wave into the beach, picked up their boards and walked up to Billy.

Billy virtually bounced up and down with excitement, "Wow! You guys were awesome, that was just so cool!"

"Remember what I told you Billy?" Hannah asked. "Surfing is all about practice and having fun."

The three of them made their way back to the surfing store. Outside Hannah took the boards and patted Billy on the shoulder.

"You did really well today, don't forget to practice your pop ups tonight, and I'll see you in the morning at ten and we'll see if we can get you riding your board standing up!"

The guys showered and changed then walked back down to the beach to hang around for a few hours so as to catch the sunset before going to get something to eat.

They'd been sat on the beach for less than half an hour, idly chatting about California, surfing, and what they would have for dinner, when Billy suddenly gasped.

"OH SHIT!"

"What is it?" Shielding his eyes with his hand Jake followed Billy's stare and saw three guys approaching them. Even though they were too far away for Jake to pick up on their scents, the fluid way they moved suggested they were probably shifters.

"I'm guessing you know them?" he asked.

"It's Garrett, my father's batshit crazy beta. That's him in the middle, and the other two are Lane and Riley. How the hell did they find us?"

"Your father's the pack alpha? Thanks a bunch for keeping that one quiet."

Billy looked at Jake apologetically, "Yeah sorry, I guess I should have said, I'll explain it all later, I promise. Besides I can guess what this is all about."

As the three shifters got closer Billy stood up, followed by Jake.

The two shifters on the outside stopped about twelve feet from Billy and Jake, Garrett stopping a little closer.

"Get your stuff kid; you're coming back with us."

Seeing Jake just about to square up to Garrett, Billy put his arm across Jake's chest blocking him.

"It's okay, I have this."

He then turned back to the three shifters.

"Listen Garrett, I make all the decisions in life now, not my father." Billy growled.

"I'm charged with taking you back and that's what I plan to do, what you want don't interest me. I don't care if I have to carry you to the car, and you ride to the airport in the trunk."

"We'll soon see about that." Billy pulled his cell out and stabbed the screen with his finger a couple of times. Somehow he'd never quite managed to get up the courage to delete his father's cellular number, despite ignoring every call, text and voicemail from the guy. And just to prove his lameness, until he met Jake he must have been the only twenty three year old in the country with just two numbers on his phone, his dad's cell and the ranch landline. These were the only two numbers his father allowed him to have. Jeez, he hadn't even been permitted to have a data allowance.

Straight after getting his first pay check he'd go out and buy his own SIM card. Well, after first buying Jake dinner in a swanky restaurant to make up for the meals Jake had bought him.

The phone rang for several seconds before the call connected.

"Get your goons outta of my face Dad. What I do is my decision and my decision alone. I have a new life now, and stunts like this will only drive me further away from you."

Jake watched the expression grow darker on Billy's face as he listened to his father.

"Then I suggest you have the balls to come down here and talk to me in person. No I don't, and I'll talk to you how I please. In the meantime you can call Garrett and tell him to leave me the fuck alone!"

He punched the screen with his finger, stuffed the phone back into his pocket and resumed his glaring. Seconds later Garrett's cell rang and he answered it before the third ring, glancing over to Jake and Billy before turning away.

Jake stood there a more than little stunned. He wasn't sure Billy getting all heavy handed with his father to be such a good idea, especially as the guy obviously didn't seem to consider himself estranged, and had sent some apparently unhinged shapeshifter and his personal posse to haul his son back home. But looking back across at Billy, Jake couldn't help but be impressed by the change in the guy's demeanor. The downtrodden pack Billy of earlier had gone, if even only briefly, replaced by a far more aggressive and confident version. Billy stood there, his arms folded defiantly across his chest, with a look on his face that Jake reckoned could quite likely burn a hole through a cinder block wall. Obviously all the shit he'd taken from his father and the rest of the pack, plus everything they'd been through over the past couple of weeks had taken its toll.

Garrett put his phone away, glanced at the other two shifters, then stared at Billy, "Alpha Thompson is flying down here tomorrow."

"He… Is… Not… My… Alpha. How many more times do I have to spell it out for you? But he is still my father, so see if you can manage some respect for his son."

"Maybe I could if you hadn't been some sort of freak." Taunted Garrett.

Enough was enough. Jake started moving forward only for Billy to yank him back.

Whoa!

The adrenalin pumping through Billy's veins had given him surprising strength, leaving Jake more than a little taken aback.

"This is my fight Jake, I need to do this."

They were brave words indeed, but Jake knew Billy was nowhere near big enough, or mean enough to take Garrett on and win if things went that far. Jake for his part had already sized Garrett up; the guy looked to be in his mid-thirties, same height as Billy but had at least thirty pounds of muscle on him.

Not only that, Garrett had a look in his eyes Jake recognized, the guy had that air about him people seem to develop when they have become truly malevolent and cruel deep inside, something Jake had not seen in a good while. It hadn't even been present in the skinwalker's human eyes, they were simply cold and expressionless, something Jake much preferred. Garrett on the other hand came across as unbalanced and thus unpredictable, and that coupled with his wolf instincts and strength made him very dangerous.

But end of day, Billy was right; if Jake muscled in to protect Billy, it would make him look weak. Not a good situation to be in, and at the moment he couldn't see a clean way out of it, not yet anyway.

"Git a move on freak! I don't have all day to waste while you say your faggoty goodbyes."

Suddenly everything caught up with Billy all in one go and his anger exploded over.

"I'm gay! Not a freak, you ignorant fucktard!"

"Same thing. Gay, faggot, freak, sicko."

Billy launched himself at Garrett, only to be instantly grabbed in a bear hug by Jake before he had chance to move more than a couple of feet.

"Let me go Jake!" Billy yelled. "I'm gonna tear that bastard's lungs out!"

As Jake fought to hold on to the struggling Billy he caught the stunned expressions on both Riley and Lane's faces and guessed they'd never seen Billy this way before. Even Garrett had a surprised look on his face for a few seconds before he regained his composure.

"Don't make us come get you kid; it'll only end up with lover boy there getting hurt."

Yep, as usual Jake had definitely spoken too soon earlier, what was it about him that attracted trouble wherever he went?

He turned his head to face Garrett. "Understand this fella, Billy's not going anywhere he doesn't want to go."

"You think you're gonna stop us pussy cat?" Garrett gestured to himself and the two guys flanking him.

Garrett's right hand casually slipping into his jean's pocket and coming straight back out again caught Jake's attention, and the furtive way he done it suggested to Jake that the guy had some sort of weapon in his hand. Then the glint of sunlight reflected by the blade of a double action switchblade as it sprung out of its handle told Jake all he needed to know. Surely, the guy wouldn't be stupid or crazy enough to use a knife on a public beach in broad daylight. Would he?

"I think you three should get the fuck off our beach. Right now!"

Garrett stopped smirking and everyone looked over to see Hannah and a small group of other surfers standing there, several of whom held baseball bats by their sides. Then down off the street came a good half a dozen more, their sprinting pace only slowing as they hit the loose sand.

Not taking his eyes off the group of surfers to his left, Garrett closed the switchblade against his right hip and pocketed the knife in one smooth motion. He then turned his head back and jabbed his finger in Billy's direction.

"You're going home, like it or not. Best you start saying your good-byes to your pet."

Ripping himself out of Jake's hold, Billy snapped at Garrett. "I go where I want, when I want and with whom I want."

Refusing to back down despite the weight of numbers against him Garrett took two steps towards Billy causing several of the group of surfers to start moving in towards him. He stopped, then after a brief pause turned around and swaggered off, signaling Lane and Riley to follow him.

After a few steps Garrett stopped again and pointed at Hannah, "I'm gonna remember you, bitch."

"You bet you should, because next time this bitch might not be so amiable."

Garrett sneered then strode off after the other two, screaming abuse at them as they'd decided against stopping with him.

Once they were out of earshot, Jake let out a whistle. "Well, that all got pretty intense."

Hannah and several of the others walked over.

"You guys okay? We spotted something bad looked like it was about to go down, so thought we'd better come over."

"Yeah thanks for that, very much appreciated." Acknowledged Jake.

"So who were those assholes?" Hannah enquired.

"Oh, three of my father's ranch hands," replied Billy, "He doesn't like the fact that I've left home to live my own life."

"Well, I think you guys should stay at mine tonight, there's plenty of space and there'll be loads of us there, so you'll be quite safe. Oh, we're also fixing to fire up the grill as its Noah's birthday."

She held her hand up in the air and waved vaguely in the direction of the group behind her.

"Can't see him, but he's over there somewhere. Anyway, there's going to be plenty of food, and loads of good company of course, just bring along whatever you want to drink."

Jake tried to assure her they'd be fine, but it was a futile effort, as she had no intention of taking no for an answer. Billy grinned, it seemed Jake had just met his match in how to be infuriatingly obstinate.

Darkness had fallen by the time Jake pulled up outside a modest California style bungalow, clad in dark horizontal siding, with a porch that spanned the full width of the house. Finding it in the dark had been easy due to all the SUV's and pickups sporting surfboards parked outside, abandoned in the driveway and on the lawn. Luckily someone must have left the party early, as a truck sized space existed in the street between the drive and another pickup. As they got out the truck Billy grabbed the two six packs from the seat, and handed one to Jake as they walked up the path to the house, judging by the hum of noise behind the house everything was happening in the back yard.

Three young lads were sitting out front on the wide steps that led down from the stoop to the path; a broad grin grew on Jake's face as he picked up the scent of what they were smoking. One of them he recognized from the beach earlier, and they all acknowledged his greeting with a chorus of "Dude" and 'hang loose' shaka hand gestures.

Rounding the back of the house the mouth-watering smell of meat and fish cooking on the grill assailed their noses and caused their stomachs to start growling in anticipation.

"There's Hannah!"

Billy put his hand on Jake's shoulder then stood on tiptoe and waved excitedly towards the crowd of people around the grill catching her attention. Waving back she gestured for them to come over.

"Hey... I'm really glad you two decided to come," Laughing she waggled a pair of tongs at them, "Didn't want to have to send some of the guys out to come get you!"

She then pointed the tongs at a mound of burgers, ribs and fish steaks on the warming rack.

"Just grab yourselves plates and some food, and once you've eaten 'til you can't fit anymore in I'll take you round and introduce to you everyone."

By the grill stood a small table loaded with condiments, flatware and a stack of paper plates and paper napkins sporting purple colored balloons each with the number 8 on it.

Noticing their amusement Hannah went on to explain that the plates were left over from a friend's daughter's birthday party a few weeks ago, and that despite Noah being twenty eight purple was still an okay color for a boy. Duly grabbing plates they got their food, and immediately became enveloped in a crush of people all wanting to know about the newest additions to Hannah's extended family.

Jake stood happily demolishing a huge chunk of seared tuna drenched in lime juice, whilst Billy attacked his second cheeseburger of the evening when Hannah walked over to them with a well-built guy sporting close cropped dark blond hair in tow.

She introduced her companion, "And this is our birthday boy, Noah."

Pointing to the boys in turn she introduced them.

"Now this one's Billy, and that one's Jake."

She lightheartedly nudged the guy forward with her shoulder, smiling awkwardly he offered his hand.

"Umm… Hi… Noah Bailey. Good to meet you."

Immediately, Jake picked up on the genuine coconut buttons on what appeared to be a vintage Hawaiian shirt, and the expensive looking diving chronograph on the outstretched forearm. Definitely not your average beach bum's wear Jake mused, but the guy's goofy smile and shyness seemed natural and genuine enough. In fact the apparent naivety behind it came across as quite disarming; the guy's face seemed to have that wide eyed, lost kitten thing about it.

After a round of handshaking a brief, but slightly awkward pause followed before Noah thought of something else to say. "Erm… So those guys from the beach left now, or do you think they're still hanging around somewhere?"

Over by the kitchen door someone called out Hannah's name; apologizing she disappeared into the house.

Jake turned back to Noah, "Hannah said you were on the beach this afternoon?"

Noah nodded. "Yeah."

Jake eyed the guy suspiciously. "I never picked up on your scent."

Glancing about Noah nodded towards an empty corner of the yard. "Let's go sit down over there."

Billy and Jake followed Noah and sat down on a low wall, under the dim red glow of a lone Chinese lantern gently swaying on its chain in the slight evening breeze.

Noah continued, "Well, that's 'cos I caught yours and the other three's first, and decided to stay downwind of the bunch of you. I reasoned if I'd got picked up on it would just complicate matters, especially as I was in with a whole bunch of 'normals'."

Over the years Jake had heard other shifters refer to non-shifters as 'normals' or 'norms'. Initially the term had amused him as it sounded like a line from some vampire movie, but more often than not, he'd heard it said in a derogatory tone that inferred shifters were some sort of elite. Plus he knew a good many shifters considered themselves several rungs higher up the evolutionary ladder than plain old Homo sapiens.

Bemused, Noah and Jake watched as Billy waved his hand in front of his mouth and made little grunting noises while he desperately tried to chew and swallow the huge chunk of burger he'd just stuffed in his mouth, finally after washing it down with a mouthful of beer he gasped for air.

"Wow! I get to sit with two cougars at the same party, that's so cool."

Both Jake and Noah shook their heads, and Noah started laughing.

"What? Why are you laughing?" Enquired a puzzled Billy.

"I know what Jake is as I've met a couple of cougars before, so I recognized his scent straightaway."

Jake looked blankly at Noah and shrugged.

Noah looked genuinely surprised, "Dude, I just assumed you knew… I'm a jaguar."

Jake's jaw fell open a little, the revelation having genuinely stunned him. Feline shifters mimicked their true animal counterparts and tended to shy away from other shifters, Jake thought maybe that had been why he'd never come across any other form of cat other than cougars.

He turned to Billy, "Well, I guess that answers your question then."

Now it became Noah's turn to look puzzled. Jake went on to explain that Billy had asked him if there were other shifter species apart from wolves and cougars. Something Jake had been unable to answer.

"Ah okay. If you guys were wondering as there's been no native Jaguars in the US for a good hundred years or so, well until very recently anyway, my family originally come from Columbia, though our bloodline has become a bit mixed over the centuries. Which I guess is my way of explaining why I look more European than Latin American. My parents came here in the early eighties to escape the violence of the drug cartels and guerrilla factions that wreaked havoc and death in our country."

Noah grinned, "You know Jake I've always been jealous of you cougars' ability to purr."

Billy butted in, "You can't purr? I thought all cats did."

"No, we physically can't, jaguars are from a different feline genus, we're the same as lions, tigers and leopards, which does mean we can roar. Now Jake's from the same family as bobcats and moggies, which can all hiss, spit and purr."

Grimacing at what he'd just said, Noah looked at Jake apologetically. "Sorry dude, I didn't mean any offence."

Jake smirked and assured Noah he wasn't in the least bit offended.

Billy laughed and patted Jake's head, "Aww, you're definitely not a moggy. Cos if you were, I might have to get you your very own kitty litter box and a little bell to wear."

Jake pouted as both Noah and Billy fell about laughing at the joke.

Once the laughing had subsided, Noah turned to Billy, "So can I ask who the three A-holes were hassling you at the beach today?"

Billy explained they were from his father's pack and that they'd come to take him back. He looked at Jake. "I know I said I owed you an explanation and I reckon now's a good a time as any before I lose my nerve."

Having checked they were still out of earshot, Billy went on to describe how ever since his mother died not long after he'd turned ten, his father had taken to keeping him close, aka 'safe' which then over time spiraled out of control to the point where his father completely obsessed over it. This meant that as time went on, the amount of freedom he'd been allowed became less and less and any protest usually resulted in him being grounded for days, or even when younger, locked in his room.

Billy went on to explain that some months after his mother's death his father had taken him out of school in favor of home tutoring effectively preventing him from any contact with other kids except those who lived within a few miles that he could cycle to, or when there were social events at the ranch like barbeques. Eventually things became so bad his father had prohibited him to leave the ranch for any reason without a 'babysitter'.

"To all intents and purposes I'd been put under virtual house arrest. And it didn't make any great difference once I stopped being a kid. And the more I complained, the worse things got, and the greater his anger at my protests."

He took another mouthful of his beer, thought for a few seconds then continued.

"I was sixteen when I first knew for sure I was gay. I never struggled with it; I accepted it and I felt completely comfortable with it. Then six months ago, just before my twenty third birthday I decided to come out to my father and a good number of the pack who happened to be in the room at the same time. Okay I know it wasn't a very tactful thing to do, and as you can probably imagine it didn't go down a storm either. It was also the first time my father had ever really slapped me hard in anger, I mean hard enough to knock me to the floor, and in front of the other pack members too. I'd shocked and embarrassed him, and he'd retaliated in the only way he knew how. Which I guess had been what I'd expected him to do, and in some ways, what I'd wanted him to do. It proved beyond all doubt that he didn't love me or respect me, it being all about him, the big pack alpha."

Noah shook his head. "That's way beyond being a 'helicopter parent', that goes straight into 'control freak' territory."

"I know, tell me 'bout it. Anyway, after he'd crushed my little 'coming out' rebellion, his attitude to me became more aggressive. I tried fighting back at first but after a while the will to keep rebelling got knocked out of me, sometimes literally, though after the time he hit me when I came out he always apologized for hitting me and told me he'd done it because he loved me. Eventually I just gave up any form of resistance, following that decision a number of the pack started to consider me their personal doormat, more often than not at the instigation of Garrett, the one with the big mouth and attitude this afternoon."

Billy stared down into his beer can and while Jake and Noah sat in silence he swirled its contents around a couple of times, before carrying on.

"So for six months I kept all my emotions bottled up, then one day everything just kinda boiled up inside me. I felt I just couldn't take another day of it and that night when all but the night guards were asleep I packed a bag, took what cash I could find in the house, grabbed my mountain bike and made off through the woods. When I hit the highway I just cycled as fast as I could until I came to a truck stop where I sold the bike for eighty bucks and managed to hitch a lift."

I an attempt at reassurance, Jake put his hand on Billy's arm, "You don't have to do this, you know."

Billy shook his head, "You don't understand Jake, I need this. Maybe if I let it all out I'll feel a little better about myself, and perhaps get some self-esteem back."

Noah held his hands up, "Maybe this is something the two of you should talk about in private."

Billy shook his head, "No, this is the first time since Mom died I've been with a group of people I trust and feel safe with."

Once Billy had finished recounting his story, Noah stood up.

"I know it's probably of little consolation, but you done the right thing, you're best off out of there that's for sure. But at least it looks like things are starting to go the right way for you now. Anyway I should go mingle before Hannah comes over and chews me out for hogging your company. But remember, if there's anything you guys ever need anytime just shout."

"Yeah will do Noah, and thanks." Jake then added. "Oh by the way, I meant to ask earlier, are you the only other one of us around here?"

"I'm the only feline that I know of, though there is a local wolf pack and a couple of wolf loners. The pack knows of me and we have little to do with each other. The two loners are roomies and both surfers, you're sure to come across them before too long. They're good guys but a real pair of stoners, and now of course there's you two."

After Noah wandered off, Billy turned to Jake.

"Noah's a great guy isn't he? And a jaguar too, that's so freakin' awesome."

Jake nodded his agreement, "Yeah, he seems to come across as pretty genuine."

"I know maybe I shouldn't have said a bunch of that stuff to a total stranger, but I felt really comfortable about saying it all in front of him. It felt like I'd known him for ages, and could tell him anything."

"Yeah." Jake agreed. "He's obviously one of those guys who can instantly make people feel at ease."

Billy bounced up and down in his excitement, "Oh and don't forget Hannah, I think she's gonna be a new best friend too. That's if we stay here. You are gonna stay here aren't you Jake? I mean it's what you want isn't it? I guess I mean that I want to stay here."

Jake grinned, "I get the distinct impression Hannah adopts waives and strays, and we definitely fall into that category at the moment."

"But settling down Jake? I need some stability. Like a place to live, a job and a bunch of friends and someone to help me learn all the stuff about things that I don't know, 'cos I know I'm pretty naïve and don't know much about how to get along in the big wide world."

"I wouldn't mind putting down roots in somewhere like here, but let's talk about it later. Yeah?"

Jake heaved a mental sigh of relief as Billy agreed and popped the ring on his fifth beer.

"I think I might be a little drunk."

"I think you might be too." Jake laughed and ruffled Billy's hair.

As the evening wore on and the temperature dropped, those who had early starts the next morning drifted off, while the others including Billy and Jake made their way to the living room and sat about chatting. After a while the alcohol and the exertions of the day took their toll on Billy and he fell asleep leant against Jake, happier than he thought he could ever be.

Jake looked down at Billy, he knew the alcohol had lowered the guy's inhibitions. But he decided to leave him where he was as no one in the room came across as the judgmental type. And it felt kinda nice in a way to have someone close to him after all this time.

The pair awoke to an empty room bathed in the energizing warming yellow of early morning California sunlight, then their noses caught the to die for smell of fried bacon, toast and brewing coffee. Billy sat up from his position of being propped up against Jake who'd ended up wedged catty corner against the wall and the end of a couch.

Jake straightened up, interlocked his fingers and raising his arms above his head arched his back, resulting in numerous joints cracking and popping loudly. He sniffed the air again then lowered his arms.

"Mmmm… something smells good. Think we should go see if we can grab ourselves some coffee before heading off."

Entering the kitchen they soon discovered après party breakfast at Hannah's was the embodiment of organized chaos. The kitchen bustled with people who'd quite clearly done this many times before. Whilst standing in what they assumed to be the queue for the coffee percolator, they each had an empty plate thrust into their hands, then before they could do anything, the plates were promptly taken away by someone else and returned filled with bacon, scrambled egg and toast. An arm from an unseen body pushed its way between two people; clutched in its hand were two knives and forks.

"Good morning!"

They looked round to see a smiling Hannah beaming back at them.

"Glad to see you got yourselves something to eat. Now let's get you some coffee or juice then you can go sit out with everyone else and eat.

A couple of minutes later, bemused and still a little shell shocked they sat cross legged out on the deck, plates in laps and tucked into their breakfast. Having eaten, they volunteered themselves to help with the washing up, then once they'd gone round and said their goodbyes they left in order to get to the surf shop by ten.

Once changed into their wet suits they met up with Hannah and walked down to the beach for Billy's second surfing lesson only to be met by four surfers they recognized from the previous night.

"Some of the guys thought they'd surf up here with us today... Just in case." Hannah grinned and winked.

The friendliness and camaraderie of the group impressed and humbled Jake. These guys were happy to spend their day on a gentle surf beach riding what to them were 'ankle busters' in order to help 'body-guard' two strangers they'd known for less than twenty four hours.

With Hannah's expert tuition and with the other surfers heaping encouragement on him, it wasn't long before Billy managed to stand on his board, and with almost each subsequent ride he stayed on a little longer as his confidence grew in leaps and bounds. His lesson flew by so fast it felt like it had lasted just minutes. Even though Hannah had to leave to teach someone else, Billy's 'minders' carried on schooling him.

While the extra lessons were going on, Jake decided to take a stroll to a nearby liquor store and buy a couple of six packs for Billy's teachers as a small way of saying thank you. Coming back out the store he'd taken one step off the sidewalk into the empty street when a dark blue sedan parked close by pulled away hard forcing him to leap backwards out of its way. But despite his lightning fast reactions, the door mirror smacked the back of his hand hard enough to make him drop the bag holding the beers.

Asshole!

He watched as the car sped up the street, only for it to stop abruptly. It then slowly turned around, causing another car to brake violently and swerve, but instead of coming back it pulled over to the opposite curb and just sat there. Jake stared up the street, debating on whether to go berate the driver. But the sun reflecting off the windshield prevented him from seeing how many occupants there were, so he decided better of it. Besides he didn't want to be away from Billy for too long, even if the guy did have his very own personal guard with him.

Jake looked at his hand, and wiggled his fingers. They all moved ok, so nothing had been broken, but it felt sore as hell and he knew he'd be lucky not get a fair bruise there by the end of the day. He stooped down and picked the beer up; at least it had escaped being run over. Keeping a wary eye on the car he crossed the street and started off back to the beach. Just before he turned a corner he took one last look back up the street. The blue sedan had gone.

Garrett! It had to be him. Damn! It was so obvious now he thought about it. His instincts were telling him just to grab Billy, bundle him into the truck and put distance between them and Billy's father's little posse. And seeing Billy's father had managed to track him down here, the likelihood of the guy finding Billy somewhere else had to be high. Actually, how did he find him? Billy didn't have any credit cards just some cash. So how in hell had he tracked him down three states over?

His cell phone! Of course! Jake gave himself a mental slap up side of the head, what was up with him at the moment? He needed to be sharper than this. The phone had to have tracking software loaded on it. The sneaky son of a bitch! Talk about lack of trust. It was obvious now the only reason Billy's father had allowed Billy to have a cell phone of his own in the first place was to track him should he ever walk out.

Jake didn't want to let on to Billy about his suspicions, as that would likely cause a total meltdown of what little remained of the tenuous father/son relationship. The easy way out would be to get his hands on the phone and delete the tracking app, and the sooner that happened the better, then they could get the hell away from here.

Once back at the beach Jake handed out the still chilled but shook up beers with his and Billy's thanks to the group of appreciative surfers.

When Billy caught Jake rubbing the back of his hand for the third time, he had to ask about it.

"Oh nothing, just hit it on the door leaving the liquor store, that's all. No biggie."

The group split up at four o'clock, agreeing to meet up the following day.

"Man I really loved today! It's been totally awesome!" Billy enthused as they walked to the surf store.

Jake laughed, "Yeah I had a suspicion earlier that I'd need to be buying a couple of suits and boards."

Billy stopped dead and grabbed Jake's upper arm, causing him to stop and turn to face Billy.

"Oh no you don't Jake! I'm going to buy my own. So I need to get a job, right?"

As Jake went to complain Billy shushed him, and to his surprise Jake actually went quiet.

"I know you want to help out and I do appreciate that, but I have to start standing on my own two feet."

Just as Jake started to speak again Billy held his hand up, and once more Jake stopped mid-sentence.

"I'll do you a deal if you like. You find a place to live, and I'll find a job, then I can start to contribute. This is really important to me Jake; I need to do this."

Jake really wasn't sure how comfortable he felt with the fact that Billy seemed to have got it into his head that they were going to live together. He knew he should probably live alone, but some company would be nice. So maybe he'd go along with it for a while, just until Billy found his feet, and a partner. However, they couldn't stay here, not yet anyway.

Jake knew they had to get away for a while, probably just a few weeks, a couple of months at the most, give the dust chance to settle over the whole business with Billy's father.

Now he just had to come up with a way of persuading Billy that they should do some more travelling before settling down. And that wouldn't be easy, especially as he himself wanted to stay. He liked the place and the group they'd started to become a part of. And besides it would mean that there were people like Hannah and Noah around to look after Billy when Jake's 'employers' wanted him next. Life looked like becoming complicated; leaving Jake wondering whether 'complicated' would be a good or a bad thing.

The little motel room seemed so quiet after all the hustle and bustle of Hannah's house and the day on the beach in the company of their new found friends, several of whom had offered couches and floors to sleep on instead of the two of them being on their own and paying for a motel room. Jake insisted they'd be fine, but eventually gave into the 'Dude... you know... just in case' persuasion and exchanged cell numbers.

Actually the atmosphere in the room went beyond more than just quiet, it had become thick enough to carve up into little gloomy chunks with a blunt knife. An uncommunicative Jake lay on his bed brooding on all things Billy related, while Billy paced the room knowing his dad would soon call, and from there onwards the day would go rapidly down-hill. He felt sorely tempted to just turn his cell off, but knew doing so would only prolong the agony. Billy decided he needed a long shower, not just to wash the salt off him but to go over in his mind what he wanted to say to his father, and what he expected his father to yell at him in return.

But his phone rang before he'd had the chance to practice his speech. Pulling it out his pocket he grimaced then held it up for Jake to see, "It's him."

He stared at the screen for a few seconds before answering with a curt 'Hi'. After listening for a short while he walked out of their room into the parking lot. From just inside the doorway Jake watched Billy wandering back and forwards, stopping every so often to tug a leaf off some poor unsuspecting bush. Although Jake could only hear Billy's side of the conversation, the steady increase in shouting and animated arm waving suggested the exchange wasn't going well.

A few minutes later Billy came back in and tossed the phone onto his bed. "He's in some hotel the other side of town. I've agreed we'll meet him tonight at eight in that Mullins Sports Bar we went to the other day. It's neutral territory and if Garrett starts anything they have doormen who'll hopefully throw his sorry ass out. And as I don't see tonight being the high spot of this year's shapeshifter social calendar and taking very long, we can go get some food straight after."

Billy stomped off to the bathroom.

Perfect! Jake picked up Billy's cell and hit the power button, only to be confronted by the lock screen. Pressing the power button once more the display disappeared. Then breathing on the now black screen he angled the phone so the greasy fingertip trail of the unlock pattern became visible on the screen.

On the second attempt the screen lit up and he was in. Going through the list of apps he found no obvious tracking ones. It could have a stealth one on it, which left just one way to make sure. He checked that the only two numbers in the phonebook were safely stored on the SIM card, and then hit factory reset. If Billy noticed anything Jake just had to say that it must have crashed or something.

They pulled up outside the bar at twenty to eight, Jake having had to rush his shower as Billy insisted they hurry as he wanted the one-upmanship of being first to arrive. However, as soon as they walked in the door Billy spotted his father already there standing by the bar with Garrett, Lane and Riley.

"Typical." Grumbled Billy, "Just typical…"

The asshole had probably been in here for ages, just so he could get one over on him.

Making their way to the bar keeping as far away as possible from the others Jake ordered their beers, they then moved towards the others and followed them over to an empty table a good distance from the bar area.

Billy's father pointed at Jake, "He needs to stay back at the bar. This has nothing to do with him."

Billy's retort was immediate and resolute, and just a touch dramatized for good measure. "It has everything to do with him. You don't want to include him? Fine, then we're both outta here, seems you had a wasted flight. Bye!"

Billy took a final slug of beer from the bottle then slammed it down on the table and turned to Jake, "We're done here, let's go eat."

Billy's father's voice boomed out, "Wait!... He can stay."

He then addressed Jake, "This is between me and my son. You have no say in it, understand?"

"That's fine by me Mr Thompson. Billy knows his own mind; he certainly doesn't need my help there."

With that Jake dragged a chair out and promptly sat down. Slapping his hand over his mouth, Billy struggled to stifle a laugh. Not only had Jake deliberately showed total lack of respect for pack etiquette by sitting down before the alpha, but where Jake had positioned himself it meant if Garrett wanted to sit down at the table he'd have to squash up next to Jake.

Knowing Garrett to be a grade A asshole, Billy knew there was no way the guy could handle that. And sure enough, the scowling Garrett propped himself up against a large brick pillar near the table and stood there arms folded across his chest glaring at Jake. Billy's father had also taken the deliberate snub personally, and gave Jake a filthy stare before sitting himself. The self-satisfied smile on Jake's face may have had a thin veneer of feigned innocence but it told Billy that Jake was loving every second of it.

Immediately, Billy's father went on the attack, "Get one thing clear right now Billy. This game or whatever it is you're playing is over. You're flying back to Colorado Springs with me first thing tomorrow morning."

Billy looked at his father and slowly shook his head. "You really don't get it do you? I'm not some little kid anymore that you can just order about, I'm twenty three years old Dad, and I decide what I do or don't do with my life."

His father's simmering silence bolstered Billy's confidence.

"And you need to understand I'm not coming back. Ever! And if I'm honest I don't care if you lost face because I walked out, you deserved it. And while you're about it, you need to come to terms with the fact that I'm gay, and if you can't deal with that, then stay the fuck outta my life."

After a distinct pause for effect, Billy's dad responded. "Have you finished being disrespectful to me in public? I'm your father Billy and your alpha. Your place is with me back at the ranch."

Billy banged the table. "Ha! That's what's really eating you up isn't it? It's the fact I walked out on you. Not the pack... You personally! The big pack alpha!"

Billy jabbed his finger at his father. "You lost face!"

"Sneaking out in the middle of the night isn't walking out. Walking out suggests you left with some degree of respect and dignity."

Billy's eyebrows shot up and his mouth fell open with astonishment.

"Respect and dignity? You're kidding, right? What do you know about either of them? When did you ever treat me with any? And besides I had no other way of leaving, you'd held me a virtual prisoner both mentally and physically ever since Mom died."

"That's not true, and why is it all of a sudden my fault? You're the one who decided you wanted to be gay then announce it to the world in an attempt to embarrass me."

"Aaargh!" Billy threw his arms up in the air. "People don't 'decide' to be gay, it's the same as being a shifter, we're born that way. It's not a 'lifestyle choice' as they say. And again it's all about you isn't it? You honestly think I came out just to spite you?"

If he was brutally honest with himself, doing it so publicly had been an attempt to get back at his father.

Jake toyed with his already empty bottle and decided he needed another beer, he could see the arguing would be going to go backwards and forwards for ages yet. Actually, thinking about it if he hadn't had been driving several beers with whiskey chasers would be better.

Billy's father, seeing Jake about to get up, held his arm up and snapped his fingers; a guy appeared from behind Garrett.

Billy watched him approach, his head held low, in typical subordinate omega style. Lucas Manning! The poor son of a bitch, Billy had always felt sorry for Manning, forever burdened with being the pack doormat. Several times Billy had begged his father to have it stopped; only to be informed it was simply Manning's role in life and nothing needed to be done about it. But what had riled Billy so much over the years had been his father's continued refusal to acknowledge the bullying and put a stop to it. Something that still appeared to be happening.

He studied Manning for a few seconds; Billy knew the guy to be in his very early thirties, a good six foot tall and solidly built, but the stoop he walked with through constantly keeping his head bowed in submission made him look like a hunched up old man. Right now, Billy couldn't hate the whole pack thing and everything it stood for any more if he tried.

"Manning, three beers." Billy's father gestured to himself, Garrett and Billy.

The guy glanced up and nodded at Billy's father, whilst avoiding any lengthy eye contact with his alpha.

As Manning walked past Garrett, he received a slap round the back of the head, "Make sure you don't spill any, shit head." Taunted Garrett, loud enough to be heard at the table.

Billy looked at his father, shook his head, then pointed at the grinning Garrett.

"I'm surprised they don't make you put a muzzle on that when you take it out in public. Or maybe you should think about getting him neutered, it might brighten his personality up a bit."

As Jake stood up, Billy frowned. "It's okay Jake; I'll buy you a beer as my father didn't have the good manners to include you."

Jake grinned and shook his head. "Don't worry, I'll get this one, you get to pay for the next round."

As Jake drew level with Garrett, he heard a 'meow' and saw the guy waggling his hand imitating a limp wrist. Instantly Jake spun round, grabbed the back of Garrett's neck with his right hand, his thumb and index finger pressing hard, and accurately into nerve points just below and behind the ears. His left hand simultaneously grabbed the guy's belt at the back to hold him up. Before Garrett could respond, his vision started fogging out and his legs buckled under him. Jake released the pressure the split second before Garrett blacked out fully.

Putting his face so close to Garrett's ear his stubble rubbed against the side of Garrett's neck Jake whispered. "That was seven seconds, if I'd have got to fifteen you'd be dead. Think carefully about that before you open your big mouth next time."

There were times the intensive and arduous combat training his employers had put him through came in handy. And although he wasn't sadistic or cruel, Jake had to admit that what he'd just done had given him a good deal of pleasure.

As Jake let go of the belt Garrett managed to grab hold of the pillar to stop himself ending up in a heap on the floor. Then as Jake started to make his way to the bar, one of the other shifters from the beach moved towards him.

Jake stabbed a finger at the guy's face.

"Don't!" he growled.

Not wanting to suffer a similar fate to Garrett, Dale Lane instantly thought better of it and smartly stepped back.

Billy's dad jumped up, and called to his beta, however Garrett had become far too preoccupied holding on to the pillar to respond to his alpha.

"Sit down Dad, Garrett's big mouth just got him into trouble with the wrong guy, he needs to suck it up and learn a valuable lesson in life, though I suspect that's wishful thinking."

Billy's father rounded on him.

"How dare you! I will not have you try and tell me what to do or what not to do, especially regarding pack matters."

Billy shook his head in frustration,

"Dad, you need to get used to the fact I'm not pack anymore, I have my own life now. And if you so desperately want my respect you need to start earning it, the same as I would expect to have to earn yours. But as it is I'm not looking for anything other than your understanding, and if you can't even manage that, then I'll happily settle for your complete absence from my life."

Still standing, Billy's father put his palms on the table and leaned forwards staring down at Billy.

"You are still my son despite whatever stupid notions have been put in your head by that... that cat. And you will obey me!"

Refusing to be put into a subordinate position, Billy leapt up, the force sending his wooden chair flying backwards and toppling over with a clatter on the tiled floor.

"I will never 'obey' you! I am not pack anymore. How many times do I have to tell you that?" His face flushed red with rage, "You drove me away!"

Billy's father reached out and tried to grab hold of Billy's arm, but anticipating the move Billy twisted away deftly sidestepping the hand.

"There's no point in us carrying on this conversation, go back to Colorado Springs Dad, our paths are never going to cross again."

With that Billy stormed off to find Jake, as he approached the still dazed and unsteady Garrett he met Manning coming the other way carrying three beer bottles. Grabbing one out of the guy's hands Billy upended it and stuck the neck into the waistband of Garretts jeans. A look of abject horror filled Manning's face, his head dipping abruptly as he carried on towards his alpha.

Billy caught up with Jake while he stood waiting to get served at the bar, "C'mon, let's go eat, there's nothing to be gained from staying here any longer."

Jake looked across to see Billy's father, and the other three standing by Garrett, all staring their way. "Yeah, see what you mean, the atmosphere in here's turned decidedly frosty. Besides, a double decker cheese burger, fries and onion rings would go down a treat right about now."

"Sounds great," Replied Billy, "Make it two, actually make it three, all this has given me an appetite."

Leaving the bar they walked along the street till they came to a restaurant they spotted earlier.

Getting a booth near the back Jake positioned himself so he could keep an eye on the door to the street.

While they waited for their food, Billy mentioned the bottle incident.

"You did what!"

Jake turned serious after an initial burst of laughter.

"That probably wasn't such a good idea; the guy is likely to hold a grudge, big time. Still I'm sure we can deal with any fall out."

"Asshole deserved it, besides he's never been happy unless he's hurting someone."

Jake held his hands up. "Not disputing that! I'm just saying it's likely to make the guy mad as hell."

Okay, Billy did kind of regret doing it now, and as usual, Jake was right, Garrett would never forget or forgive. But boy it had felt so good at the time.

Jake sucked hard on his milkshake straw letting the artificially sweet banana taste flood his mouth.

"So why is your dad so keen to take you back to Colorado?"

"I have no idea. I'd become a major embarrassment to him after I came out, so your guess is as good as mine."

"Hmm, it might be a good thing to find out."

"No way, I'm not interested, I'm not going back to the ranch, Colorado Springs, or anywhere he is. Ever!"

Their server arrived with their food and after having plonked Billy's plate down in front of him she walked round to Jake's side. As she leant in to set his plate down in front of him, Jake noticed that between taking their order and bringing their food, another couple of buttons had become undone on her white blouse allowing a clear view of her lacey bra. Placing his napkin and flatware down by his plate she'd managed to lean across even more, virtually thrusting her more than ample cleavage in his face. Jake had now lost sight of his plate and most of the table.

As he tried to avert his eyes the overpowering smell of cheap perfume hit him and started to make his nose burn and his eyes water; he realized she must have doused herself in it just before coming back to their booth. Standing back up she laid her fingers with their huge purple false nails on his left forearm and asked if she could get him anything else. Jake smiled and assured her he'd be fine. With that, she insisted that if he needed anything else he just had to ask for Kelly, she then smiled sweetly and left.

Billy watched until she'd disappeared out of sight, then leant forward, fluttered his eyelashes at Jake, and impersonated the waitress.

"Oh hi, is there anything else I can do for you? Extra cherry for your milkshake, or maybe you'd like to try my milkshakes."

With that he held his pecs and wiggled his chest from side to side.

Billy leant back and roared with laughter.

"Dude, she SO want's into your boxers."

"Come on, she was only being friendly."

"Friendly? Yeah right. Tits in your face, drowned in gallons of fresh scent. Oh not flirting at all then?"

The waitress's not so subtle attempt to come on to Jake had definitely lightened the mood, but Jake knew he needed to carry the original conversation on. He stared down at his plate and stabbed a couple of fries with his fork.

"Look… about your dad. I'm just worried that he will do something stupid."

The fact that Jake had dragged this particular topic back up left Billy less than best pleased, especially as he had just started to put the earlier events of the evening out of his mind.

"Jake I really don't wanna talk about him. I know he's a single-minded son of a bitch, but I don't think he'll do anything now."

"I'm not so sure. I mean he sent those three thugs out to get you, and somehow I'm pretty sure they wouldn't have taken no for an answer if Hannah and her friends hadn't have turned up when they did. I really do think you should find out what's driving him so nuts."

Billy shrugged, picked up his burger and took a huge bite from it, filling his mouth to capacity, he then proceeded to chew it with a deliberate slowness. The action may have been childish, but it's meaning abundantly clear; the topic wasn't open to further discussion.

The next day passed remarkably non-eventful, No psychotic shape shifters, or irate fathers, just a pleasant day spent on the beach hanging with some of Hannah's friends. 'Happy Billy' was back and had begun getting all best friends forever with some the surfers, and that made things difficult for Jake. He knew they needed to move on right away but after Billy's reaction at the restaurant the previous night Jake decided to take the risk and leave things well alone until the evening as he felt convinced that it wouldn't take Billy's father long to realize the cell phone's tracking software had stopped working. And he knew that little discovery would go down like a lead balloon.

Having bided his time, Jake eventually broached the matter back at their motel room.

"I'll book us out of here tomorrow and we'll drive up to the other side of San Francisco and check out the surfing up in Northern California. We'll even get to see the Golden Gate Bridge on the way. Cool eh?"

The look that fell across Billy's face didn't bode well, a mixture of dismay and disbelief, topped off with a good serving of anger.

"Why do we need to go anywhere else? We've starting making friends here Jake."

Jake tried to back pedal a little in order to recover the situation.

"We'll come back here. I just think it'll be good to go see some other places."

"Jake, I like it here just fine, I don't want to go anywhere else. What I want is to settle down and get a job. I've told you this so many times, you don't seem to hear me. Or maybe you just don't want to hear me, I'm not sure which."

Jake started to get exasperated, he couldn't tell Billy about the car incident, the tracking software on his phone, or how unsafe he thought they were if they carried on staying here, as Billy would simply dismiss him as being paranoid, or go completely the opposite way, lose his temper and confront his father or Garrett causing even more hassle.

A growing part of Jake desperately wanted to walk out the door, get in his truck and put as much distance between himself and everything that was happening around him as possible, it wasn't his fight anyway, and he didn't need to get involved. But something buried deep inside kept gnawing away telling him he had to stay with it at all costs.

Aaarg! It was enough to give anyone a headache!

"We can settle anywhere, maybe you'll find somewhere you like better than here. At least check some other places out first." Jake argued.

"No Jake! I'm happy here."

"How do you know 'til you seen some other places?"

Billy didn't respond.

"Billy?"

No answer, just an angry look and a deliberate sullen silence. Oh! That's it! Jake had had enough of it all.

He wasn't prepared to be drawn into a fight over it, and turned away from Billy in an effort to stave off the potential argument that threatened to erupt any minute. Unfortunately his action had the exact opposite effect to what he had intended.

"Don't turn your back on me!" Yelled Billy, "Just because what I want doesn't fit in with your plans you don't want to hear it!"

Jake turned back round to face Billy again. But before he could say anything Billy stepped straight into Jake's personal space and leant in to face off against him.

"How many times do I have to tell you I don't want to go anywhere else? Maybe if you just listened for once instead of always expecting me to fall in with what you fucking want to do!"

The last thing Jake needed was for the situation to escalate into a full blown confrontation but his cat's fiery temper had already started to get the better of him once again. Instead of turning away his eyes narrowed as his expression darkened, and his top lip curled up one side exposing overdeveloped canines as the anger inside him started to boil over. At that moment Billy's self-preservation response kicked in and he backed off in face of the far more powerful and increasing aggressive adversary.

Despite Billy's rapid withdrawal Jake's anger had already started to put words into his mouth that otherwise would never have been there if he'd been more capable of reason.

"Whoa! Who do you think you are trying to square up to me? Unless you want a fight, drop the attitude Billy. And don't have a go at me about turning my back. You refused to answer my question, that's even more disrespectful!"

Okay, that really, really wasn't helpful. Jake could feel things starting to fall apart around him, but he knew it would happen, it always did. He simply couldn't deal with it anymore, he had to get away before he made the situation any worse.

However, Billy had no intention of being forced into backing down totally, he needed to stand up for the things he wanted in his life. He'd had too many years of being controlled and dominated, and he certainly wasn't prepared to start taking it from Jake as well.

He fisted his hands as he held them down by his sides.

"If I've got 'attitude' it's 'cos of you! You're starting to act like just my father. You really don't get it do you Jake? I don't have your wanderlust. Or maybe it's just your inability to settle down and become part of something? Whichever way, I'm not being pushed around anymore. Not by my father, and certainly not by you!"

As Jake turned to the door he snatched his keys and wallet off the nightstand. "I'm going for a drive!"

"Oh yeah that's right, just walk away! At least I'm man enough to want to try to sort things out. If I'm given half a chance!"

"I'm not walking away!"

"Then what are you doing?"

"I don't know! I just… I need to clear my head."

Jake yanked the door open letting it crash into the chest of drawers behind it, and stormed out of the room to his truck.

Billy stood and stared briefly at Jake's disappearing back through the open door before slamming it shut rattling the adjacent window.

Grabbing his bag off the bed he hurled it against the wall in frustration. Tears started to well up in his eyes, but he stubbornly refused to cry. He'd done feeling sorry for himself, and he refused to be anyone's doormat anymore, for them to walk all over.

After recovering his composure, he sat on his bed feeling righteously angry when a series of rapid knocks on the door snapped him out of his reflections. Billy walked over and peered through the viewer only to see Lucas Manning standing outside. Had his father now resorted to sending messengers to speak to him? Something about the urgency of the knocking and Manning's presence really didn't feel right so he slipped the safety stay on, then opened the door and spoke through the crack.

"Manning, what are you doing here? Has my father sent you? 'Cos if he has you can tell him I'm not interested… Whatever it is!"

"No! Nobody knows I'm here. I really need to talk to you." Implored Manning.

"Come to think of it, nobody knows we're here! How'd you find us?"

"I heard your father tell Garrett you were here and that everyone had stay away."

His father knew where he and Jake were staying? Jeez! As if he wasn't in a bad enough mood already, it now it seemed his father had been spying on him! No way would he allow that, and first thing in the morning he'd be telling his father just that.

"You sure you're alone?" The words had hardly left Billy's mouth before he realized the stupidity of his question.

"Yes, I swear! You gotta let me in." The ever desperate sounding Manning begged.

The pleading tone in the guy's voice, suggested a good degree of desperation.

"I don't know, I'm not interested in pack matters."

"Please?"

Looking into Manning's face Billy saw the hollow look of someone well and truly crushed. Taking the safety latch off he opened the door fully, Manning glanced backwards before entering the room, his back hardly clearing the door before Billy hurriedly shut and locked it. Billy put the safety latch back on; he didn't want anyone else getting in, and at the moment that included Jake.

"What is it Manning? Why are you here?"

"I want out of the pack. You've done it. I need you to help me get away." Manning blurted.

The unexpected revelation stunned Billy, who had to think for several seconds before he felt able to respond.

"I think the events of the last couple of days shows I'm not nearly far enough away from it all as I'd like yet."

"I can't take anymore. After you left the ranch things got much worse"

Then to prove his point Manning pulled his sweat shirt up to reveal a mass of bruising over his torso. Billy walked round Manning and saw the bruising continued over his back. He knew only too well that the range of colors from red, through purple, green and yellow meant the beatings were regular and probably ranged over several weeks old. Billy gently touched one of the worst bruises causing Manning to flinch.

"Sorry. Who did this to you?" As if Billy didn't know the answer to that question already. "And why haven't you shifted to heal it?"

"Mainly Garrett, but he encouraged a few of the others to hit me; he then wouldn't allow me to shift so I could heal."

About to ask why no one had reported it to his father, Billy realized Garrett would only have come up with some bullshit cover story to the contrary, and as his father's beta, Garrett's version of events would have been automatically believed over that of a mere omega's.

Damn it all! Billy had become almost beside himself with rage at the brutal and callous treatment Manning had been subjected to. He needed Jake; he'd know what to do for the best. NO! Billy needed to sort this out on his own, and not rely on other people.

"Look, you need to stay here just until I can get you away to somewhere safe. Where are your clothes?"

"I had to leave everything back at the hotel. I pretended I was going to get some more ice. Then when I got to the ice machine I dropped the ice bucket and ran out of the hotel and came here."

"Ah right... We need to go get your stuff in the morning."

The words had hardly left Billy's lips when Manning started shaking his head vigorously.

"I can't go back, I really can't. And besides, Garett's up to something bad, I know he is. He'd been gone most of the afternoon, then when he came back Riley only asked where he'd been and Garrett lost it with him totally and started screaming that what he did had nothing to do with anyone else. Once everything had calmed down Lane asked Garrett and me if we wanted to go to the movies with him and Riley this evening. But Garrett said he was taking the rental and then another huge row started between Garrett and Lane and Riley."

None of this was Billy's problem anymore, but he felt sorry for Manning and needed to think of a way to help get him safely away from the pack and if that made matters worse between himself and his father then the old man would just have to suck it up.

"Well that's Garrett for you." Billy said as nonchalantly as he could, trying to defuse the situation.

"You don't understand. Garrett pulled a knife on Riley when they were arguing about who would use the rental and threatened to cut him up. Garrett then grabbed the keys and left again."

It looked as if Garrett had finally lost it, and Billy had no doubt that the episode in the bar the previous night had finally tipped Garrett over the edge. Threatening to stab a fellow pack member over something as simple as who used a rental car would be regarded as a very serious matter, even more so if the pack alpha's beta happened to be the one doing it, they were charged with keeping order and ensuring everyone adhered to pack etiquette and rules.

If reported it would cost Garrett dearly, and Billy knew if the complaint came from Lane, Riley and Manning his father couldn't simply dismiss or ignore it. He'd have to take action and it would need to be seen by the rest of the pack as just and proportional to the seriousness of the offense. At the very least, Garrett would lose his beta's position, and would be lucky not to get kicked out of the pack.

Billy's cell phone buzzed in his pocket telling him he had a text. He hesitated briefly before taking it out; it would be either Jake or his father, and he didn't know if he wanted to hear from either one of them just right now. No, he'd made his mind up to take control of his life, and facing up to unpleasant things and dealing with them was part of that. He unlocked the screen and saw the message from Jake.

Sorry 4 earlier. I'm just trying to do what's best but as usual not making a very good job of it.

I'll get pizzas if you still want to eat.

Will go to that place you like by all the car dealerships. Text back.

A couple minutes later as Jake sat in the truck leant over the steering wheel brooding, his phone chirped.

K. I understand. cu soon. btw bring extra pizza we have a hungry guest. Explain all when you get here. x

Well at least Billy was still talking to him, he typed his reply.

Cool. Be about 30 min

A guest? He decided it must be one of Hannah's crowd, probably Noah, which would be cool. It seemed to be getting difficult nowadays to find another shifter who didn't want to shoot you, tear you limb from limb, run you down or just generally be a complete asshole.

Plonking himself down heavily on a plastic chair Jake toyed with his phone while he waited for the pizzas. Hmm, maybe he should have a quiet word with Noah about it all, so the guy could help him convince Billy getting away for a while would be the right thing to do.

He'd also come clean with Billy about the tracking software and the car being driven at him when he got back. Why did life always have to be so complicated, and why did he always manage to screw everything up so badly?

Letting his head drop he clasped his hands between his knees. He still wasn't convinced he could live like this, he had enough on his plate worrying about when he'd be contacted next and required to 'work' again. And if he and Billy lived together how would he explain having to disappear every so often? But whichever way it went, he needed to decide finally one way or the other tonight.

Leaving the pizza place Jake climbed in the truck and put the pizza boxes on the seat. He was just about to drive off when he noticed the piece of paper stuck under his windshield wiper. He leant out through the door window and managed to snag it, thinking it to be an advertising leaflet he was just about to toss it when he spotted the handwriting on it. Levering himself back into the cab he flicked the interior lamp on, and as he read the scrawled note, his blood ran cold.

YOUR LITTLE FAGGOT BOYFRIEND IS WITH ME

I'LL TRADE YOU FOR HIM

OLD FACTORY DOWN PAST THE GRAVEL PLANT ON MITCHELL ROAD

SPEAK TO ANYONE AND HE DIES

COME ARMED AND HE DIES

BE ALL YOUR FAULT PUSSYCAT

'PUSSYCAT'! THAT MEANT ONLY ONE PERSON. GARRETT!

The pickup left two black rubber stripes on the asphalt as it pulled away in a cloud of pungent white tire smoke. If Garrett had harmed Billy in any way Jake would rip the guy's head off with his bare hands and shit down his neck, doing everyone a big favor. Running a red light in his blind rage Jake suddenly realized his haste could get him pulled over by the cops or have a wreck, he needed to calm down and drive fast, not suicidally.

Finding the turning by the gravel works Jake backed the throttle right off slowing right down to a fast walking pace. After a few minutes, the truck's headlamps picked up the dark blue sedan from the liquor store incident parked outside one of the old buildings. So it had been Garrett who'd tried to run him down!

Jake turned the headlights out, dropped the truck into neutral, killed the engine, and coasted the last few hundred feet in darkness. Without the glare of the headlights, Jake could see that from a building behind the sedan, dim yellow light glimmered through a dirty window and spilled out an open doorway. Getting out the truck, he gently pushed the door to, so the latch just clicked the once. Taking several deep breaths, he proceeded to walk over to the building. Stopping outside he studied what he could see of the inside through the open personnel door.

The interior looked to be devoid of anything meaningful, instead the only reminders left of the building's previous life were broken wooden crates, piles of rubbish, and odd lumps of old, long disused machinery. Every so often light bulbs under tin shades hung on long chains from the roof trusses threw circular splashes of weak yellow light onto the dusty floor, leaving the rest of the building in varying degrees of darkness. He could see no obvious sign of Billy, looking up Jake saw a mezzanine floor with what had obviously once been offices; one of the rooms had a light on in it.

He stepped through the door and walked a few paces into the building, looking back up towards the mezzanine he called out to Garrett.

Someone grunted behind him. Jake never even managed to turn round to face the noise before a sudden, blinding pain exploded at the back of his head. Staggering forward the pain struck again causing a flash of bright white light behind his eyes. Then everything went dark...

Jake came to with the mother of all headaches. He went to lift his hands to rub his head but was unable to move his arms. The pressure on his wrists suggested they'd been tied together behind him. Now as he became more compos mentis he could smell Garrett close by. Slowly he opened his eyes and could see his own legs and those of a wooden chair.

Lifting his head he couldn't make any sense of the blurs, but gradually his eyes focused to reveal a smirking Garrett sat in front of him.

"'Bout time you woke up for me pussycat."

"Okay Garrett, you've got me. Now let Billy go, this only needs to be between us."

Garrett's grin widened and took on a manic quality as he scooted the wheeled typists chair in so close that Jake could smell the guy's breath.

"Oh I lied, he ain't here yet. But he soon will be. Once I've let him worry a while about you missing I'll call him and tell him where you are. You see you're the real bait in my trap, I followed you and when you went to in to get pizza I left the note on your windshield. Both of you are gonna pay for what happened in the bar. And I want him to watch you suffer before I make him decide how I'm gonna kill you."

Garrett's hand shot out and slapped Jake's face hard enough to cause his head to snap round, and blood to trickle from the corner of Jake's mouth where his upper lip had been driven into his teeth. Then putting his fingers under Jake's chin Garrett lifted Jake's head so that Jake could see the mock sad expression on his face.

"Poor pussycat, did that hurt?"

Garrett's fingers softly stroked Jake's cheek where he'd slapped him, he then ran his fingertips through the blood under Jake's bottom lip. Pulling his hand away Garrett studied his fingers as he spread the blood around by rubbing it with his thumb before wiping it off his hand onto Jake's jeans.

"Then after he's watched you die it'll be his turn to suffer, but you ain't gonna be around to see that."

The sad expression left Garrett's face to be replaced by a cruel sneer. "You reckon he'll piss his pants just before I kill him? I hope so. 'Cos I want the last thing he ever feels to be humiliation like I felt in that bar."

Jake spat blood out onto the floor, "You can't kill him Garrett, his father knows he's here, and you're charged with taking him home."

Garrett pulled a plastic bag out of his pocket and waggled it at Jake.

"No one will know 'cos all they'll find are your charred bodies along with some drug paraphernalia. Everyone will assume you came here to drink and smoke crack, and then managed to set fire to yourselves and the building whilst OD'd. Just another couple of druggies who done the state a favor and off'd themselves."

As Garrett got up and pushed the chair away Jake knew the guy was going to hit him and he could do nothing but just sit there and wait for the pain. He didn't have long to wait; Garrett's short throw punch to his temple actually had Jake seeing stars.

Shit! That hurt.

An hour and a half to get pizza? Where the hell had Jake got to? Billy prayed to no one in particular; please don't let him have had an accident. No, it was more likely the pickup had broken down, that was it. The long drive to and from the Navajo Reservation had been too much for the old truck. However, his reasonable explanation didn't help any, as he became ever more increasingly worried.

He rang Jake's cell, no reply, eventually it went to voicemail. Billy checked his own phone for messages, nothing. He'd never been in this situation before, how long were you meant to give it until you started calling all the hospitals and reported a missing person? He barely managed to wait another fifteen minutes before ringing again, still no reply. Going outside he scanned the motel parking lot, still no pickup.

Once back inside he straightaway rang Jake's number, it started ringing.

Don't go to voicemail…Please don't go to…

The call connected. Oh man, at last!

"Where are you? I was worried stupid something had happened to you and… Jake, are you there? Hello? Jake?"

The laugh at the other end of the phone didn't need any introduction.

"Hey little fag boy, you lost something?"

Lost something?

It took a few seconds for Billy to fully grasp what it meant.

"Where's Jake? If you've hurt him Garrett I swear I'll fucking kill you."

Garrett's deranged laugh filled Billy's head, "Your pet's with me, we're just here having a friendly chat. And I've not hurt him... well not much."

The laughing stopped and the voice then went flat and expressionless. "You two assholes made me look stupid in that bar, and someone is going to fucking pay for it. So it can either be you or him, it's your choice."

"Garrett, just tell me where you are, I'll come if that's what you want."

"Good choice. Go south along Mitchell Road, past the gravel sorting works, there's a turning with a bunch of old buildings at the end. You'll see boyfriend's truck outside one."

"I'll get there as soon as I can."

"Best you hurry then. You don't want me to start getting bored, or I'll be needing to find ways to keep amused. Maybe I'll take up carving, on his face."

Garrett laughed and the call cut off.

"What's happening, that was Garrett right? I could hear his voice. He's coming here isn't he?" Demanded a fearful Manning.

"Garrett's got Jake, I think he's gonna kill him."

"Where is he, back at the hotel?"

Billy grabbed his hoodie and turned to Manning, "No. He's says he's in some old building down by the gravel works on Mitchell Road. Look, I gotta go. You'll be safe as long as you stay here. Just keep the door locked, kay? And only let me or Jake in, nobody else."

Flinging the door open Billy ran out into the middle of the parking lot then just stood there as it dawned on him he needed transport. Unseen behind him Manning slipped out of the room and quietly closed the door. Then moving to the shadowy side of a parked SUV he proceeded to watch Billy through the windows.

Frantically Billy looked round the lot. Damn it! He simply couldn't think straight. How the fuck was he going to get to Jake? He ran over to a couple of parked cars and in sheer desperation tried the door handles. Then looking around, spotted the two mountain bikes neatly tucked away between a dumpster and the back of the motel reception office.

He ran over and listened, he could make out three voices inside the small building, and there was no discernible scent of anyone outside. Luckily, and boy could he do with some luck just now, the owners had obviously thought their bikes would be safe hidden like they were and hadn't bothered securing them. He quietly picked the top bike up and made off on it, standing up he pedaled frantically in the direction of the gravel plant, the bike rocking from side to side as he pushed his leg muscles to their limits. Shit, he reckoned it had to be a good three or four miles, plus he wasn't too sure of how to get there, as he'd only ever seen the place through the truck windows.

Luckily several large sodium lamps lit the steel latticework of the colossal elevator tower up bright orange, making it visible from a good distance. Billy cycled past it and down to the old buildings. He spotted Jake's truck and a sedan parked outside a large building. A little way behind the vehicles, a dim light shone through a partially open door.

Deciding to stop a good distance away from the building in case his brakes decided to squeal, Billy quietly lent the bike against a wall and made his way over to Jake's truck. Walking alongside it, he put his hand on the hood, which still felt warm to the touch. By pressing the driver's door handle button slowly and holding the door closed the latch released almost silently. Once he'd opened the door he looked around inside, there had to be something he could use as a weapon. The cab yielded nothing of any use; he needed to look in the lockbox. He checked the ignition lock, the keys weren't in it, he pulled the sun visor down to see if the keys were above it, again no luck. Maybe Jake kept a spare set of keys somewhere.

He had only just started searching under the bench seat for hidden keys when he touched something chunky and odd shaped. Running his fingers over it, he froze as he realized what the object was. Gingerly he pulled the object out from its holster under the seat and stood there with a silver snub nose revolver in his hand. Mesmerized at the sight of a gun in his hand, he managed to do no more than stare at it for several seconds. It felt a lot lighter than he expected it to be and it had a distinct oily smell to it. The thought that he might have to use it shortly scared him so much he almost put it back. But he had to rescue Jake and if that meant having to shoot Garrett, he was damn sure he could do it.

Billy studied the gun, carefully turning it over in his hands; he then closed his right hand around the black rubber grip and slid his finger through the trigger guard, the crook of his finger resting lightly against the trigger. Even though he'd never fired a shot in his life with a real handgun, he'd stood and watched pack members shooting cans, and seen enough cop shows on TV to know you had to take the safety off before you could fire. He looked around for the safety lock, he really didn't want it to go off accidently and end up shooting himself.

Finding a button on the left side he pressed it causing the cylinder to promptly swing out. Two of the five bullets dropped onto the cab floor then rolled under the foot pedals. Cussing quietly at his clumsiness, he picked the bullets up and reloaded them, as he pushed the cylinder back in it made a satisfyingly solid click. Not being able to find a safety lock, or even a hammer, which he felt sure it should have one of too, he became a little concerned. But he couldn't see Jake having a gun that didn't work, and besides, maybe just pointing it at Garrett would do the trick and he wouldn't actually have to use it.

He put it in his hoodie pocket to start with, but the weight of the gun made the pocket bulge out making it obvious he had something in there. So he stuffed the gun into his jean pocket leaving the butt sticking out so he could pull it out without too much fumbling around if needed. After tugging his hoodie down to hide the gun butt, he felt reasonably confident Garrett wouldn't know he had it.

He pushed the truck door to and walked up to the small personnel door, stopping, he cautiously pushed it all the way open. As he stepped inside the horror of what he saw stopped him dead in his tracks and sent a cold shiver racing down his spine. Jake sat on a wooden chair in the middle of a pool of yellow light from a light bulb directly above him.

His head hung down and lolled to one side, Billy prayed Jake was just unconscious and not anything else.

"There you are. We'd nearly given up on you, hadn't we pussycat?"

Billy followed the voice and spotted Garrett aimlessly digging the tip of his switchblade into a packing crate just outside the circle of light.

As Billy tentatively walked closer, Garrett moved across to Jake, Billy stopped about twelve feet away.

"Sorry he's not very talkative, but I'm sure he'll be back with us in a minute or two."

"If you've hurt him Garrett, I'll make sure my father hears about it and you'll pay for what you've done."

Billy wished he had the courage to simply pull the gun out and shoot the bastard dead there and then, leaving him free to rescue Jake. But right at this moment that would be a physical impossibility, as he felt his whole body trembling like a leaf in the wind.

Ignoring the threat Garrett shook his head,

"Boy do these cats have thick skulls. Had to hit him twice before he'd shut up and sit nicely. Couldn't have him yelling out and warning you could we?"

Garrett smacked Jake round the back of the head.

"Fucking dumb cat."

Grabbing hold of Jake's hair, Garrett yanked Jake's head up.

"Look who's come to see you, it's your little faggot boyfriend."

Jake groaned.

"Oh good, I think he's waking up for us."

Garrett let go of Jake's head and proceeded to untie him. Jake crashed to the floor taking the chair with him. Billy stared in disbelief, why untie Jake? Surely Garrett wasn't just going to let him go, was he? It couldn't be this easy, could it?

Whether it was or not was irrelevant. Billy couldn't let Jake get hurt anymore, not over the stupid bottle incident.

"Okay! I'll go back to the ranch with you. Just let him go."

Garrett took a couple of steps towards Billy who's right arm tensed as he readied himself to draw his gun.

"You think this can be settled just by you going home to Daddy? Oh no… It's too late to get out of it that easy now. You two are both going to pay for what you did to me in that bar."

Garrett jerked his thumb over his shoulder, "Starting with him!"

Jake still felt a little groggy but could hear everything being said, and through half closed eyes could see both Garrett's and Billy's legs. He knew he had to do something as he knew both he and Billy were in grave danger. He could only hope that Garrett thought him still out for the count, and was preoccupied concentrating on Billy and not him.

Slowly he reached his arm out and closed his big hand around one of the legs of the chair. Then summoning up all the strength he could muster, he swung the chair round at floor level into the back of Garrett's legs below the knees.

The force of the unexpected blow took Garrett's legs clean out from under him and he landed on his back. Billy felt physically sick at the loud, almost hollow sounding 'thud' Garrett's head made as it hit the cement floor with some considerable force.

Jake despite feeling unsteady and disorientated desperately struggled to stand, but Garrett had beaten him to it, and had already managed to get back up.

Seeing Jake attempting to stand, Garrett bellowed like a bull and rushed at Jake knocking him back down and landing on him in the process. Garrett threw punches wildly, seemingly content with hitting Jake anywhere about the head and upper body.

With one concerted effort, Jake managed to shove Garrett off, sending the guy reeling backwards and crashing into some crates. Garrett howled in pain as a long piece of shattered wood pierced his cheek. Jake willed himself to get up, and lurched towards Garrett who was now knelt on the floor trying to pull the splinter from his face. As it came out he spotted Jake coming at him and slyly slid his hand into his pocket and took the switchblade out, concealing it in his hand.

Jake stopped, making sure he stood far enough from Garrett not to be taken by surprise.

"Come on asswipe, get up!" Bellowed Jake.

Garrett held his left hand up, palm outwards.

"You saying you had enough already?" Inquired a highly skeptical Jake.

"Yeah, okay, okay… just let me get up eh? I know when I'm beat."

Christ Jake thought, it would be great if Garrett turned out to be just another gutless bully who caved in when on the receiving end of something, but he didn't trust Garrett one inch, and as such the guy's unconditional surrender would likely turn out to be a feint. The guy was nothing short of a certifiable psychopath, and in Jake's experience people like that didn't just unexpectedly give up.

As Garrett stood his eyes never left Jake, while all the time blood steadily dripped off his jaw from the jagged puncture wound in his cheek. He drew his forearm forwards along the jawline and studied the red streak on his arm and back of his hand. As he looked back up he grinned, showing off teeth and gums covered in a thick translucent film of blood.

Jake watched puzzled as Garrett slowly tilted his head back and held it there. What the fuck was the guy up to now?

Then fast as a snake striking, Garrett's head snapped forward and he spat a spray of blood at Jake's face.

The bizarre act left a stunned Jake unprepared for Garrett's follow through lunge, and unable to get completely clear. The pair fell heavily to the floor; just as Jake struggled to his feet, he saw the switchblade in Garrett's right hand. Desperately he tried to twist his body out of the way, but the evasive action was too little, too late. As the three inch blade plunged deep into Jake's thigh, he felt his leg give way and he collapsed back to his knees, his leg bleeding heavily. As he went to pull the knife out he failed to see Garrett grab a nearby piece of two by four and swing at his head.

Once again Jake fell to the floor unconscious.

Garrett tossed the length of lumber away, stooped down and yanked the knife out of Jake's thigh, sadistically twisting it at the same time. He wiped the blood off the blade onto Jake's jeans before pocketing it.

Garrett walked a few paces and picked something up off the floor before turning to face Billy.

"See this? You see this? It's the beer bottle that you emptied into my jeans. I've been keeping it for just this moment. Garrett held it by the neck and swung it against some nearby machinery smashing the bottom half off, leaving a deadly jagged edge.

"Thought it funny didn't you? You fucking little brat!"

He waved the bottle at Billy. "Well just for that I'm gonna ass rape your boyfriend with the broken end. Then we'll see how funny you think that is."

Garrett moved towards Jake's motionless body.

"B-back off Garrett! Or I swear I'll s-shoot you."

Garrett wheeled round to see Billy shakily aiming the revolver at him.

"Oh, the little sissy boy has a little sissy gun. I'm. So. Fucking. Scared... Where'd you get it? You know I'm sure your boyfriend wouldn't like you playing with guns."

Billy kept the gun trained on Garrett the best he could, he couldn't be sure he'd actually hit him first shot as he couldn't keep the damned thing steady. But he had five bullets, and at such close range, at least one or two had to find their target.

Unexpectedly dropping to one knee and catching Billy out, Garrett pulled Jake's head back and held the jagged glass to the side of his throat.

"Drop the gun down and kick it to me, or I swear I'll shove this into his throat and you can watch him bleed out nice and slow all over the floor... Drop it!"

Garrett's eyes narrowed as his expression turned to a snarl. Billy knew the guy was just seconds away from doing what he said. Billy opened his fingers and let the gun fall to the floor. However, his deliberately fumbled kick sent the weapon skidding across the floor away from Garrett and into the shadows by a nearby mezzanine staircase.

Standing back up Garrett sighed, "You useless little shit! Are you so pathetic you can't even kick straight? I should have done your old man a big favor and drowned you a long time ago. But oh no, his precious little boy always had to be kept safe and away from any harm."

"My father's never given a damn about me, so don't waste your time trying to psych me out Garrett, it won't work."

"Well see now, that's where you're wrong. After mommy dearest died, he took to keeping you close all the time. Then one day the pair of you went for a nice little father and son outing and he managed to lose you in the middle of downtown Colorado Springs. The whole pack ended up on the streets looking for you. After that everything had to be done to protect you, so much so he got all cranky about it, and still is. That's when he started protecting you from the big bad world."

Tossing the bottle away, Garrett retrieved the switchblade from his pocket and made a show of releasing the blade.

"I'm going to teach you something else now about the big bad world. You know what that is? No? Well I'll fucking tell you. Never trust anyone, especially me. 'Cos now I'm gonna slit your pet's throat and you can watch him die. Then it'll be your turn, and that I'm really looking forward to."

Billy had to go for Garrett; he could see no other course of action left open to him. He just needed to ignite the overwhelming rage that had exploded from deep inside him in his room once, and again when he and Jake had fought the coyote shifter. Ever since he'd first seen Jake on the floor his whole body had become so swamped with adrenalin he had the jitters. He needed to save Jake, he just needed to...

But nothing happened. No uncontrollable fury, no wild anger. He couldn't make it happen; the capacity to erupt in a violent manner was in him, in both his human and animal forms, he knew that, he just didn't seem able to channel it at will. He'd managed it when they'd fought the coyote, so why not now? Jake's life was at stake once again, and Billy needed the strength the rage gave him.

Nothing... He had no choice but to go for the guy anyway and try to get the knife away from him.

At a hair's breadth away from launching himself at Garrett, Billy froze as he spotted movement in the deep shadows by the stairs. He could smell...

No, not possible. He had to be mistaken.

Without warning a deafening crack and simultaneous yellow flash startled Billy causing him to flinch.

The gunshot hadn't finished echoing around the empty building before Garrett roared out in pain and spun round to face the source of the shot.

Over by the mezzanine stairs, at the edge of where the weak yellow light from the ceiling lights hadn't quite lost its fight with the darkness, Billy caught sight of a hand holding the revolver he'd discarded just a few minutes ago. Despite his ears ringing like mad from the gunshot, he gazed transfixed at the gun, captivated by the small wisp of smoke curling up from the short barrel. Then out from the darkness stepped Lucas Manning.

Garrett stared in silence for a few seconds while the fact he'd just been shot by the pack omega sank in.

He snapped to and screamed out, "You goddamn shot me! You fucking little prick!"

Garrett held his left arm up and watched as blood dripped off his elbow and splashed onto the dust covered cement floor.

He looked back to Manning.

"I'm gonna cut you up bad, you son of a bitch!"

Turning round he booted the unconscious Jake hard in the ribs.

"Don't run away pussycat, I'll be back for you in a minute."

Having studied the bullet hole in his upper arm again, Garrett pushed a finger into the entry wound, causing himself to howl in pain. Billy shuddered as the look on Garrett's face sent an icy coldness shooting down his spine for the second time in just a few minutes. It went way beyond the scowl of simple anger; this was the look of a man now consumed by overwhelming hatred, his desire for vengeance fuelled by pain and pure malevolence. For the rest of his life Billy would always swear that for one brief moment Garrett took the form of something else. He could never quite describe what he saw, apart from saying that for a second or two Garrett became the personification of evil incarnate.

And now, totally incandescent with rage, Garrett started towards Manning.

"I'm gonna make you sorry you were ever born Manning, I'm gonna slice you into dog food, one little piece at a time."

Garrett strode forward. He'd taken four paces, almost half way to Manning, when a second shot rang out. This time the bullet's impact caused Garrett's whole upper body to jerk, breaking his stride. He staggered a step backwards then stopped.

As Garrett looked down, the knife fell from his bloody hand, clattering onto the cement floor. Slowly he brought his hand up to his chest. Even in the poor light Billy could see blood flowing freely from between Garrett's fingers, causing a dark, almost black stain to spread down his tee shirt towards his jeans. As Garrett slumped to his knees, he looked up at Manning, the expression of hatred never leaving his eyes.

Rooted to the spot by both shock and fear, Billy watched as Manning lowered the gun slightly and aimed straight at Garrett's head. Billy looked back to the glaring Garrett, his eyes still fixed on Manning. Christ! The guy actually appeared to be daring Manning to pull the trigger again. Something in Garrett's fucked up mind must have still thought Manning didn't have the balls to shoot a third time.

Silently someone else appeared from the shadows alongside Manning and put their hand on top of Manning's and gently pushed down so the revolver pointed at the floor.

Noah spoke softly, "It's okay dude, he's dead, or will be in a few seconds. Besides, the more shots the more chance someone might hear and call the cops." Gently he eased the gun out from Manning's sweaty and trembling hand.

Billy, Noah and Manning all turned and watched as Garrett took one last rattling breath, swayed a little then fell forward, his eyes never leaving Manning until they saw no more.

As Billy dashed over to Jake, Noah stuck the gun in his waistband, squatted down, picked the knife up then proceeded to wipe it clean where he found a dry patch on Garrett's tee shirt. Getting back up Noah made his way over to Jake. He knelt down and studied Jake's injured leg, then carefully slid the knife blade into the hole in Jake's jeans and cut the blood sodden denim open and examined the wound in Jake's thigh.

Billy became even more alarmed as Noah blew his breathe out noisily between pursed lips, it signaled the first sign of any emotion the guy had shown since appearing.

Noah looked up at Billy, "It's a deep jagged wound as the back half of the blade is serrated, but luckily I'm pretty sure it's missed the femoral artery, otherwise he'd have bled out by now."

Using the knife again Noah cut Jake's tee shirt up one side and gently pulled it off him. Ripping a piece off, he folded it into a large pad.

Placing the pad over the wound through the hole cut in Jake's jeans, he looked at Billy.

"Can you press down on this for me, while I fix it in position?"

A still shaking Billy did what had been asked of him, while Noah tore the tee shirt into strips and used them as a bandage to hold the pad firmly against the wound.

Noah examined his handiwork, "The bleeding has almost stopped on its own, Good thing about being a shifter eh?" Not getting a reply from Billy, Noah carried on. "The dressing will keep the wound clean and help prevent anything from getting in. What we don't want though is for the wound to open up when we move him, in case it ruptures the artery."

Pointing at Billy's waist, Noah asked, "What sort of belt do you wear?"

Confused, Billy stuttered at the unusual question, "W-why?"

"I ideally need a belt with a sliding buckle to wrap round his leg to hold the wound together when we move him, I don't want to put any undue strain on the artery."

"Oh, right. Yeah, I've got one of those."

Noah held his hand out.

Billy released the clasp on his canvas belt, pulled it out of the loops and passed it to Noah.

Once Noah had secured the belt, Billy asked him how Jake seemed apart from the leg wound.

"I think he's just out cold, he has a nasty gash to the back of the head but I'm no doctor. Look, we need to get Jake and the other guy out of here. Who is he anyway? I mean I know he's a wolf but…"

Instinctively, Billy looked across at Manning who was still stood staring down at Garrett's lifeless body, not having moved since Noah had taken the gun off him.

Turning back to Noah, he explained. "His name is Lucas Manning he used to be an omega in my dad's pack, but he came to see me earlier this evening at the motel to ask for my help to get away from the pack. He was with me when Garrett phoned saying to come here, I guess I must have told him what Garrett had said and he followed me here."

Having wrapped the rest of the tee shirt around the wound on the back of Jakes head, Noah stood up. "I'll bring my truck closer, but it'll take the three of us to get Jake into it so we don't put too much strain on his leg."

Billy wasn't really listening. This whole thing just had to be a really bad dream, he'd wake up in a minute and he'd be safely back in the motel room with Jake eating pizza.

"Right, I need you to drive Jake's truck to my place. You okay with that?"

Noah snapped his fingers twice in Billy's face, "Dude, you need to stay with me here."

"I… I can drive, but I don't have a license. I've never driven on real roads before, only around the ranch."

"Jeez!" Noah put his hand across his forehead for a second while he thought. "Okay. Do you think you can do it if you follow close behind me?"

"Yeah, I'll be okay. I can do it."

"Good, I need to get a doctor I know to come check him out. Jake can then shift at mine once he comes round."

"A doctor? Is that wise? I mean you know what if..."

"It's fine, the guy's local pack, but he's happy to treat all shifters, no questions." Noah reassured Billy.

"But what about Garrett, what we going to do with him?" Billy asked, aware they couldn't leave the body there.

Noah thought for a second, "Do you have a number for the other two guys who came with him? Would they help us get rid of the body?"

"They might, but I don't have their numbers." Billy felt way out of his depth; this was all too much for him to deal with. He couldn't think straight.

Then it came to him. He went over to Garrett, knelt down and trying not to look at the guy's face managed to roll the body over onto its back, and then patting down Garrett's pockets, found what he'd been looking for. Having pulled the cell phone out of Garrett's jeans Billy wasn't entirely surprised to find it had no PIN set on it, probably too complicated for Garrett to setup.

Going through the phonebook he found Dale Lane's number, called it and after a couple of deep breaths explained in brief what had happened and that they needed to do something with the body. To his complete amazement, Lane simply replied that 'The asshole had had it coming to him'. Lane agreed that he and Riley would come over after speaking to Billy's father to see if he could arrange for some help from the local pack to get rid of the body permanently.

Billy took some comfort in the fact his father would now owe the local pack alpha a significant debt. But there again there would be no way the local pack would want the body ending up on a coroners slab. A blood test and any subsequent DNA testing would throw up all sorts of issues and likely bring unwanted attention from certain elements of the authorities, so their cooperation in the matter was pretty much guaranteed.

Once Billy had finished the call Noah held his hand out, "We need to get rid of Garrett's phone too. Probably be easier if I do that."

After entering Lane's number into his own cell, Billy handed Garrett's phone over to Noah.

After thirty long minutes waiting at a window, Billy saw a large dark colored SUV with its lights off drive up to the building and pull up outside. As he watched, the rear doors opened and both Lane and Riley got out. Billy went to the personnel door and opened it; Lane came in first and straight away asked Billy how he was holding up. Although Billy had always thought of Lane as one of the friendlier pack members, the unexpected show of concern left Billy a little taken aback at first, but Lane's smile seemed genuine. Even Riley who had been a little standoffish at times with Billy, patted him on the back in a show of camaraderie.

Lane put a reassuring hand on the still shaking Billy's arm.

"Man, sorry it took so long to get here but Garrett took the rental so we had to wait for someone from the…"

Suddenly spotting Noah, Lane stopped mid-sentence, Billy guessed why he'd gone quiet, "It's cool, Noah's a shifter too."

"Ah right…" Lane turned back to Billy, "So anyways, we had to wait for a couple of the local pack to pick us up. They're sat outside waiting for some of the others to get here."

"Oh man, its bad all this shit going down." Observed Riley. "I mean everybody knew Garrett was one seriously fucked up son of a bitch right? But who'da thought he'd go this far? Always acting tough 'cos he had the power of the beta rank and knew no one had the balls to call him out."

Billy scoffed inwardly at the word, 'rank'. It all seemed so lame now, trying to make it sound all military like. But that summed the whole pack thing up nicely for him. Hell, he'd even heard pack members refer to themselves as 'soldiers' before. Boy! He felt so glad he'd finally escaped all that macho BS.

Now looking over at Noah, who still had the gun tucked in his waist-band, Riley acknowledged him with a nod. "Best thing you could have done, shooting that bastard, he was destined to kill someone sooner or later."

Then gesturing at Jake, Riley added. "Is he gonna be alright?"

Noah shrugged, "I think it's just concussion, plus he's got a nasty stab wound to the inside of his thigh that just missed the artery. And by the way, I didn't shoot him. That guy there did."

Riley hadn't even noticed Manning until then.

"Manning? You're shitting me right?"

Assuring Riley he was shitting him not, he led Lane and Riley over to Garrett.

Lane peered down at the body, furrowed his brows and shook his head, he then turned to Billy.

"Seems your father and the local pack alpha know each other from way back, which kinda sped things up by cutting out some of the usual pack protocol crap. I need to call him again in a minute; he wants to be regularly kept up to speed on what's happening. Or do you want to talk to him?"

"No way!"

Noah checked Jake's dressings were still okay then spoke to Lane. "Once you've made your call, can you help us get Jake into my truck then wait here for the rest of the local pack while we get Jake and Manning away? Oh, and someone needs to take Garrett's rental back."

Lane replied, "Yeah, no problem, we'll take the rental, we need it to get back to the hotel anyway."

It had become all too clear to Billy, Lane and Riley that some serious repercussions would follow Manning's shooting of the alpha's right hand man, irrespective of the reasons or justification behind it. Billy knew he and he alone needed to sort the Manning situation out. Yep, it was high time he grew a pair and started to behave like an alphas son. He just hoped it would be as easy to do it, as say it.

He announced to Lane and Riley that, "When everything's calmed down in the morning I'll speak to Manning. He told me earlier that he wants out of the pack, so if I can get him away it should help keep things from getting too fraught. I hope."

Lane shrugged, "Can't say that Manning wanting out is going to come as a great surprise to anyone, life's been pretty shitty for him recently. Garrett and several of his cronies have really had it in for him of late, Garrett, the asshole, even arranged a mock trial and lynching for Manning last week when your dad went away for a couple of days. Poor guy pissed his pants as they put the noose around his neck."

"How the hell did Garrett get away with that?" Exclaimed a stunned Billy.

"Nearly didn't." replied Riley, "A number of people started making noises about reporting it to your dad, but they were… let's say, 'persuaded' to keep their mouths shut by Garrett and some of his buddies."

Beside himself with rage, Billy laid all the blame squarely at his father's feet. The man's arrogance and total blind trust in Garrett had caused hurt for too many people now. If only he was bigger, tougher and meaner Billy would go back and challenge his father for the role of alpha. But being none of those things, he'd have to be content with putting the guy straight on the phone in the morning.

Lane chewed on his bottom lip, "Look I'm really sorry Billy, we should have stood by you when all the crap was going down after you came out, but… Well, you know how it is."

His words tailed off and he hung his head, shamed by his apparent lack of courage.

"It's okay Lane, I understand. I'd probably done the same thing in your position."

He'd liked to have been able to say quite the opposite, but he knew in his heart he'd have settled for the quiet life too.

"Garrett was going around voicing his hatred of you to everyone. You see after your Dad's bad reaction to your coming out, Garrett found it easy get the pack to side with him."

"So what you going to do now?" Billy asked Lane, "Surely this makes you next in line to be Beta?"

"Well I guess, but there needs to be some changes. To start with all Garrett's accomplices need throwing out, or severely disciplined at the very least. To be honest Billy if your old man's not willing to change things I'll leave myself."

Billy looked shocked, "A lone wolf?"

"Not a loner, I'll be going with him" Chipped in Riley. "Besides I'm sure the two of us can find some other loners to team up with or a pack in another state that'll take us in."

Walking over to the three of them, Noah took hold of Billy's elbow, "I hate to break things up here but we need to get these two out of here. I've spoken to the doctor and he's going to be at my place in about forty minutes, so we really have to get going."

Billy started to panic, "Shit! What about the bike I stole from the motel to get here? Its outside, what happens if it's found? They could trace it back to the motel."

Lane thought about it for a second, "Don't worry, I'll see if the guys outside can dump it somewhere else in town, if not we'll do something with it."

Once Manning and the still unconscious Jake had been loaded into Noah's SUV, a somewhat reassured but not a lot calmer Billy got into Jake's truck and cautiously followed the tail lights of Noah's Ford Explorer as they drove through the darkened streets. Several times cars came up behind Billy causing him to grip the steering wheel even tighter as he expected any minute to see the red and blue flashing lights of a police cruiser in his rear view mirror. But each time they turned off after having gone a few blocks. Then after what seemed like an eternity to Billy they made it safely to a one story Mediterranean house on the outskirts of town and Billy parked the pickup outside in the street. Noah had already pulled his truck up in front of the garage, and sat waiting as the automatic door opened.

By the time Billy entered the garage Noah had already parked and stood waiting by a switch on the wall, as he flipped it the door closed behind Billy.

"I thought it best to get them out in here, away from any prying eyes."

Noah led Manning inside the house via the connecting door, then came back to help Billy with a now semi-conscious Jake who was doing his utmost to be obstinate and refusing to budge from the back seat. Leaning in Noah checked out Jakes wound, and decided it should be okay if Jake walked as long as he and Billy took the guy's weight so not to put any undue strain on the injured leg.

After another fruitless round of trying to get Jake out of the truck, Noah laughed, "Typical stubborn cat."

Eventually they managed to coax a grumpy Jake out of the truck and half carrying him between them they walked Jake to Noah's bedroom, where Noah had already laid several old beach towels on the bed. The pair of them helped Jake onto the bed who then promptly curled up into the fetal position with his back to them. Billy sat down on the edge of the bed and just watched Jake lie there, their spat of earlier washed from his mind by his continued concern for the guy's wellbeing.

Hearing a noise behind him, Billy turned to see Noah with a some-what overweight guy in his late fifties wearing a straw trilby and carrying a large brown leather bag, in Billy's eyes the guy even looked like a doctor. With just the briefest of introductions the doctor removed all the wound dressings and after Jake had struggled out of his jeans got on with giving the now wide awake Jake a once over.

"If you were human, I would have you transferred to the ER straight away. It sounds like you've sustained a concussion, twice from what I hear."

"Three times I think Doc, though not absolutely sure on that one, I lost count."

The doctor's curt 'Humph' implied he was less than impressed with Jake's quip.

"Anyway," the doctor continued, "You also have a couple of nasty lacerations across the back and side of your head. The stab wound to your thigh is deep but fortunately missed the artery. I would imagine you've lost a fair amount of blood, but from your general demeanor I don't think it's enough to be unduly alarmed about or warrant giving you plasma, and I don't think it will prevent you shifting. But, I strongly recommend you change to your animal as soon as you can. Do you think you can do that?"

"Yeah, no problem."

"Good, you should also try to get several hours' decent sleep in your animal form; it will do you the world of good. Then when you wake, shift back to human again and make sure you eat well afterwards and stay hydrated."

Jake propped himself up a little higher, "Okay Doc, sounds good to me, I have the headache from hell to get shot of too."

Billy announced he'd stay with Jake, only for the doctor to forbid it, stating Jake needed proper rest not company. The doctor took an brown plastic pot from his bag, shook a couple of capsules out into his hand and gave them to Billy.

"Now young man, you take these; they will let you get some sleep tonight too."

Then led by Noah the doctor went to see Manning.

Billy sat on the bed next to Jake and started to speak, "I've been so worried I…"

Jake interrupted and cut Billy off mid-sentence.

"Can we talk about it in the morning, I really need to know all what happened, but right now I just really want to shift and sleep."

Billy started as Jake reached out and put his hand on his knee.

"But thank you for coming to rescue me, I did kinda see you there, then I don't really remember much else until I got here. But you shouldn't have done it. It was way too dangerous a thing to do just for me. Now I really have to shift, I feel like road kill that's been run over by an eighteen wheeler."

Once Billy had left the bedroom, Jake took his boxer's off, curled up into a ball, and started his shift.

Needing something to do in order to take his mind off everything, Billy quietly opened the bedroom door and seeing Jake had already started the transformation to cougar, picked Jake's jeans up off the bed thinking he should take the wallet and cell phone out in case Noah washed them. Not that he seriously expected Noah to start doing laundry at stupid o'clock in the morning, but he needed to reestablish some degree of normality back into his life. As he pulled the phone out a piece of crumpled blood stained paper fell from the pocket onto the floor, picking it up he put the phone and wallet on the nightstand. Billy walked out of the bedroom and closed the door behind him. Looking at the piece of paper, he decided to open it before the blood dried completely and stuck it all together, if it wasn't important he'd throw it in the trash.

Gently unfolding the piece of paper, he read the handwritten note.

Billy wasn't sure how long he'd stood there staring at it before he heard Noah's voice.

"What's up?" Noah enquired.

Billy passed the piece of paper over, then spotted one of Noah's eyebrows shoot up as he read it.

Looking at Billy to pass the note back Noah saw the tears streaming down his face.

"I feel so awful." Billy wept. "He went there prepared to trade himself for me, knowing it would be a trap."

"Why do you feel bad? He'd have done it without giving it a second thought, and yeah, I've no doubt he'd been fully aware it would likely be a trap. So it was no different to when you went to give yourself in exchange for him."

"But we'd had a huge row just before, and I thought he…"

Noah put his arm round Billy's shoulders and led him out of the bedroom turning the light out behind them. "C'mon, the doc's just giving Manning a shot of some heavy duty sedative, then he's done with us."

Noah pointed Billy in the direction of the kitchen. "Grab yourself a beer or something from the refrigerator and I'll be back in a moment."

Billy leant back against the countertop with a soda and watched Noah and the doctor as they conversed quietly for several minutes outside the front door. While they chatted, Billy discretely dropped the two sleeping tablets down into the garbage disposal unit. After seeing the doctor off, Noah came into the kitchen grabbed a small brandy snifter and a bottle of Extra Añejo tequila from a cupboard, then proceeded to pour himself a good two fingers worth of the pale gold spirit.

Billy watched as Noah swirled his glass then after taking the merest sip, closed his eyes and ran his tongue over his gums and lips, delighting in the first taste. He followed this with a larger sip, again savoring the flavors.

Noah sighed, as the stress and tension of the night's events eased away, he then turned to Billy. "As the third bedroom is my gym there's no bed in it. So you and I are going to have to sleep on the couch, but it makes into a pretty comfortable double bed. I'll fetch us some blankets, but first I think we should get you out of those clothes and cleaned up."

Looking down, Billy saw blood liberally smeared over his hoodie and jeans. He held his hands up in front of his face, and for the first time noticed the dark reddish-brown stain of dried blood covering them. As the enormity of what had gone on hit him, the color drained from his face and he started shaking like a leaf.

Noah took one look at Billy, grabbed the soda can out of his hand and hauled him into the bathroom where they just made it to the toilet before Billy violently threw up.

After he'd finished heaving, Billy flushed the toilet and stood back up.

Noah grimaced, "It's okay, you're in shock, which isn't surprising really. I'll find you some fresh clothes and leave them outside the door. When you feel up to it take a good long hot shower, I'll be in the living room when you're done."

As Billy showered and scrubbed away at the blood some of the details of what had gone on earlier started to come back to him, and he tried desperately to make sense of it all. Man! He had been so relieved when Noah showed up and started to sort everything out. The guy was really something, never once had he lost his cool, or appeared unsure, he just seemed to know precisely what to do. Noah and Jake were straight out of the same mold. Then it dawned on Billy, why had Noah turned up at the old factory? Had Jake called him? And come to think of it what on earth had Manning been doing there too?"

It was all too much to deal with at the moment. Leaning back against the shower stall wall and out of the spray he blinked as salty tears stung his eyes. A hollow aching pain burnt deep inside his chest, he knew the crying wasn't out of self-pity, he'd shed so many tears over the last eleven years he knew exactly what that felt like.

No this felt different, real heartache, and he was crying because he knew his stupid actions could so easily have cost Jake his life, and all because he shoved that dumb bottle into Garrett's jeans. He shook his head and clasped it in his hands; maybe he was some sort of jinx on Jake. The guy had been right that time in Vegas, he didn't need any help getting into trouble. Billy started to wonder if somehow he made things worse for Jake just by being around the guy. He'd run away from the home he hated, the life he hated, and the father he hated, everything should be simple now.

So why wasn't it? And why was he so drawn to Jake?

He just had to stop screwing himself up like this over some guy who would never reciprocate what he felt for him. But he still wanted to be with Jake despite everything, and that presented the next problem. Jake needed to travel more while he wanted to stay right here. Could he wait until Jake got back from where ever it was he needed to go, and more importantly, would Jake even come back?

And he needed to make good on his promise to get Manning to somewhere where he'd be out of harm's way, the guy's safety had to take precedence over everything. Then once he'd sorted that out he'd decide what to do about him and Jake. And on top of all that, there would be the

227

inevitable fallout from Garrett's death, which would mean having to deal once again with his father. Yes, he had an agenda now, and responsibilities. He needed to man up, get on with it, and stop constantly doubting himself and his abilities.

Having set his mind straight he returned to showering, holding his hands up he studied them closely, no trace of blood remained, though the skin on the back of them looked red raw from the obsessive scrubbing they'd received from a loofa. However, he was convinced he could still taste the coppery tang of blood in his mouth. He tilted his head up and opened his mouth allowing it to fill with water from the shower head, then after swirling it round and round he spat it out. After repeating the exercise several more times, he finally convinced himself he could no longer taste it anymore. Now at last, he felt clean.

Next morning Billy sat at the small round kitchen table eating toast and watching the small TV on top of the refrigerator as the local news channel showed footage of the smoldering remains of what had once been the building they were in the previous night. The reporter at the scene stood interviewing the senior fire fighter who claimed that the fire had most likely been caused by an electrical fault in old wiring and muttered something about vagrants.

Billy assumed that had dealt with any evidence like blood. And he really didn't want to think about what had become of Garrett's body, but he knew it would never be found. Just then Noah entered the kitchen. As Billy attempted to smile at him round the slice of toast hanging out of his mouth Noah pointed at the TV. "I take it that's our factory on the news?"

Billy set his coffee mug down on the table and pulled the toast out of his mouth, "Yeah, the fire chief said something about faulty electrical wiring."

Noah laughed, "He would do. He's local pack."

Billy looked quizzically at Noah, "Really?"

"Yeah, probably him who set the fire in the first place. Anyway, Jake's shifted back to human and is awake proper now, and Manning is slowly getting there too. So how about we fix them both a good breakfast? Jake especially needs to eat plenty of protein after two shifts in relatively quick succession."

"How is he?" Billy asked.

"Jake? Hmmm... Grumpy."

Billy laughed, "Oh he's feeling better then."

Once they'd cooked breakfast they took a tray each for the two patients.

Sitting on the bed Billy started to explain the missing bits from the previous night to Jake while he ate. Just as Jake finished Noah joined them.

Billy turned to Noah, "By the way I keep meaning to ask, how come you where there last night?"

Noah went on to explain how Jake had passed him going like a bat out of hell and he reasoned something was wrong, so decided to follow him, but then lost sight of the pickup.

"I'd been driving around for ages and had just about to give up when I spotted you peddling furiously towards me on a mountain bike, which seemed odd as well. So then I followed you guessing you were heading for where ever Jake had gone. And Manning just told me he took a mountain bike from the motel as well and followed you."

Then Billy with some help from Noah finished explaining everything that had gone on, from Billy getting the call from Garrett, finding the gun hidden in the truck, Manning shooting Garrett, and the building now being nothing more than a pile of smoldering rubble.

Jake looked at Billy and shook his head.

"You shouldn't have come, Garrett had set a trap and once he'd got us he meant to torture and kill us both."

"Well you came for me!"

"That's different."

Billy shut up and refused to be drawn into some *'Yes you did- No I didn't'* argument on the matter.

Jake leant over and picked up his jeans now caked in dried on blood, then put his fingers though the large slit in the leg. Not again! How come he only needed to be out of it for a just a few short minutes in order to wake up to find his clothes shredded, and where was his tee shirt?

"What's everyone doing here? Why's Jake in your bed? And whose are those bloody jeans he's holding? And who's the guy in the other bedroom?"

Noah and Billy turned round to see an exasperated looking Hannah standing in the doorway, hands on hips. Jake, all of a sudden racked by modesty tugged the comforter up from his waist to his neck.

Noah tried to reassure her. "It's nothing, Jake got into a fight with that Garrett guy from the beach. But Manning, the guy in the spare room, he saved Jake from serious harm. So everything's fine now."

Hannah pushed past Billy and Noah to get to Jake.

"Are you sure you're okay?" she said looking at the jeans, "That's heck of a lot of blood."

"Honestly Hannah I'm fine, it looks worse than it actually is. And a doctor's checked me out. He says I'll be fine."

"Are you sure? And who's this Manning guy?" She turned to Noah. "And why's he in your spare bed?"

Billy tried explaining that Manning used to be a worker on his dad's ranch, and one of life's genuinely good guys, hence him saving Jake's life.

Noah face palmed and groaned.

"Saved his life?" Hannah rounded on Noah. "Noah Bailey, You just said 'It's nothing'. That doesn't sound like 'nothing' to me!"

Then right on cue Billy's phone rang, and everyone turned and looked at him.

Uncomfortable with all the sudden attention he looked down and pulled his phone out his pocket before scowling at the screen. Then glancing back up at Jake, he wiggled the phone, "Wanna guess who?"

Jake shrugged his shoulders, "You're on your own with that one, good luck."

"I'm not sure I need this right now." Grumbled Billy, "I'm not as angry as I want to be."

Pursing his lips he exhaled noisily through his nose then accepted the call.

After a few mostly subdued yeses and noes, which Jake took as a good sign, at least they weren't having a shouting match straight off like last time. Finally Billy said, "If you're serious, then we have a lot of things to talk about. Plenty has changed in the last twenty four hours. Text me when you land and we'll sort out where to meet."

With that he ended the call and pocketed the phone.

Noah broke the ensuing silence by saying Billy was more than welcome to use his house for the meeting with his father as everyone would be here. Taking Noah up on the offer Billy announced he needed to go speak with Manning, in order to try sort out getting him away before his Dad flew in.

Entering the other bedroom he found Hannah sat on the bed trying to coax Manning into talking about the previous night.

Getting off the bed Hannah grabbed Billy's hand and led him back out the room into the hallway pulling the door to behind her.

"What's up with the guy? I've tried to talk to him but all I get is mumbled one word replies and he won't look at me."

Billy explained that Manning was very shy by nature, and had been heavily sedated the night before, plus he was probably still in shock.

Billy didn't like lying to Hannah, but knew a few white lies were necessary just right now. He went on to explain that Manning had left the ranch as he'd been badly bullied. When he cited the mock lynching as an example, Hannah put her hand over her mouth and stared wide eyed at Billy.

"Oh my God! The poor guy, no wonder he's like he is."

"Yeah, well any way I'm going to talk to him, see what I can do about getting him to a place of safety."

Hannah thought for a second, "If it helps I can make some calls, see if I can find somewhere for him to stay around here where he'd be safe. But what about that Garrett guy? What if he comes back?"

Billy said it would be great if she could find somewhere local for Manning to stay, even if only until he sorted himself out. Regarding Garrett, he simply stated that the guy wouldn't be coming back.

"Well I'm going back talk to Jake; see if he'll be more forthcoming about what's gone on."

With that Hannah strode off into Noah's bedroom.

Billy chuckled. *Yeah, good luck with that.*

He then went back in to see Manning.

As Billy spoke to him, Manning still did his best to avoid direct eye contact.

Billy placed his hand on Manning's forearm, "Lucas, you can look at me, you are my equal, you're any man's equal, you don't have to go on putting yourself through all this torment anymore."

"You don't understand, this is what I am."

"No it isn't. You are so much more. Look what you done last night; you saved both mine and Jake's lives. Your pack days were over the second you pulled that trigger. You are your own man now, free to live your life your way."

"No, they will find me where ever I go, your father will drag me back and punish me for leaving and shooting Garrett. I know he will."

Billy attempted to reassure Manning that no one was out to kill him or kidnap him, especially Billy's father, and that now Garrett had gone things would change for the better. Billy went on to explain that Hannah said she'd try to find somewhere safe and friendly for Manning to stay. And then when he and Jake came back they'd be there for him too. After some more reassurance from Billy, Manning started to calm down a little as he finally accepted that he was probably in the safest place for him right now, then he suddenly realized what Billy had said about going away.

"Come back? Where are you going?"

"We're only going away for a short while, and then we'll be back."

"But why do you have to leave?"

"Jake thinks it would be good if he and I got away from here for a bit in order to help forget everything and let the issues between me and my dad calm down."

Billy surprised himself with his own words, when had he decided all that?

It seemed that as much as he was determined to settle here, he'd somehow come to the subconscious conclusion that Jake was probably right when he said they should get away for a little while. But it would only be for a few weeks at most, just until the memories of the previous night faded and his father had seen sense. Then they'd come back and stay.

Billy told Manning he'd arrange for Lane and Riley to collect his stuff from the hotel and bring it over when his dad turned up. At hearing his ex-alpha would be arriving Manning physically scooted up the bed and away from Billy.

"It's okay Lucas; he's coming to see me. I'll tell him you're not going back, no arguments. He won't even know you're here, you don't have to talk to him or get involved at all if you don't want to."

"But Riley and Lane will try and force me…"

"No they won't. Look Manning, things need to change big time in the pack if it's to survive, and I'm pretty sure they will if Lane becomes beta and my old man sees just how wrong he's been, but it will take time. Personally I think Lane is the obvious choice for the next beta, he's a good guy. And I'm one hundred percent convinced he'd have no truck with anything like forcing you to go back against your will."

In the other bedroom Hannah had decided she was fighting a losing battle trying to get any more information out of Jake or Noah. Giving up on them she went off to arrange accommodation for Manning. Billy, having left Manning to mull over the things he wanted from his new life, went out to the pickup and fetched clean clothes for both him and Jake. Once showered and changed the pair sat on the bed sorting things out between to two of them. Billy agreed that their getting away from everything for a little while seemed a good idea, but he wasn't going all over the country, just up the coast for a short while, and nothing more.

Jake agreed with going for just a few weeks, and said that once they got back they'd both start looking for a place to live, and jobs. Jake knew he could get by without one but renting somewhere big enough for both of them to live in would mean they could do with some extra income, and of course having a visible source of income would avoid potentially awkward questions about where his money came from.

As Billy left the bedroom to sit with Manning again, Noah took the opportunity to go in and talk to Jake. After learning Jake felt a lot better he took the Smith & Wesson out of his pocket and held it out to Jake.

"Do you want this back? I know the chances of Garrett's body ever being found are pretty much zero, but still, it has been used in a homicide. I can get rid of it for you if you like?"

Jake thought it over for a few seconds, then reached forward and took the gun from Noah's outstretched hand.

"Like you say, no one's going to want him found in a hurry so I'm guessing it'll be safe to keep hold of. Besides it's not registered to me."

"If you're really sure? I mean it's no problem." Noah assured Jake.

Jake swung himself off the bed, thanked Noah for his offer then stuck the .38 in his jeans pocket.

Billy had been sat staring out of the window in the living room waiting for his father to arrive for what seemed like an eternity. He looked up at the wall clock for the hundredth time, it had just gone one thirty, his father's flight into Santa Ana had landed just before one and they'd exchanged texts, so he should be due any time now. As Billy turned back to watching the street, a dark blue sedan slowed down and pulled up the other side of the driveway outside the next door house. As Billy got up he saw the lone figure of his father get out the back of the car.

Walking into the kitchen where Noah, Jake and Hannah stood talking, Billy announced his father had turned up. Noah offered him the use of the living room if he wanted somewhere private to talk. Billy thought for a moment, it made sense to do it inside, it meant he had the advantage of home territory too. Plus Jake, Noah and Hannah were in the house, he felt more confident today than he had for a long, long time. He opened the door and waited for his father to walk up the path. After a brief, nodded greeting he showed his father into the living room.

He steeled himself. *Right, best form of defense is attack.*

"So, have you accepted that I'm not coming back to the ranch? Because if you haven't then there's little point us sitting here having this conversation."

His father somewhat stunned by Billy's directness hesitated slightly before answering.

"Yes, I can understand why you don't want to come back at the moment."

"No Dad! There's no 'at the moment' about it. I am NOT coming back to live at the ranch. Period! Jesus! I thought from our talk on the phone earlier you'd got that."

"Sorry, bad choice of words."

"Manning's not coming back either. His spirit's gone and he needs time and the care of friendly people to mend. His days with the pack are over."

Billy's father once more became the Alpha "You keep telling me you want nothing more to do with the pack, and here you are trying to make decisions for it, and for me. I'm sorry but you can't have it both ways son."

Waiting until his father finished, Billy told him about the mock lynching and some of the other degrading things he'd found out Garrett had been responsible for and encouraged. Billy found himself suitably impressed with the look of genuine shock he'd caused to appear on his father's face.

"I… I honestly didn't know those sorts of things were going on. He should come back, we can get him some sort of help."

"Some 'sort of help'? You still don't have a clue how to deal with people and their emotions do you? The best help you can give him is to let him go. He's of no use to you or the pack anymore dad. He's a broken man, and that's not all Garrett's doing, you have to take a lot of the blame for being so unapproachable that people were scared to report it to you and for blindly trusting in Garrett."

After a few seconds deliberation his father agreed that maybe Manning would be better off away from the pack, at least until he'd got himself straight and could decide better what he wanted. Billy was genuinely stunned, he never expected his father to give in that easily, he decided to follow through right away while he seemed to be on a winning streak.

"And I think you need to give him some money, enough to tide him over 'til he's well enough to get a job."

Again, Billy's father surprised him as he took his wallet out and counted the bills in it, then leaning forward in his chair he handed a wad of them to Billy.

"There's six hundred. I'll arrange to wire him some more once I get back to the ranch, plus I'll also get his belongings shipped here via Greyhound. Do you want I should wire you some money too? I'm guessing you're broke too as there wasn't much more than a few hundred in the house."

"Pretty much yeah. Jake and I are going away for a sort while, when I get back I'll text you about sending the money."

Billy's father took the last three hundred dollars out of his wallet and offered them to Billy who happily took them. He decided if his father expected him to be pig headed and turn down the offer of money he was badly mistaken, after all it was the very least the guy could do for him.

"Will Manning be alright here on his own if you're going away?"

"He'll be in the company of lots of good people, plus there's a lone feline shifter here to keep an eye on him, besides we'll not going be gone long."

An uncomfortable silence followed, Billy could see from his father's expression the guy seemed to be struggling to find the right words for something.

"I never meant for anything like this to have happened, I just wanted you back home safe."

Billy just stared at his father for a few seconds, incredulous at his revelation, "How did you think it was going to play out sending Garrett and a posse here? Are you honestly trying to tell me you never had any idea what he was like?

"I knew he could have a temper on him and could be a bit heavy handed at times, but no one ever complained officially, and obviously now I see why. But a pack must have discipline."

"Heavy handed? Talk about understatement. The guy was an out and out bully Dad, plain and simple."

Billy carried on, "But I did gather from Garrett that everything you'd done had been to protect me. Quite what from I'm not sure. And in a way I do appreciate the thought behind it, but not the fact you became so obsessed over it you made me a prisoner in my own home. But sitting here, I get a feeling you're not ready to give up on all that just yet are you? Because I'm getting the impression now you're trying to buy me back."

Billy's father looked mortified. "No! No! It's nothing like that. I'm just trying to make amends for all the wrong I've done to you, and that I inadvertently let others do."

Billy sensed genuine remorse in his father's voice, now that had to be a first!

"Well I have my own life to lead now Dad, and in the way I want to. So if you can live with that then we'll keep in touch, maybe you can come down to see us from time to time. And then one day, if and when the trust has been re-established between us, I'll come to visit you at the ranch, but that's a long way off right now."

"You're my only son Billy, and I love you, probably more than you'll ever know. All I've ever wanted was for you to be safe and happy."

"Look Dad, like I said, I appreciate that somehow you thought you were doing the right thing, but after Mom's death I so wanted and needed to be able love you and to have your unconditional love back, but the love that should be inside of me for you has been driven out, by you.

I'm sorry if that hurts, but it's the truth, and I won't hide it. But if we can start having a normal father and son relationship I hope that'll change in time."

Wringing his hands Billy's father looked down. When he looked back up there were genuine tears rolling down his face. The sudden disappearance of the powerful alpha and its replacement with a normal father worried sick about his son wasn't entirely lost on Billy. Part of him wanted to go to his father and hold his hands, look up into his eyes and ease the hurting. But he couldn't make such a forgiving gesture, not yet, he had too much pain of his own.

"As for being safe and happy, trust me I am. I want to live my life here, and I hope in time you will accept that and want to be part of that life and we can be family again."

His father looked up, anguish written across his face. He wiped his tears away with his palms, "I do son, I want that more than anything."

Regaining his composure, Billy's father stood up, "I think I should be going now. I'm acutely aware my presence here is a strain and I don't want to risk jeopardizing anything. Plus if we don't leave soon there'll be no chance to eat before we catch the flight back and I don't think I could bear Lane and Riley whining all the way home."

Billy smiled politely at his father's joke. The one thing his father had never been was an actor, and the man in front of him, despite his attempt to try to lighten the atmosphere was hurting bad. Sensing his old man was in his own way genuinely trying to put things right, Billy stood up, walked over to his father and hugged him, an act returned without a second's hesitation.

"It'll be okay Dad, everything will work out right in the end if you just keep working at it."

He buried his face in his dad's neck and briefly squeezed him tighter before letting go and stepping back.

Jake had just finished stowing the gun back under the seat when he spotted Billy's father walking down the driveway. The guy looked so wretched Jake almost felt sorry for him. Seeing Jake looking his way, he carried on walking towards the pickup.

Jake nodded, "Mr Thompson."

"Please, call me Jeff."

Jake wasn't sure he really wanted to be on first name terms with a guy who only a few short days ago had barely acknowledged Jake's existence, and then, only begrudgingly. Getting some satisfaction from the fact his lack of reply had obviously caused Billy's dad to feel awkward Jake continued to stay silent.

Realizing a response wouldn't be forthcoming Jeff Thompson carried on.

"Jake, I'm not too big to admit I've been stupid beyond all belief and managed to drive the one thing I care most about in this world away from me. And I pray that one day Billy will truly forgive me. Lane and Riley have updated me on what happened last night and I've been told of some of the things Garrett had been doing back at the ranch. All things I have no excuse for not knowing about. But most importantly I can never repay the debt I owe you for saving my son's life, especially as you risked your own life to do it."

Further silence. Okay maybe he was being childish and mean, but Jake didn't see why should he help the guy out. If he wanted to atone for what he'd done he'd have to do it without Jake's help.

"If there's anything either of you need, you only have to ask, I'm just a phone call away."

Jake relented slightly, and thanked him for his offer.

The tone in the guy's voice suggested a genuine remorse and a heartfelt desire to make amends. Now feeling a little mean how he'd just treated him, Jake offered his hand in friendship and the pair shook.

"I'll make sure Billy stays in touch Mr Thompson, and I'm sure if you're true to your word about rebuilding bridges then everything will end up being as it should."

"Thank you Jake. I know you don't trust me, that's plain to see and I guess I can't really blame you. If I'm being honest, in your position I'd probably feel the same way. But I am sincere, Billy means the world to me, and I will do anything to protect him and keep him safe."

Yeah like incarcerating him, tracking his whereabouts and sending people out after him, Jake mused.

The conversation stopped as they both spotted Noah come out the house, closely followed by Billy who walked straight over to Jake and his father, leaving Noah standing where his path joined the sidewalk. As Billy reached the truck Hannah led Manning out of the house and the pair of them stood together just outside the front door. Then to complete the gathering, Lane and Riley got out of their car, Riley walked round the back, popped the trunk and pulled out a backpack, the pair of them then stood by the car looking at everyone else.

Jake studied the surreal scene with some amusement. It seemed like they were all pieces on some bizarre chess board with everyone waiting for the next move to be played. And it didn't take long before the moves started to come thick and fast. Jeff Thompson moved away from Jake and Billy and stood at the end of the driveway for no apparent good reason, well none that Jake could think of.

Lane and Riley moved next and came over to Jake and Billy. Riley handed Manning's bag to Billy, explaining he'd thought it best to give it to Billy, as he didn't want to risk freaking Manning out by trying to give it to him.

Then everyone stared as Jeff Thompson slowly walked across the lawn to Manning and stopped in front of him. Hannah sensing the tension edged up even closer to Manning so they were touching shoulders. And although unsure of what Billy's father's intentions were, she knew that if he even looked funny at Lucas she'd be between them before the guy had chance to draw his next breath. As Manning stared for several seconds at Jeff Thompson's outstretched hand before gingerly shaking it, Hannah tried to figure out what hold Billy's father had over Lucas in order to turn him into a complete nervous wreck.

"You take care of yourself Manning, I know my apologies will never be enough to make amends. I should have been aware of what was happening. I let you down badly, and for that, I have no excuse to offer.

But should you ever want to come back to the ranch you will always be welcome."

As Manning stood there silent, seemingly frozen to the spot, Jeff Thompson smiled awkwardly, patted Manning twice on the shoulder, and then walked off towards the rental. As he reached the back of the car, he turned, looked at Billy one last time, raised the fingers on one hand then got in and shut the door. Lane and Riley exchanged phone numbers with Jake and Billy, the four of them agreeing to keep in touch. Then having said their goodbyes Lane and Riley nodded at Manning before returning to their car.

Billy walked up the path to Hannah and Manning and handed the wad of bills over and tried one last time to convince Manning that everything would be fine now and that his father would be wiring both of them some more money soon. Hannah informed Billy that she'd sorted the accommodation side of things out. Cody and Ryan, two of the surfers who'd been Billy's unofficial bodyguards, had been looking for someone else to share their apartment for a while, and were more than happy for Manning to stay with them. She went on to explain that Manning would stay the night at her house then move in to the apartment the following day, once the boys had cleared their junk out of Manning's room.

As the sedan pulled away and headed off to the airport Noah came and stood alongside Jake. Shrugging his shoulders Jake announced, "Well... I guess it's our turn now. Want to get up to Hollywood Hills tonight so Billy can see the sign all lit up and get his first glimpse of Tinsel Town."

In a tone of mock disbelief, a bemused Noah laughed. "I thought you two would have wanted the quiet life now. But here you are, going out and looking to have more adventures."

"That's what I thought too."

They all looked across to see Hannah, Manning and Billy standing there.

"I really hoped you guys had decided to stay here." Said a dejected sounding Hannah.

Billy smiled at her, "Of course we want to live here, and we're going to. It's just we have some more exploring to do first."

He stepped in closer to her and grabbed hold of both her hands then beamed a huge grin at her. "But once I've got that out of Jake's system we'll definitely be back to stay."

"Oi!" Jake tried his comic best to look shocked and hurt.

Hannah said she'd managed to come up with few good leads on some jobs already. They carried on chatting, discussing the various merits of the potential jobs. After a couple of minutes Billy realized Manning wasn't just standing there quietly, he'd actually joined in on the conversation, albeit mostly monosyllabic replies. But it seemed the guy had obviously started to feel a little more at ease by having people around him who were looking out for him.

Jake leant over and quietly whispered in Noah's ear, "Is it my imagination or does Hannah seem to be taking an unusual amount of interest in Manning's wellbeing?"

"Hmmm…" Noah whispered back. "I'm not a hundred percent sure, but I'd say something could well be developing there. And if I'm right, that is going to present a serious problem down the line when it's time for her to know."

"Yeah, been there, seen it and done that one. Not an easy thing to do."

"Are you two conspiring?"

Jake and Noah both looked at Hannah who now stood by them, the pair shook their heads emphatically. The action reminded her so much of her two kid brothers when they were little. If the boys got caught out by their parents having been up to no good, the two of them would stand there and shake their heads denying having been bad.

No… She didn't want to remember, not now. She needed to keep this a happy moment, it wasn't a time for grieving.

The mock quizzical look on her face said she didn't expect a truly honest answer from either of them.

"Honest." Replied Noah, "We weren't doing nothing."

Oh God. The words hit Hannah like a sledgehammer blow. It was word for word what Jack used to say. While Joseph the quiet one just used to stand there shaking his head and would instinctively reach out and hold his twins hand. She could feel the tears starting to well up in her eyes.

She gently shoved Jake away, "Will you two just go already? Before you make me lose all composure and start crying in public."

After one final round of hugging, Jake and Billy finally got in the truck.

Billy poked his head out the window, "We'll call you when we get to Frisco."

"I'm gonna hold you to that." shouted Hannah, "Or I'll come find you and bring you back! You both have my number, so there's no excuse not to stay in contact."

"We will." Yelled Billy as Jake pulled away.

Hannah, Manning and Noah waved as the pickup drove off up the street with both Jake and Billy waving back out of the windows. Hannah put her hand on Manning's shoulder who sheepishly returned her smile, and the pair of them went back into the house.

Noah stood alone on the sidewalk watching the pickup. Just before it disappeared from view he raised his arm above his head and waved one last time knowing they were probably too far away see him.

Dropping his arm and his smile, he slipped his hand into his jeans pocket and pulled out his Blackberry. After typing a message he re-read it, and then hit the send button.

15:23 PDT. Rabbits 1 & 2 on route to S.F travelling on Coastal Highway 1.

GPS vehicle tracker confirmed active.

He stood kicking the heel of his sneaker against the curb while he waited for the reply. A minute or so later his phone chirped alerting him to the incoming message.

Your intell relayed to intercept teams.

Geotracking of both cells now real time.

Good job.

Await instructions regarding your new target, now designated Rabbit 3.

I.R

He deleted both messages and pocketed the phone. Shoving his other hand into his jeans he turned and sauntered back towards the house.

FOR INFORMATION ON
OTHER SEAN CATT
BOOKS
PLEASE VISIT

WWW.SEANCATT.COM

Lightning Source UK Ltd.
Milton Keynes UK
UKOW06f0213040915
258000UK00008BA/125/P

9 780992 904685